DOLLHOUSE

DOWN WE GO BOOK ONE

KYLA FAYE

Dedication

To the little girl who dreamed of one day writing a book.
You did it. I'm so proud of you.

WARNING

This book contains adult content, including language, violence, dub and non-con, blood and knife play, and other situations that may be uncomfortable. Proceed with caution and at your own risk.

PROLOGUE

For as long as I can remember, I've been fascinated with death. I've seen it a lot in my life, and I'd be lying if I said I hadn't thought about it often, wondering how I'd die.

Would it be painful?

Would I be old and gray?

What happens afterward?

I was seven when I started thinking about my death after watching my mother die by her own hand. The needle she'd shoved into her vein containing her 'medicine' killed her. When I was eight, I continued to think about death when I saw my father paint our musty yellow walls with chunks of his brain.

My fascination with death bloomed, growing into an obsession when I was thirteen and witnessed my foster brother kill our foster father. He painted my face with his bloody hands, and I'd never seen anything so beautiful. The sight of me in the mirror with blood on my face stayed with me throughout the years.

Every time I closed my eyes, it brought me back to that moment, a memory I've always been fond of. No one has ever protected me the way that he did. When I think of my childhood, few memories light up my face, but his bloody hands touching me is one that I've always cherished.

I was jealous of him—of the blood on his hands.

To say I was obsessed with death was an understatement.

The only thing that mattered to me was how I'd die. For years I mulled over it, and never once did I expect my death to be at the hands of someone I loved. Someone I took vows with and promised my forever to. My husband, the very man who vowed to protect me and love me, was taking the 'til death do us part' a little too literal.

Now once again, the question was replaying in my head. What would death be like? I was all too eager to experience it.

Would I go to heaven, or would I go to hell? Knowing myself, hell was more than likely the place I'd go. Fuck it. Maybe I'd have a dance with the devil while I'm there.

My abnormal fixation with death was the only thing giving me the strength to endure this moment. My body was numb, and I wished he'd make my death painful so I could go out feeling something. I'd been a shell of a person for so long that the lines between dying and living were becoming blurred.

If I die painfully, at least I'd know the feeling of being alive.

I didn't fight back against his grip on my throat. Why should I fight to save myself from an inevitable death that I've longed for? If I didn't die today, it would be tomorrow, or the next day… One of these days I was going to die, so I might as well make it today. It's as good as any.

I got exactly what I wanted, and now, I was going to die a happy woman. A stupid woman who signed her death warrant the day she laid eyes on the blond-haired, blue-eyed sinner.

My feet dangled beneath me. He had me pinned against the wall with both of his hands wrapped around my throat. I was giving him permission to kill me, but I wouldn't let him get away with it. He was signing his own death sentence just as much as mine. My head was becoming heavy, and it took every ounce of strength I had to scratch any part of flesh I could reach: his arms, his neck, his perfect face. I could feel his peeling flesh getting stuck underneath my fingernails, bringing a sinister smile to my lips.

I wasn't fighting against my death. I only needed his DNA.

Bright dots crept in, and my vision blurred until eventually, all I saw darkness.

Darkness.

This is it. This is how I die.

"I became insane, with long intervals of horrible sanity."
– Edgar Allen Poe

ONE

Lee

Don't do anything stupid.

Don't say anything stupid.

Don't speak unless spoken to.

I chanted the list of rules in my head like a mantra. I'd obeyed every single one like I always do, yet Sebastian was still as angry as he always was. The car ride is silent, and I already know what is to come once we arrive home. His actions on the way are always the tale indicator of what I could expect.

When he yelled, that meant he'd fuck me rough to get his anger out of his system, and then he'd move on.

Silence meant he'd use me as his punching bag, but it wouldn't be as bad. It would be tolerable, and that's what I preferred. Based on his silence, that's what I would be getting.

Tonight, my husband is going to add to my collection of bruises.

Sebastian never gives them time to heal before adding a new one, so I always seem to have bruises somewhere on my body.

This time, it's my arms that have been permanently bruised for weeks, which is why he chose a floor-length long sleeve dress for me to wear tonight. The dress was beautiful—blending hues of powder pink and made of velvet. I hated pink, and I looked like a Barbie doll wearing it, but it matched my nails and made him happy. My fingernails and toenails were always painted a shade of pink, but I learned my lesson early on about what happens when I try to go against him. It's just not worth it to end up with broken fingers again. And honestly, I think he likes me wearing pink because it makes me seem even more like a Barbie doll living in his fucked-up dollhouse.

Tonight was the first night in months I'd felt beautiful, and my dress was too pretty to get blood on it, so all I had wanted was to keep him happy.

The night had been fine until his boss, Sean, decided to get handsy. Obviously, I didn't ask him to touch me or give him any sign that I was interested, but I knew by now that everything was my fault. Anything that angered Sebastian was my fault, even if I had nothing to do with it. In this case, his boss touching my ass when he hugged me was all my fault.

If I would've pushed Sean's hand away, Sebastian would've been upset. So, I accepted the hug and smiled like a good wife, but it was never enough to appease him. It was a lose-lose situation. I look like a whore, and that's why his boss touched me. He'd told me himself that if I didn't look like temptation, then his boss would have never touched me. As I said, it's always my fault.

The closer we get to our house, the worse my nerves become. I should be used to his temper and my punishments by now, but I'm not. Can you ever really get used to being abused? I know what to expect, yet I still get nervous every time.

Will he take me by surprise, or will I see the first lash coming? He's unpredictable, and he never does the same thing multiple times in a row. Sometimes he'll lure me into a false sense of security until I let my guard down, and that's when he'll strike; other times, he'll jump me right away, and I'll see every blow coming. I prefer to watch his lashes that's coming at me. His element of surprise… I just hate it.

Our over-the-top, custom-built glasshouse comes into view. It's situated in the suburbs of the city, devoid of any neighbors. Part of me often feels that's intentional. There was a time when I loved our place. I basked in the security it gave me, but now it feels like my own version of hell.

Pulling into the driveaway, Seb parks inside the garage right next to my car. He'd bought me a brand-new car for our fourth wedding anniversary a few weeks ago, and I know it's equipped with a tracker, even though it's not necessary. He already keeps tabs on me, tracking my every move and even phone. But I guess tracking my car gives him further control over me; something that he seems to crave. I've tried leaving him before, escaping this hell, and that was the first time he'd beat me as severely as he could.

The night that changed everything for us. He'd warned me before that he'd beat our baby out of me if I ever left, and that was the first promise to me he'd ever kept. Clever bastard, this one. I was wheeled into the hospital even, where he claimed I was in a car accident, and that's it. No further questions were asked. But who would question the loving man who feeds the homeless in his free time, buys toys for underprivileged children, and literally saves lives? Oh, and let's not forget that he's the son of the chief of police and the grandson of a senator. He could kill me and get away with it. One day, I'm sure that's exactly what will become of me.

He could've cared for me in the privacy of our own home like he usually does since he's a *doctor*, but he needed to have witnesses as he played the role of the perfect husband. When the ER doctor confirmed I'd suffered a miscarriage, the bastard even teared up, and the nurses swooned over the grieving father, who was excited for our first child. He was a good liar, I give him that. The moment I healed though? He'd seen to it I got an IUD to prevent any further *mistakes* from happening. He'd made it clear that we weren't going to have children, and that was one thing we both agreed on. There was no way in hell I'd have the child of this monster.

Seb's words are as good as gold. To the outside world, he walks on water and is damn near God himself. Everyone worships him and his family.

To me, he's the devil. He's my tormentor, a sinner, and my husband.

Once he parks inside the garage, next to my car, he turns off the engine, climbing out of the car. I don't have permission to get out yet, so I remain in my seat. That was another lesson I'd learned early on. When I was with him, I wasn't allowed to open my door. Most women would think that's sweet, but not me. I still remember the first time I made that mistake, and I shudder at the memory. Something as simple as opening my car door set him off. Everything I do triggers him. I walk on eggshells around him daily, careful not to detonate the bomb that he is.

Sebastian opens my passenger door and holds his hand out to me. After removing my seatbelt, I place my hand in his, and he yanks me out of the car so roughly I could swear he pulled my arm out of its socket. Fuck. He's not even going to wait until we get inside.

In times like this, I hate living outside of the city and not having neighbors. He could do whatever he wanted to me; I'd scream until I coughed up blood, and no one would ever hear me. This has happened many times. I think that's the reason he chose this house. No witnesses.

There, in the dimly lit garage, he shoves me against the side of the car. With my front facing him, I'm able to anticipate his hand flying at me. He backhands me with his right hand, and even though I saw it coming, it still hurt like hell. My head snaps to the side, and instantly the taste of copper floods my mouth. I swallow the blood from my freshly cut lip. "Dammit, Lee! Why the fuck can't you listen?!" my beautiful monster screams in my face, and even when it's asked as a question, he doesn't expect an answer. In his depraved mind, he's convinced I have done something wrong, and nothing I'd say or do would change his mind otherwise.

"Is it your goal to fucking embarrass me? That's my fucking boss you were throwing yourself at, Lee!" He grabs a fistful of my hair and brings my body flush to his. "You're a fucking whore. Do you want him to fuck you? Are you that fucking needy for a cock?" He drags me inside the house by my hair, and instantly I can feel the burn in my scalp and the sting from the strands that are being ripped out.

"You're so fucking desperate you couldn't even wait until we came back home. If you needed a cock so badly, all you had to do was ask." He throws me on the couch, and I watch as he works quickly to remove his belt and free himself from his black slacks. "Suck it, whore." Gripping my hair tight once again, Seb yanks me off the couch and throws me down to my knees, shoving his cock into my face. He's already hard, and I can smell the perfume on him and see the remnants of red lipstick. My lips aren't painted in red lipstick, and I haven't sucked his dick tonight either.

Ironically, he calls me a whore, yet he had his dick sucked by someone else tonight. No doubt it was his assistant. I knew he'd been sleeping with her, likely since the first day she started working for him.

It was the night of my twenty-fourth birthday when I found out he was having an affair. I wanted to celebrate with him since he was working late that night, so I took dinner to his office. His office door was unlocked, and there on his desk, he was fucking her. Luckily for me, he didn't see me, and to this day, he still has no idea that I'm aware he's having an affair. Bastard.

Seb shoves himself in my mouth, and like the good whore he wants me to be, I take him down my throat. For a second, I contemplate biting his dick off but decide against it. He fucks my mouth ruthlessly and holds my head against his crotch, my nose touching his skin as his cock fills my throat. My eyes water as I gag and struggle for air, fighting against his tight grip on my head. He grabs my forearms roughly and yanks me up to my feet, then pushes me over the back of the couch so I'm bent at the waist. Lifting my dress, he pulls it over my head, trapping me in darkness with the thick velvet fabric over my head. My breathing quickens, and my other senses are now heightened. With rough fingers, he pushes my thong down my legs, spreads my ass cheeks, and I already know what's to come. He spits between my spread cheeks, his thumb spreading the saliva around my puckered hole, and then in an instant, he shoves his cock into my ass so roughly it knocks the air from my lungs. The stretch is painful, and my insides burn with the intrusion. It's so fucking painful I want to weep, but why should I give him the pleasure to see my tears? I should've been used to it by now, but how could I be? Does anyone ever get used to this? He has no mercy for me as he fucks my ass. I'm whimpering, biting my bottom lip so hard I taste blood. I refuse to let him hear me cry and beg.

My asshole stings from being stretched so full. I can feel the wetness between my legs, but I don't have to see to know that I am bleeding. Seb's fingers circle around my ass, wetting them in my blood before they trail down to my pussy and then he shoves four fingers inside of my dry entrance without warning. "You can get wet for someone else, but not for me? Come on, whore. Get me wet." But how can I? This is pain, not pleasure. My pussy is drier than a fucking desert because I am not aroused. I loathe his touch. At least in the bedroom, he'd lube me up before he fucked me.

Even though my vision is dark from having my dress wrapped around my head, I still close my eyes.

Luckily for me, Seb can never last long. Three more pumps into my asshole then he pulls out, removes my dress from my body, and shoves me down to my knees. He pumps his cock in his fist a few times then shoots his load all over my face, adding to the whore aesthetic. Pulling his pants up, he spits on me and wipes his mouth with the back of his left hand, looking down at me with pure disgust. "Clean yourself up, fucking whore." He strides away, leaving me kneeling on the floor— burning, bruised, and battered. I remain kneeling until I hear the sound of his office door closing from down the hall, then I quickly run up the stairs toward our bedroom.

A mirror never lies, they say. As I stare at my reflection in the mirror, I no longer recognize the person staring back at me. But did I ever truly recognize myself? I'm trying to remember a time in my life I truly felt like Lee but come up short. My black mascara is running down in streaks, my eyeliner is smudged, my mouth is bloody, my pink lipstick is smeared across my chin and cheeks, with *his* cum dripping down my face. What a fucking sight I am to behold.

I remove my ruined clothing with slow and steady fingers and step inside our large, marble walk-in shower. I turn the water on, not flinching at the hot temperature.

I'd taken longer than usual in the shower. The hot water feels so good on my bruises. The bathroom is the one place where Sebastian never bothers me, and day by day, it has become my sanctuary, my safe place. I wash my face over and over again until I feel clean enough. I am pretty careful while washing my body, not wanting to disturb my already fragile skin.

After showering, it takes another twenty minutes for me to complete my nighttime routine of moisturizing my freshly exfoliated and shaved skin, brushing and braiding my long blonde hair. Seb likes me looking my best, and that takes time. He knows that once I step out of the bathroom, I'll be the perfect wife he wants.

With freshly lotioned skin and a face full of serum, I step out of the bathroom and into our massive bedroom. I can't help the smile that spreads across my lips when I find our room empty. Even after I emerge out of the closet, dressed in a fresh pair of panties and a matching silk chemise, the room's still vacant.

Without that brutal monster in sight, I go to sleep alone, and for the first time in weeks I sleep through the night, uninterrupted, and dream of what it would be like to live any other life except my own.

TWO

Lee

t's been three weeks since the night of the charity gala for Sebastian's hospital.

We'd spent these last two weeks in perfect bliss. Not one cruel word was spoken, and for once, my bruises had time to heal.

But, as we all know, all good things come to an end sooner or later.

Sebastian had been under immense pressure at work, and when he lost one of his favorite patients, a nine-year-old girl with cancer, it set him off. He'd come home that night and took his frustration out on me. That was four nights ago.

Now we're back to our regular routine of abuse. He gets upset by something at work, or by his father telling him he's not good enough, and I'm the one to get the brunt of his anger. He considers me as his own personal punching bag, after all.

Sebastian has always lost his temper over the slightest thing, but these days, it only seems to get worse. I hate his family for triggering him so much. I'm a coward for allowing myself to live day after day in my own personal form of hell, living with the devil himself. *God, why am I so pathetic?*

How sad is it that I'd prefer this over living in bliss? When we're getting along, I never know what's going to happen next. At least when we're following our typical abuse cycle, I know what to expect and when.

After being bruise-free for two weeks, I'm back to having permanent scars, and I've returned to wearing long sleeves and applying concealer to the visible bruises on any bare part of my body.

I find it odd to have a bizarre fascination with blood. It's my twisted little kink—the warmth it oozes, the crimson color of it. But I don't enjoy bleeding from the hands of my husband. I should be used to pain and bleeding, given the life I've lived. I should hate blood because of it. I'm used to receiving pain, both physically and emotionally, so living with Sebastian isn't any different.

When he fucks me raw until I bleed and cry in agony, I want to curl up and take my last breaths in my own puddle of blood, and it disgusts me that I find blood so damn beautiful.

Something is severely wrong with me.

Sebastian uses objects on me. Anything he can get his hands on he'll force inside me. If I'm being honest, I'd prefer to be hit than to have him violently fuck me.

Is that even rape? Is he raping me every night? I often struggle, but then he tells me that he has a right to my body because we're married.

It is rape, right?

The lines between right and wrong have become so blurred while living in Sebastian's dollhouse of horrors.

Every day I feel myself drifting further and further away from sanity and the person I once knew myself to be.

Seb is changing too. Each day I see his anger take control over him more and more, and I know one of these days he'll end me. And I'm preparing for it. For my inevitable death.

You could say I'm even poking the bear to speed up the process.

I'm tired. So fucking tired.

Tired of living in the hell that I allowed myself to end up in.

Wondering if it's my karma for the sins of my past.

I must've sold my soul to the devil, and at this point, I'd give anything to be set free.

I hate Sebastian, and one day, he's going to pay for hurting me the way he has.

Love makes a person do crazy things.

Hate makes them do even crazier things. When fueled by hatred, you'd do the unthinkable—the unimaginable.

I've been walking the thin line between love and hate for far too long. Now there's no more gray area; there's only black. Darkness, fueled by my hate for him.

Hate for the man I married.

Hate for the life I was given.

Hate for myself for being so weak.

It's the only thing keeping me going these days.

The thought of my death brings a sadistic smile to my face. My thoughts keep taking me back to it as I sit at the nail salon in the pedicure chair, getting my nails and toes done, like I do every Saturday.

My best friend, Delilah, is beside me this week. We had lunch, and now we're getting our nails done. She picked a neon purple, and as usual, I chose pink.

Wearing pink fits the Barbie doll aesthetic. I'm the perfect little blonde Barbie doll wife for Seb, and he's the devil himself.

"I swear, you're the only girl I know who's so obsessed with pink," Delilah chirps, holding her hand out in front of her to admire her new neon purple gel nails. Her nails are always different colors, and I won't lie but I'm envious of her for it.

How fucking sad is that? It's a god damn nail polish, and here I am, too afraid to even try anything different because I know how Sebastian will react. God, I'm so pathetic I actually laugh at myself and at what has become of me.

Delilah raises her perfectly threaded eyebrows, looking over at me.

"Oh, girl, I hate pink," I answer with a smile, holding my hand out in front of me to inspect my freshly painted nails as I lose myself, remembering what happened the first time I disobeyed Sebastian.

"Where were you? I called, but you didn't answer." Seb's dark eyes stared at me from across the room. I jumped, startling in surprise. I didn't hear him when I entered the house. He was perched at the kitchen table, polishing his golf clubs to prepare for his colleagues' weekend golf trip.

"I'm sorry, Seb. I was at the nail salon, and then I went grocery shopping. My phone must've been on silent." I set the brown paper shopping bags on the kitchen island, cautiously unloading the bags of groceries. The darkness in his eyes chilled my skin, and I kept one eye on him as I put the items away in the fridge and pantry.

"Must've been on silent," he mocked with an amused laugh, clearly not believing a word I was saying.

"It won't happen again. I'm sorry." I turned to face him, watching his jaw clench as he stared at me.

"Good, you know I worry about you." He stood, walking toward me with a stoic expression. He took me in his arms and stole a kiss that left me dazed and breathless. His fingers raked over my hair, and a satisfied smile spread across his lips.

"Do you like it?" I asked, raising my own hands to smooth out my freshly colored hair. We decided, well, Seb decided that I should trim my hair and go a lighter shade of blonde. So, I did. I had an inch cut off, and my blonde hair was even blonder and fell into perfect layers.

He nodded his approval. "I like your hair." A pause, then his eyes followed the movements of my hands. "What's this? I told you to get pink." He grabbed my hand, inspecting my freshly painted cherry red nails. "I wanted to try something new. You know I don't even like pink." He shoved my hand away so quickly you'd think it burned him. "Only whores wear red. Are you a fucking whore, Lee?" I gasped, staring at him in disbelief. "Answer me. I said, are you a whore?" I didn't respond. I kept staring up at him speechless, watching his face contorting into something demonic. "Answer me!" he roared, the back of his hand catching me by surprise. With wide eyes, I stood there silently, my hands covering my now stinging cheek.

"N-no, Seb. I'm not a whore." My voice was so small, so pathetic. In a flash, I was on the floor on my back while he straddled my waist. His bruising grip on my wrist caused me to cry out. One hand wrapped around my wrist while the other squeezed my fingers together. Screams filled the air along with an audible pop. Those screams were mine. I was choking on my tears, my voice aching from screaming like a woman possessed.

"That'll teach you to do what the fuck I say next time. Do you understand?" I couldn't speak, and that angered him further. He left me for a second, and then I felt the coldness of the golf club connecting with my skin. "You are a dirty fucking whore." The cold club trailed underneath my dress, and I felt it against my core.

"I'm not a whore! Don't touch me!" My protests and screams were useless at that point.

Seconds later, my panties were gone, and the metal club was shoved inside of me, and he fucked me ruthlessly with it while I screamed and cried.

Meanwhile, he got off to my screams. Sebastian jerked himself off as he violated me with a golf club.

"Who wears red?" he asked calmly after he spilled his cum on my face.

"Whores! Whores wear red!" I screamed.

"Are you a whore?"

"No! No! No! I'm not a whore!" He stilled, his lips stretched across into a sinister grin, and then he removed the club from my aching pussy.

"You, my wife, will wear pink, and do as you're fucking told." He tossed the club next to my head. *"Clean yourself up, you dumb cunt."* He spat on me as if to show me how truly beneath him I was.

I lay there, on our kitchen floor, curled in a fetal position, my core bloody and aching, and my hand throbbing, as my ring and pinky finger were limp.

The first time he'd used something other than his dick to assault me.

The first time he'd broken my bones.

It was the first, but not the last time.

I snap out of the unwanted memory with tears in my eyes, taking in a deep inhale of oxygen into my greedy lungs.

"Lee? You okay?" Delilah's soft voice sounds full of worry. We'd already paid and were standing outside, but I was too lost in a flashback that I didn't even notice her dragging me from the chair. Losing track of time and getting lost in the past seems to happen a lot lately.

"Yeah, sorry, I'm fine." I shake the memory off, giving her a reassuring smile.

"You know that you can talk to me, right?" Her eyes showcase sincerity, and I believe her. God, I wish I could talk to her, tell her everything I've been keeping bottled up, but oh well. I can't make her a part of my fucked-up life.

"Thank you, but I'm fine." I smile to seal my lie. She nods, dropping the subject for now, and I appreciate the fact she didn't pressure me for any further answers. We resume our girl date without another thought or mention of Sebastian.

It's Friday night, and tonight we're going to Seb's parents' house for dinner. I'm not particularly fond of my in-laws, Nate and Lucille.

Actually, I hate them as much as I hate their son. His father doesn't know how to keep his eyes to himself, and his hands are out of control. He likes to touch me at any given chance. Sometimes it's a lingering hug, or he'll brush against my arm on purpose, and when no one's looking, his hands would meet my ass. I've never told Seb. It would be pointless to let him know how uncomfortable his father makes me. His mother is a different story. She's never liked me and has made that known since the day we met. She thinks I'm after her precious son's money, and despite our prenup, she still doesn't trust me.

Newsflash, you uptight plastic Botox bitch, I don't care about your son or his money.

Her hatred for me is humorous, considering we're similar. I've seen the bruises she tries to hide beneath her concealer and long clothing. After all, I do the exact same. I've witnessed the fights between her and Nate when they thought they were alone. And even Sebastian has told me stories from his childhood; how he would hide when his father would lose his temper and beat the crap out of his mother.

I remember Sebastian narrating the story of when he was six and tried to defend his mother for the first time. Nate had come home drunk off his ass and started hitting Lucille when she tried to get him to sober up. Poor six-year-old Sebastian was hiding in his room listening to his parents fight, and his mother crying in agony. Desperate to end their fight, he'd ran out of the room and begged his father to stop.

Of course, Nate didn't, and ended up throwing a vase at Seb instead of Lucille. Sebastian still has the scar on his forehead that required five stitches.

You'd think that after growing up in that type of environment, he'd want to break the cycle instead of allowing history to repeat itself.

He's turned into his abusive father, and I'm Lucille, a weak woman standing beside an abusive bastard.

After showering and putting my makeup on, I am now standing in our walk-in closet, dressed in only a thong and a strapless bra, debating on what to wear.

Before Sebastian speaks or enters the closet, I smell him. My nose tickles at the familiar scent of his cologne, mixed with the cheap perfume his assistant wears.

Instantly, I know he was with her tonight, and that's the reason he's coming home later than usual.

"Wear the green dress. It'll cover these nicely." He stands behind me, stroking his fingertips along the handprint bruise that covers my left bicep. His finger trails over the single bruise, like he's admiring his handiwork. *What a bastard.*

Maybe if I'm lucky and pray really hard, he'll get in a car accident one day on his way to work and die. That would be a dream come true.

"Yes, Seb," I mumble, taking the emerald dress from the hanger. I step into it, his fingertips brushing along my spine as he zips it up. "Thank you." I step into my black heels, turning to face him. He looks me over, nodding his approval.

"Let's go." And just like that, he walks away, without a second look at me, and I follow behind him, the feeling of unease churning in my belly.

It takes us forty minutes to get to his parents' house, and thankfully, the entire drive has been silent.

When we arrive, his parents greet him with wide smiles and big hugs. His mother greets me with a fake smile and a wave, which I return, because I'm a perfect wife. And as usual, his father greets me with a lingering hug that results in having my ass grabbed.

Gross.

Dinner goes by painfully slow. Per tradition, I sit there silently, pushing food around on my plate and taking a bite here and there while the three of them are chattering and laughing without a care in the world. They speak as if they've forgotten I am even in the room, minus his father, of course. I have always wondered why I have to attend these biweekly dinners. I'm never included in their conversations anyways, and surely, they wouldn't miss me if I don't attend. I make a mental note to fake an illness before next month's dinner if I'm still around by then.

Dinner's uneventful until Lucille makes the mistake of taking the wine bottle back to the kitchen instead of leaving it on the table for Nate. He immediately snaps at her with a "What the fuck do you think you're doing?" and it all goes downhill from there.

They fight, and my husband suffers the consequences of it. Despite being well educated and having achieved so much in his life, none of Sebastian's accomplishments are good enough for his father. He's the best doctor in the state, and still can't please his father.

While they are arguing and then making up over a game of football on TV, I slip into the kitchen to help Lucille clean up the dinner mess.

We take care of it in silence, but I feel her judgmental eyes steal glances at me and her huffs of annoyance.

Lucilla is the first to break our silence. "Don't upset him when you two get home tonight, he's always on edge."

My eyes snap to hers, and my brows pull together in a frown. "He's upset because of Nate. We were fine before we arrived." *Lie.* He's never fine. "We're the same, Lucille, and it's sad that you can't see that. We're both trapped in abusive marriages. Except, you encourage your son to act the way he does." Suddenly I have a loose tongue. I've never spoken to her so freely before.

"Excuse me?" she snaps. "Listen, little girl, my marriage is fine and is none of your damn business. You and you alone are the reason that my Sebby is so angry all the time, and if you tried to make his life easier, you wouldn't have to suffer the consequences." Right. Her precious son being an abusive dick is all my fault.

I scoff. "I know you don't like me, but don't assume his attitude is always my problem. His behavior issues come from you." I narrow my eyes, giving her a deadly glare. Silently patting myself on the back, I take a step closer to Lucille, grip her wrist, and yank up her sleeve to reveal the purple and black bruise on her forearm.

"We're the same, Lucille. This isn't on me." She pulls away from me, her blue eyes looking over my shoulder as a slow smirk forms on her overly injected lips.

This is not good. My stomach drops at the sight of her smirk.

I don't have to turn around to know that Sebastian's standing right behind me.

Fuck.

I'll be in for it when we get home.

THREE

Lee

"**G**reat job today, everyone!" Delilah claps her hands, praising our students for our final class of the week. I've been missing more and more classes lately, and the classes I do attend are beginning to take a toll on my aching body. I'm exhausted all the time because I don't sleep at night anymore. I'm so afraid to sleep during the night ever since the huge fight we had the night we returned home from dinner at Sebastian's parents' house.

Sebastian didn't touch me when we got home like I expected him to. Instead, he waited until I was sound asleep in our bed. I should've slept with one eye open, but I was too exhausted. The smell of lighter fluid is what awoke me. My pajamas were damp with the liquid, and Sebastian sat stoic at the edge of the bed flipping a zappo.

That was two weeks ago, and I've been terrified to sleep since then. Afraid that he will fulfill his promise of lighting my ass on fire.

Lucille convinced him that I'm a liability, that I'm going to leave him and ruin his reputation with accusations of being abused. He's been so paranoid that he's watching my every move and calling me every second that he's not in surgery, which has been a lot lately.

After the last of the students clear out of our classroom, I close the door and take Delilah by the arm, dragging her toward my desk in the corner of the studio, maybe a little too roughly.

"Did you mean it when you said I could talk to you about anything?" It's been a few weeks since that day at the nail salon when I lost myself in memories, and she had noticed that. We haven't been out together since that day because Sebastian wouldn't allow it. He doesn't like for me to have friends, and I know it's because he fears that I would either tell someone about the abuse or that someone would see the bruises that permanently decorate my body. Little does he know, Delilah has already seen the bruises he's left behind many times.

"Yes, of course. Are you okay?" Her eyes shine with kindness, and I know I can trust her. She's my only friend, the only one that I have to trust. "God, Lee, you're scaring me. What's going on? Is it about Seb?" *Yes. Everything's about him. Always.*

My body still aches from last night's beating. I don't remember what caused our fight, but we'd gotten into an argument, and well, now I have a black eye that, thankfully, the concealer is covering along with a split lip. I needed to get away from him, so I went to work today, lying to everyone who asked what happened to my face. They didn't need to know that my husband used me as a punching bag. Delilah was the only one who had seen past my lies and knew the real source of my injuries.

"Listen, you can't say or do anything, not yet." I inhale, taking a large sealed manila envelope from my purse and handing it to her. "Don't open it, don't tell anyone you have it, don't do anything." She takes the folder from my hands shakily, looking at me with wide, fearful eyes.

"What's in there, Lee? What's going on?"

"If anything happens to me, I need you to give this to the police."

"What! What's going to happen to you? Are you in danger? Do we need to go to the police right now?" Too many questions, but sadly, I can't answer either of them.

"No, I can't. But please promise me that you'll take this to the police if anything happens to me."

"Like what, Lee?" I sigh, collapsing down into my seat.

"If I disappear"—her eyes widen—"or if I turn up missing or dead, you must take this to the police. Don't ask questions, just promise me." I straighten up with a frown, wiping the tears away from her face that streams down her cheeks. She wraps her arms around me and hugs me tightly, and even though the bruises hurt, I squeeze her gently. *This might be our last hug, who knows.*

"I promise, Lee. Please, let me help you if you're in danger."

"You can't help me. Thank you for being a great friend."

The words that tumble out of my mouth are true. No one can help me or save me from that monster. Only I can help myself, and that's what I'm doing.

Sebastian's anger is getting unbridled with every passing day. His abuse has become a daily occurrence. Maybe it's my fault, because lately, I seem to have found my urge to fight back. And fight back, I do.

I'm going to fight him until I die. A death that I'm anxiously waiting for, and knowing it's getting closer with each passing day, has me even more anxious than usual.

Death is calling for me. I can taste it.

"Happy birthday, honey." Sebastian's lips press against my temple. "You look beautiful." He takes my hand in his and spins me around, fully admiring my attire for the evening. I'm wearing a floor-length navy satin dress that accentuates every curve and dip in my body perfectly. The formfitting dress is tighter than any dress I'd usually wear, and the crisscross straps leave my back exposed. I'd worried it would be too revealing for Seb or not the right color, but to my surprise, he likes it. He'd taken me shopping last week, and when I stepped out of the dressing room wearing this dress, I expected to find rage brewing in his eyes. Instead, I found lust, and that's the same way he's looking at me right now. With pure lust in his devilish blue eyes. My heart skips a beat at the way he's looking at me, and I can't yet tell if that's a good thing or not.

Today is my twenty-sixth birthday, and he's taking me to a fancy new restaurant for dinner in the next town over. The restaurant is two hours away, so he got us a hotel room for the weekend.

I handed the folder of evidence to Delilah on Monday. Today is Friday, and all week long, Sebastian's been spoiling me. He's been surprising me with endless gifts, morning breakfasts, and peppers me with kisses every now and then. If I didn't know any better, I'd say he's showing me *affection*. But I know him too well to fall for his nice guy facade. It's only a matter of time until he flies into a rage, and I'm the one who'll suffer once his inner demon is unleashed. But for now, I'm going to enjoy a weekend away and being worshipped. I deserve it. I'm walking on eggshells, but I'll try and enjoy it for as long as possible. I'd like to have one final good memory together before everything goes to shit.

Seb is dressed in a navy suit that matches my dress, and as usual, he looks flawless with minimal effort. Sebastian Riley has the looks to sweep any girl off their feet. I would know because that's exactly what he did to me.

"Happy twenty-first birthday, bitch!" Zoe, my best friend, yelled over the loud music. I'd never been much of a drinker and didn't want to celebrate tonight, but after practically begging me to come out, along with a few of our other friends from Ciel, I gave in. A group of us went out to the new club in town to celebrate my birthday.

"Drink up! You're drinking until you black out." Lola giggled, shoving another shot of tequila in my hand. I already felt tipsy enough, but that didn't stop me from downing the shot of amber liquid and relishing in the warmth it provided my body.

I'd lost count of how many shots we'd taken and was drunker than I'd ever been, but I still knew the exact moment he entered the club. The air shifted, and my skin tingled, not from the tequila but from the feeling of sharing the same space as him. He dominated any room he entered. Even in the crowd of people, my eyes were able to find him instantly.

As if he could sense me gawking at him from across the room, he looked up, and our eyes met. Out of everyone in the building, our eyes were drawn together like magnets. A spark of electricity shot through my veins as I watched a slow, sultry grin form on his lips. My mind wandered to places it shouldn't, and then I was thinking what it would be like to have those lips on mine.

"Your hot stalker is here." Zoe chuckled, nudging me forward, closer to him. "Go talk to him!" I rolled my eyes and took the drink from her hands. They'd been teasing me for far too long about the mystery man who always appeared at my recitals with a bouquet of red roses addressed to me. He never said a word. He'd watch me dance, bring the flowers backstage, and leave before I even had a chance to thank him or introduce myself. I saw him all the time, and every single time he looked at me with those arctic eyes, he stole the air from my lungs. I didn't have the heart to tell him how much I hated roses.

"Okay, I will!" I announced, shocking my friends as well as myself. Zoe

looked at me with wide eyes, clearly not having expected that I would agree. I've asked around about him, but none of the other girls knew who he was. My friends called him my stalker.

My hot stalker, for whom I was crossing the room to talk to for the first time, hoping he wouldn't run away like he normally did.

With a smirk, his eyes raked down my body, causing an unfamiliar throb between my legs. This man was pure sex on legs. He was tall with broad shoulders and had a white dress shirt on that happened to be too tight around his muscular chest.

Oh God, I was already wet just from the sight of him.

"My friends think you're stalking me," I blurted out instantly, the tequila I consumed giving me the courage to speak to this beautiful stranger.

"Do you think I'm stalking you?" he rasped out smoothly with a hint of amusement. Holy fuck, even his voice was sexy as hell.

I lifted my left shoulder up in a shrug. "You seem to always be at my recitals," I accused. He didn't deny it. No, he just kept looking at me with a delicious smile that I wanted to lick off his face.

Woah, where were these thoughts coming from?

It was several pounding heartbeats later when he finally spoke. "When I see something I like, I make a point to continue seeing it and then claiming it." His fingertips stroked along my jawline, a shiver creeping down my spine. "And I like you, my little ballerina."

Three months later, I was married to Mr. Sex On Legs and was head over fucking heels in love, ignoring every single red flag.

"Where did you go just now?" Sebastian's voice pulls me away from my thoughts. He's standing behind me in the elevator; his arms wrapped securely around my waist.

"I was thinking about the night we met," I answer honestly, a small smile pulling at the corners of my lips. He kisses my temple, his fingertips trailing up and down my exposed back.

"You were wearing an awful gold minidress that you kept pulling down every few seconds because you hated being exposed. Your friends surrounded you, yet your smile never met your eyes. The only time you would dance and laugh was when you thought no one was watching. You were a girl who hated attention, yet you were the lead role in every recital. You'd lose yourself in dance but shy away when you realized people were watching. You danced for yourself, not for anyone else."

With wide eyes, I turn around in his arms to face him. Staring into his deep blue eyes, I gasp. The eyes that were staring back at me were the same eyes of the man I met at the club all those years ago—the man who made me fall in love on our second date.

"How hungry are you?" I ask breathlessly. I hadn't realized he'd noticed all those things about me or would even remember, but hearing him say those things about me melts me into a puddle right at his feet.

I am a red-blooded human, after all. It's okay to be turned on by the right words. Even if those words are coming from the devil.

"Right now, I'm only hungry for you." Sebastian picks me up and tosses me over his shoulder with a devilish grin, like I weighed nothing. In an instant, we are back inside of our hotel suite.

Sebastian lay me down on the bed and worships my body as he did years ago. He makes love to me, and for a night, I allow myself to forget about the devil hidden underneath those beautiful blue eyes.

Our weekend is spent tangled in the sheets and consumed with each other. We never make it to the restaurant we came here to try, the spa appointment he booked for us, or any other activities he planned. We drink wine, order room service, and explore each other's bodies fully. Sebastian behaved like a lover, not once raising his hand at me.

I am not foolish enough to forgive all the damage he's caused and all the shit he's put me through, or believe that he could ever change. But for a moment, for just a single moment, I want to forget and allow myself to have a good time before everything changes. I'm not overlooking his abuse, but for once, I deserve to have a good day. His kindness will not last; I know that. But temporarily, I'm going to be worshipped, and pretend that my husband loves me and that I love him.

After all, I'm great at pretending.

The weekend is indeed perfect. The perfect ending to our twisted love story. It's only a matter of time until our spell is broken and we're back to reality. I'm just waiting until we get home before I break our spell.

The weekend isn't about him or forgetting the shit he's done to me. It was about me, and me wanting to have one good moment before we're over. For once, I'll be selfish.

We spend the two-hour drive home laughing and sharing memories from our dating life, and discussing plans for our fifth wedding anniversary that is coming up in three months. It's humorous really. I'm planning a trip I know I won't be there to attend with this monster.

"Let's go to Bora Bora for two weeks," he suggests, intertwining our fingers and stroking the back of my hand with his thumb. I look over at him, expecting him to tell me he's joking or he's too busy, but all I see is a genuine smile that has lit up his eyes.

"I'd love that. Are you sure you can take time off of work?" *Lie*. I wouldn't like that. And I wouldn't be around much longer.

"Anything for you, my love." His eyes turn back to the rode, and we finish our drive in perfect peace. I don't know what's happening to him, but whatever it is, I am not complaining. We had a perfect weekend together.

When we arrive home, Seb takes my hand and helps me out of the car. He picks me up bridal style and carries me into the house while we both erupt in a fit of laughter. He doesn't get our luggage right away, instead, he carries me straight to our bedroom and tosses me on the bed, making love to me until I see stars.

It's after midnight now and we're laying on the floor in the living room in front of the fireplace. Tomorrow is Monday, but neither of us has made any attempt to move or get back to bed. He has work tomorrow, yet we're lying here, drunk on each other and sharing endless laughs and stealing glances. It's perfect.

I'm relishing in the warmth of being wrapped in Sebastian's arms. The arms I once found comfort in but haven't in a long time. I want to soak up this feeling for as long as possible and enjoy our bliss before the inevitable happens. "Sebastian…" I start, running lazy circles over his forearms.

"Hmm?" He kisses my temple, his lips trailing down to my jawline and brushing against my exposed shoulder.

With a deep breath, I give myself encouragement to ruin our moment.

"I want you to stop sleeping with Sara," I blurt out and hold my breath, not knowing how he will react. We'd never talked about his affair, and I don't think he's even aware that I know, but I've turned a blind eye to it long enough. Am I a total idiot for bringing it up now of all times when we're getting along? Abso-fucking-lutely.

His body stills underneath me, his breathing slow and steady. He doesn't deny it; his fingertips continue stroking over my bare skin. "How did you know?" he pries. I pull away from his grip, covering myself with the blanket, and turn to face him.

"I've known for a while. You weren't very discreet about it, and I've seen you two together." Assessing me silently, his eyes never leave mine. "Do you love her?"

"That's enough, Lee," he speaks through clenched teeth, and I know I'm provoking an angry bull, but I can't stop. Not until I get the outcome I am hoping for.

"No, I want to know. Do you love her?"

"It's just sex." I feel nothing hearing him admit his affair to my face. I've had enough time to deal, and now I feel nothing. No anger or resentment toward Seb or his mistress.

"Why? You get sex from me anytime you want. With or without my consent," I snap, crossing my arms over my chest. A loud, unpleasant snicker leaves his mouth. The bastard fucking laughs in my face.

"You are my wife. Do you think I need your permission to fuck what belongs to me?" He cups my bare pussy that's still wet from his cum.

"It's rape. All those times you fucked me until I bled, and I begged you to stop, all those times you shoved objects inside me, it's fucking rape!" That does the trick. Seb's like a rubber band that I keep pulling on, and soon he'll break and snap at me.

"Watch your fucking mouth," he growls. "Don't forget who the fuck you're talking to." I open my mouth to argue, but my words are cut off by him grabbing my jaw in a vise grip and bringing me nose to nose with him. "Is this what you want to talk about right now? The fact I like to fuck Sara? Do you want to hear all the things that she likes?" He grips my jaw tighter, and I know I'll have a bruise. "She gets so fucking wet when I kiss her neck. She's a little loose, her pussy isn't nearly as tight as yours is, and she's not as sweet as you. But she has a warm body and gets me off. Don't worry, I use condoms. My cum is only meant for you." He shoves me away, looking at me in complete disgust.

Yes. He's angry and giving me exactly what I want. "How would you like it if I had an affair? If I let someone else kiss my neck and let them fuck my tight pussy that you love so much? Taste how sweet I am and feel how wet I can get?"

"Shut the fuck up now, Lee. I'm not playing around!" Sebastian yells, but I keep fucking pushing because I do have a death wish.

"What if someone else kissed that spot on my thighs that gives me goosebumps?"

"You fucking bitch!" In a flash, I'm on my stomach face down, his hands tangled in my hair. He straddles me as he pulls my head back toward him. "You fucking cunt can never keep your god damn mouth shut." He smashes my head down into the carpet, one hand holding me while the other delivering blow after blow to any part of my body he can reach. I reach a hand back and claw at his thighs, feeling his skin collect underneath my fingernails. He roars, stopping his assault and removing his body from me. With him away from me momentarily, I'm able to stand and run up the stairs, noticing the blood on my fingertips from scratching him.

Once I reach our bedroom, I lock the door and run to our closet, shutting myself inside. With all the strength I can muster in my throbbing body, I shove the dresser in front of the closet door, blocking myself inside. Pounding comes from the bedroom, and I know it would only take mere minutes for him to break down the door. Sebastian yells inaudible words as I busy myself with dressing. My heart's beating so rapidly I could hear it. My head is pounding, my body aches terribly, and in the back of my mind, I know this is it. This is our final fight. All that we are is ending tonight.

"Lee!" Sebastian's voice and bangs from outside the closet startle me. I jump, my hands flying to my mouth to muffle the scream when the dresser comes crashing down, and the door flies open. I've never seen him as angry as he is at this moment. He stands in the doorway fuming, his fists clenched at his sides, and his chest rising and falling quickly. His skin is flushed red, and his usually blue eyes are now black as sin.

I don't cry. I don't beg. I don't plead. He doesn't deserve my words or my tears. Not when his fist connects with my face, or when he gut-punches me and takes the air from my lungs, and not when he pins me against our bedroom wall and holds me off my feet by my throat. "Why do you make me do this to you, huh?! I love you, Lee. Yet you continue to fucking push me, and now look!" he yells, beads of saliva hitting my face as he yells. His grip on my neck is tightening. I kick my legs and scratch at his hands and arms, any piece of him I could get my hands on. This isn't what I intended. I didn't expect my death like this.

They say when you die, your life flashes before your eyes. That's how I know I'm dying. My life plays in my head like a slideshow, and I can see all the times in my life that I've been happy, which hasn't been often. I have regrets for how I've lived my life—all of the things I once wanted to know and do but now will never get to. The day I met Sebastian was the day I signed my death warrant. There was never any chance of walking away from him, not then and not now. Was this my fate all along? To die at the hands of someone I loved?

I stare into the eyes of the man I once loved and see a stranger staring back at me. An unfamiliar monster, not my husband who once made me chicken soup when I was sick and spoon-fed me, or the man that carried me for miles when our car broke down and my feet ached from my shoes, or the man that would massage my tired bloody feet when I'd push myself to dance too hard. No, that wasn't the man that was staring back at me. The cold emotionless eyes I stare into belongs to the man who beat me into a miscarriage, who broke two of my fingers when I didn't get the nail color he chose, who threw me down the stairs because I complained about wearing the shoes he liked, but I could hardly walk in; who beat me without mercy for nearly five years.

Honestly, I'm surprised I've been alive this long. I'd thought I would've died long ago by his hand, but here I am. I lived for almost five years being subjected to his abuse, only to die when he decided it was time for me to.

He wasn't God, and he didn't get to decide when I'd die. Yet, here he was, making that decision. We've been dancing on a thin line between life and death for years. At any moment, he could've taken my life, and I guess he chose now to take it. But I was ready for it. I've been waiting for the moment when he went too far and did something he'd never be able to come back from. Would he even care that I'm gone? Not likely. I would guess that he'd be grateful he didn't have to deal with me anymore, and he could find someone else to replace me. Perhaps he can marry Sara next, and she can deal with his shit. Fuck Sara; she can have my bastard of a husband.

Sebastian loves control. He craves it, and he needs it. Everything he does, he's in complete control. The only reason he hasn't killed me in the past is that he didn't want to. And now, he wants to. I can see it in his eyes.

The lights are dimming. Darkness is clouding my already blurry vision, my head too fuzzy for me to be able to hear what he's saying to me. I can see his lips moving but can't tell what he's saying. I'm sure it's profanities. It always is when he's angry. My body feels limp and weightless, my eyelids too heavy to keep open. I'm in a plane of total and utter numbness.

Cold.

This isn't how I planned it.

I'm so cold.

I'm floating.

Down, down, down.

I stare into his cold blue eyes until I reach the abyss.

The darkness of meeting my death.

I'm finally free.

FOUR

Sebastian

Lee is gone.

I could feel the difference in the air. The emptiness. The cold.

Gone is the sweet scent of her perfume that greets me every morning I open my eyes. Her honey vanilla scent has been replaced, and the smell of rust has taken her place.

I'm lying face down on my pillow, and when I extend my hand to reach for her, my hand touches her cold pillow.

Gone is the warmth her presence brings, that always made our house feel like a home.

She's gone. And emptiness is her replacement.

But something's wrong.

My hands itch. My arms itch. My chest itches.

Why am I itching so much?

Something isn't right.

I figure that out the moment I roll over onto my back, examine my hands that have been clawed up. I scratch at the itchy, dry blood.

I press the heels of my palms into my eyes and scrub away at my distorted vision, blinking several times to clear the fog.

With clear eyes, I see the scene in our bedroom and gasp.

I'm staring at the bloody mess that awaits me.

Images from last night play in my head on repeat like a slideshow.

My hands around her delicate throat. Warm blood on my hands. Scratches down my arms and chest that fucking itch.

I can still feel the throbbing vein in her neck on my fingers, and the exact moment the throbbing stopped, and cloudy blue eyes stared back at me.

My wife is dead.

I knew it the second I woke up this morning.

My wife is dead.

And I killed her.

But there are questions on the tip of my tongue that no one seems interested in.

Where is her body?

Where did the blood come from?

She wasn't bleeding during our fight.

I believe I killed her, I know I killed her, and that's why I didn't fight when I was arrested and read my rights... but they're wrong about one thing.

I didn't make her bleed.

"You will surprise yourself one day by havingthe strength to so something you never thought you could."
— Smita Maharana

FIVE

Tate

nother day.

A cheerful morning awaits me, along with the bitter aroma of coffee in the air. Every morning, it's the aroma of Folgers coffee and fresh breakfast that wakes me, a breakfast I don't have to prepare. It calls to me like a siren, and before I know it, I'm floating down the hallway, drooling over the bacon that I know I'll find. Cassie, my roommate, is awake before me every morning. While I prefer to sleep in, she likes to be productive way too early in the morning.

As I walk into our small kitchen, I notice the fresh bouquet of flowers in the crystal vase she bought from the thrift store. I hate flowers; they're a waste of money. They're pretty for a moment, then they die. However, Cassie loves them, so there's always a fresh bouquet somewhere in the house. It's familiar and comfortable for me. The small things she does make our shitty apartment seem less shitty and more like home.

"Good morning, sunshine!" She directs her bright smile at me just as she sets a plate of hot breakfast in my hands. She's always trying new diets and experimenting with new recipes to make things healthier.

Today, it appears to be French toast, and knowing her, I know it's not made with bread. I've learned to stop questioning her food choices because she's a bomb-ass cook, no matter how weird things can get.

"Thanks," I respond with a smile, setting my plate on the counter while I pour myself a cup of coffee. I take my plate and mug to sit at our small two-seater kitchen table.

"It's egg loaf French toast. Keto," she explains, taking her plate and sitting across from me at our table. Keto, paleo, vegan, low calorie, whatever other diets are out there, she's always on a new one every week. Cassie doesn't have a pound on her to lose. She's in better shape than I am and stays active, but she sure does enjoy dieting. She struggles with an eating disorder, so as bizarre as her diets might be, I'd never say anything to her about it.

I love Cassie. She's my best friend and the only one I've ever felt comfortable enough to be myself around. We're complete opposites. She often jokes that she's the light to my darkness, and I guess it's true. She's a bubbly, happy, go-lucky blonde, and I'm the dark, gloomy one with hair as black as night and clothing to match.

"Stop getting lost in your head and join the land of the living," she teases, throwing a piece of bacon at me that I fetch from my hair and stick in my mouth, flipping her off with a smile. She knows that I'm not much of a talker. I prefer my own company rather than the company of others. I'm not a people person, never have been, and in this life, never will be.

"I was actually thinking that you should never make this again." I gesture to my plate of half-eaten egg mystery loaf. Even drenched in syrup, it tastes like death. Guess, not every new recipe experiment she makes can be great.

"Fuck right off. It's low carb and low calorie." She giggles, brushing her shoulder-length blonde hair behind her ears.

"Well, next time, use bread." I stand up from the table, take my plate with me, and scrape the remaining food into the trash. No way in hell I'm saving this as leftovers. "Are you working tonight?" I ask, loading my plate into the dishwasher along with the pile of dishes that consume our counters from her cooking breakfast. Cassie can cook, but she sure can't clean.

"Yeah, Jamie asked me to cover her shift. You can ride with me." She walks off toward her bedroom, leaving me to clean up the mess from her failed breakfast concoction.

Cassie and I have both worked and lived together for months now. We met during my interview, and ever since then, she's taken me under her wing and decided that we're friends, and we've been inseparable ever since. On my first night at work, I was glued to her side, and she taught me everything she knows. Now we're roommates, and she's the sister I never had. Crazy how someone can mean so much to you in a short amount of time.

Even with the walls I'd put up to protect myself, she bulldozed them all down. I'll forever be grateful for her.

"Cassie, let's go! We're going to be late!" It was truly amazing how this damn girl could take so long to get ready before work, only to get there and spend another hour getting ready.

"Hold your fucking panties, sunshine," she says, walking into the living room with both middle fingers in the air and a grin on her pink lips. We share a giggle, and arm in arm, we leave our apartment and make our way outside toward her car.

Our apartment building isn't anything fancy, but it's perfect for us, and it's become home. The only place I've ever truly felt comfortable and the only true home I've ever had. It's ours, and no one can take it from us. Even if it's run-down and could use a fresh coat of paint, it's our home.

The minute Cassie starts the car, she connects her phone to the Bluetooth. Joan Jett and the Blackhearts instantly blast from the speakers. We both sing our hearts out, and by the time we arrive at the club, I'm pumped up and ready to start my shift.

It's nine at night on a Monday, and I'm sitting in the dressing room with the other dancers doing my hair and makeup to get ready for my first set of the night. I know it'll be busy despite the fact it's a weekday.

Sinners is the most popular strip club in the city. It's not your typical strip club either. This place is upscale and has an elite client list four miles long, with an even longer waiting list. Every member must be thoroughly vetted and sponsored by an existing member. There are security guards everywhere to protect the dancers. We're not allowed to be touched; we can only be touched when the client has paid for it in the VIP rooms. Even then, security stands guard outside the door, ready to interfere if needed. Thankfully, it's never gotten to that point with me. All of the members are respectful and know the boundaries. If they ever did cross the line, they'd be at risk of losing their membership.

Yeah, I know. What type of strip club has memberships with monthly fees? Sinners.

As I said, it's not your typical strip club.

"Welcome Raven to the stage!" the MC announces, and the crowd goes wild with roaring cheers. Every time Dustin, the club's MC, introduces me, I get the same response. I'm an absolute crowd pleaser, a favorite for our clients.

Every night my makeup is the same. My eyeshadow is a dark smokey eye with winged eyeliner and a deep red lipstick, and I tie the lace masquerade mask around my eyes.

Again, as I said, Sinners isn't your typical strip club. All of the dancers wear a masquerade mask at all times, and when the clients enter, they wear theirs. We're never allowed to remove our masks, never to reveal our true selves. When you're here, you're someone else. That's partially why Sinners is as popular as it is.

Tonight, I'm dressed in red lace lingerie with black fishnet stockings that go up to my thighs and connects to my garter with a pair of red bottom stilettos. With applause from the crowd, I make my way to the stage as "Pour It Up" by Rihanna begins playing. Both men and women are seated in front of the stage, their complete attention on me when I wrap my hand around the pole. My body moves in perfect sync to the beat of the music. I swing on the pole and roll around the stage, all eyes on me, and never once do they stray. I hold them in a trance, all the while losing myself in the music and rolling my body against the pole.

I dance through two songs, and not once does my clothing slip. Another thing about Sinners—fully nude is not allowed on the main stage. The only way to see a dancer nude is to purchase a VIP room.

Our naked bodies are reserved only for those who pay the extra fee, and the strip show is only done by the girls comfortable enough to be fully nude, which not all of the dancers are, myself included.

"Hey, Raven, there's a request for you in VIP room six. Check in with Bobby when you're ready," Cecelia, the floor manager, says as soon as I exit the stage. Around here, we don't use our real names. We shed our names and true identities at the door the moment we step inside the darkness of Sinners. The name—Raven—was given to me on my first night because of my hair.

My raven-colored hair falls halfway down my back, and my bangs curtain my eyes. Finishing my look are my turquoise eyes, even brighter, paired with my pitch-black hair, making them almost neon and unreal.

The clients can request whichever dancer they want for their time in the VIP rooms, but they're given a list of rules and are made aware of what we will and will not do. Personally, when a client requests for me, they know I won't reveal my entire body to them. I don't like being nude, but they want to watch me dance anyway, and I like to put on a show. Sometimes they'll even pleasure themselves, which I don't mind. They get off to the sight of me dancing. I'd rather have them do it to themselves than try to touch me.

With a nod, I do as Cecelia says. I make my way to VIP room six, where Bobby, one of the bodyguards, is already standing outside the door, where he will remain until the client's appointment ends. "Hey, Raven, how's it going tonight?" he greets me with a smile. He's always friendly, and I feel safe with him when I get to have him posted outside of my room for the VIP dances.

"Hi, Bobby. I'm tired but good. How's Meg?" His wife is seven months pregnant, and last week, Bobby told me about her massive swollen ankles and how her hormones made her a nightmare to live with.

"She's doing fine. Still wants to cut my balls off for knocking her up, though." He laughs, throwing his thumb over his shoulder. "You've got three guys in the room. They're aware of the rules and know what they're getting with you." I look up at him with wide eyes. I've never entertained more than one person at a time before. It's always been singles that requested me. Groups never request me because I wasn't willing to do even half of the things the other dancers are comfortable with doing.

"Are they regulars?" I ask, and he shakes his head.

"I don't believe so, but you know the drill. Press the alarm or holler if you need me. Good luck, kid." With a nod and a wave, I open the door and step inside, pulling apart the sheer curtains that greet me after stepping inside the door. The room is dim, matching the same ambience as the rest of the club. In the center of the room is a small stage with a pole; to the left, there's a red sectional against the wall, large enough to seat twelve. To the right of the stage is an open minibar. The members can make their own drinks or request to have a bartender in the room to make their drinks. Walking further into the room, I stop in my tracks when the first set of eyes connect with mine.

Deep chocolate eyes stare into mine, and time stands still. I pull my gaze from his intense stare, and next, I'm staring into emerald eyes that glow underneath his mask. Next was the final man in the room. The third set of eyes were a beautiful hazel. I took in the sight of all three men that stood before me, my eyebrows pulling together when I realized they wore full face masquerade masks; all that was visible was their eyes. Each set of eyes is completely captivating in its own way. They're all wearing suits, and they drip dominance with every passing second. The air in the room becomes thick and suddenly feels small and stuffy. My heart hammers in my chest. I've never felt intimidated by clients before, but I do standing in front of them. I feel small next to their large presence and appearance.

The three men are tall and tower over me; even wearing heels, they are much taller than me. Not so subtly, I let my eyes roam over their bodies, and I don't need to see them without their jackets to know they're muscular. These men are powerful, and here they stand in my room, requesting me specifically.

Weird.

We stand in a stare-off for who knows how long until the brown-eyed guy takes a seat and the other two follow his lead.

Hmm, okay, so brown eyes must be the alpha.

They sit in silence, their eyes following my every move and never once straying. With shaky legs and sweaty palms, I walk toward the stage just as the music begins. One of them must've turned it on, and I don't bother looking back to see which one is responsible for the music choice. I inhale a deep breath and let it out slowly, calming my nerves.

I've done this plenty of times over the last few months, yet standing in the presence of these three, I feel more nervous than I've ever been. Why? They're no different than any other man I've danced for.

That's a lie, and I know it. I knew they were different the moment our eyes connected. They are nothing like the men who've come here to watch me in the past. But I'm not going to let them see how much they affect me. No man will ever intimidate me again, and it's time I remember who the fuck I am and stop acting like a cowering child.

I am Tate fucking Dawson, and no man defines me or intimidates me. I have all the control over myself and my feelings.

I give myself a mental pat on the back for the internal pep talk.

With a slow smirk spreading across my lips, I straighten my posture and step onto the stage. "Bad Girlfriend" by Theory of a Deadman plays loudly as I grab the pole with my right hand, wrap my leg around it, and spin myself around, throwing my head back as I swing.

My body moves perfectly with the song as I give them the show they came here to see. Sliding down the pole, I land on my knees. I lean back toward my heels and throw my head back, running my hands down my body painfully slow. I could feel their intense eyes on me, and suddenly my body ignites, and I feel like a powerful fucking goddess as they devour and undress me with hungry eyes.

Their eyes warm my skin, and I want them to watch me for much longer than their allotted time.

Something sparked within me just from looking in their eyes when I entered the room. I could feel their inner darkness; it radiated off of them.

These men are not good. They are not the type that you'd bring home to meet your parents. No, these are the type of men that your parents warned you to stay far away from. They'll take whatever they want, whenever they want, without taking no for an answer; and they're in my room.

Of all the dancers available, they chose me. Why? That was the burning question.

I dance around the stage provocatively for song after song, losing myself in the music and losing track of time.

I feel so alive. I haven't felt this alive in months. So, why do I feel that way now? Why do I feel free and fucking alive because of them?

I lay on my back, high on euphoria, my chest rising and falling rapidly, my eyes snapping toward the now-empty couch.

They're gone, and I'm alone in the silence of the room.

I was so lost in dancing that I didn't realize the music had stopped, and the three men had already left. They didn't say anything; they only watched for who knows how long, then they left.

They set my soul on fire, then left me alone to burn in the flames.

With a smile on my face and a rapidly beating heart, I exit the room and go on with my night.

Dance after dance, client after client, I finish my night off, happy, and with newfound confidence.

And that night, I go to sleep thinking about the three guys with beautiful eyes that lit fire to my soul.

SIX

Tate

I t's Friday, and all week I've been dreaming of those three men.

I don't know what it was about them, but every night that I close my eyes, I see their eyes staring back at me, and I'm instantly reminded of the way I felt when they were in the room with me, their eyes trained solely on me. God, I'm like an obsessive teenage girl. It's ridiculous.

I'm beginning to think I need to get laid. That's got to be the reason why I can't stop thinking about them. It's my hormones that are speaking to me. Quite some time has passed since a man has touched me, so it's normal to get horny and have wet dreams... that's got to be the reason.

I'm lying on the couch, flipping through the channels aimlessly when Cassie comes in carrying a plate of what appears to be cookies, but knowing her, it's probably some vegan, gluten-free, sugar-free, low-carb, low-calorie version of a cookie that will taste like dirt. She holds the plate out toward me, and I shake my head, sneaking a peek at it. "If they're sugar-free, I don't want them," I deadpan. She giggles and shoves the plate toward me again.

"Try them. I've made a new recipe." With a roll of my eyes, I hesitantly take one of the still warm cookies from the plate and bite into it. There's a warm gooey chocolate explosion in my mouth from the first bite, and I welcome it, moaning at the deliciousness. After the week I've had, now wasn't the time to cut carbs. Not that there's anything wrong with those who diet or have special restrictions, but I need to be in a sugar coma.

I take another cookie from the plate and groan in relief when the caramel and chocolate meet my tastebuds. "These are your best ones yet."

Cassie gives herself a proud pat on the back and lays down opposite of me on the couch. I shift to allow her space, putting my hands behind my head. "Are you working tonight?" she asks while setting the plate of cookies on her stomach and shoveling them into her mouth.

"I'm not sure. I should, but I also really want to stay home and be a lazy fuck."

"Translation, you want to stay home and mope around because of those hot guys you were with on Monday night." My eyes shoot toward her and my brows pull together.

"First, I'm not moping. And two, I don't know that they're hot. In case you've forgotten, everyone wears a mask."

Cassie rolls her eyes and leans up on her elbows. "I heard a few of the other dancers talking about the group of mystery giants in the white masks. They said that they requested you, so I'm guessing they're the reason for your behavior. What happened in the room?" She wiggles her eyebrows at me, and I roll my eyes.

"Nothing, you already know my hard limits. I danced, and they left."

"That's it?"

"That's it." They have stolen a piece of my soul with the way they looked at me, but she didn't need to know that.

"Go to work. It's Friday night, and you know how much money you can make tonight." She has a point. Weekends are the busiest, and I always make the most on weekends. Yes, the club's still popular during the week, but weekends brought in much more money. I've worked every night so far this week, and I'm exhausted. My sleep schedule is more fucked up than usual, and I could desperately use a day off, but I could also use the money. It doesn't take me long to decide what to do. "You're right. I'll go for a couple of hours and take the weekend off." Cassie nods, taking the remote, and switches it to Netflix to play *Gilmore Girls*.

It's three in the morning, and I have been going nonstop ever since I started my shift. I've been spending my time between dancing on stage and in the VIP rooms. It seems to be guys night out because I've danced for several groups of men, something I've never done up until Monday when I danced for the three men with full face masks that looked at me like I was their next meal. Fuck. I can still feel the flutters in my stomach when I locked eyes with each of them.

I've just finished dancing for a bachelor party and am walking out of the room when Cecelia waves me down and hurriedly approaches me. "You're requested in room six. Go, and then take a break." A break. I love the sound of that. My feet ached, and I desperately needed to sit and chug at least a gallon of water.

As usual, Bobby was standing outside of VIP room six and greeted me with a smile and a quick "How are you doing tonight?" to which I returned the smile and said, "Good." Before entering the room, I adjust my mask to ensure it covers part of my face and ruffle my bangs.

The music blasted when I walked inside of the dim room. Each room had controls on the end table near the couch to allow clients to play whatever song they wanted and control the room's lights. The room could be as bright or as dark as each client wished.

This room has been darker than most of the rooms I've had tonight. The stage glows red, and right in front of the stage, I find my client sitting in a chair with his back toward me. But instantly I recognize the hairstyle. Tonight, his dirty blond hair looks something like a low man bun, and I know it's him before I even step on the stage and face him.

The most intense hazel eyes I've ever seen stare back at me, his face covered by the white mask, same as it was on Monday. My eyes do a quick scan of the room, only to find that we are alone. His friends aren't here this time.

He's close, too close, yet it doesn't make me uncomfortable. The last time he was here, he sat across the room on the couch beside his friends. Now he's alone and in my personal space—sitting right in front of the stage.

I grab the pole and wrap myself around it, our eyes locking with each other like magnets being drawn together.

Elbows resting on his knees, I take in his appearance just as his hazel eyes dance in mischief. He isn't wearing the suit that he'd worn last time. Tonight, he's dressed in all black. His jeans, t-shirt, leather jacket, and boots. All black. The only thing that stands out is his white mask that nearly glows in the dim room.

I dance while he watches me closely, his eyes never once straying from me. I've never wanted to remove a client's mask more than I do right now. I want to see the man behind the mask that has awakened my soul, whose eyes have taken control over my dreams all week long.

How is it that I feel this way about a stranger? I don't know him from Adam, yet I'm drawn to him more than I've ever been drawn to anyone before. I tell myself it's the mystery about him. His aura screams danger, and that both excites and terrifies me all the same.

God, what's wrong with me? He's a stranger. He could be utterly unattractive under that mask, but I have a feeling that's not the case with him. Something tells me that he'll be as good-looking as I imagine.

Hazel Eyes doesn't say anything, nor does he move. Not at first anyway. He sits there simply watching me, but each time I steal glances at him, I see the way his hungry gaze is following me around the stage.

I drop to all fours, giving him the perfect view of my ass that is covered only by the fishnet tights that go all the way up underneath my breasts. The black thong I'm wearing is irrelevant, and when I spread my knees further apart, I know he can see me. See all of me.

With a low smirk, I look over my shoulder at him, gasping when I see his position. He's leaned back in the chair with his knees spread wide and his massive cock in his hand.

What. The. Fuck. His cock is in his hand. I repeat, his cock is in his hand! He's busy cupping his balls with one hand while the other is thrusting up and down his shaft, and I'm entirely aware that I'm drooling and eyeing it like it's a science experiment.

Good god, that thing is huge.

My eyes have adjusted well enough to the dimness of the room that I can see every vein in his angry-looking cock. My mouth salivates at the delicious sight. His grip looks painfully tight as he pumps the massive piece of meat from thick root to tip, my lips parting involuntarily when a piece of metal in the tip of his cock catches my eye. This fucker has his dick pierced! Looks painful, but very fucking sexy. I wonder what it would feel like to have that metal bar dragging along the soft tissues of my insides or how it would feel hitting the back of my throat.

Slowly, I crawl to the edge of the stage, lean back on my elbows, and spread my legs wide to give him a pleasant view. I can feel my panties shift, and I know that he can see my bare pussy. This is not something I'd normally ever do, but I have a whole new level of confidence around him.

His eyes rake over my body, feeding the already burning flame within my core. His breathing is heavy and ragged as he jerks himself quicker. My tongue darts out to lick my lips, his hazel eyes following the movement. I am so fucking turned on right now and can already feel my wetness dampening my thin panties, knowing he'd likely be able to see my exposed parts glisten, but I don't care. For one night only, I'm stepping out of my comfort zone.

His masculine groans are feeding my hunger. His left hand squeezes his balls, his right using the beads of cum as lubricant to wet his shaft. I bet he'd taste like salt and silk underneath my tongue.

With a loud groan, he shoots thick cum out of his engorged purple head; the white delicacy covers his hand. I resist the urge to lick him clean and suck him dry. My throat's aching for a taste of him. I watch transfixed as he brings a cum-coated finger to his lips and sucks it clean.

Holy, sweet mother Mary. That's the hottest thing I've ever seen.

He uses a dry washcloth from the bar to clean himself up, then shoves his still semi-erect cock back into his pants. He doesn't say a single word to me, even as we end up in a stare-off, neither of us blinking while I wait for him to speak, wishing to hear his voice.

I'm too afraid to blink thinking he might vanish, and none of it would've been real. And I want him to be real. This is the first time I've ever felt truly alive, and I want to hold on to this feeling for as long as possible.

It only lasts so long because he breaks our spell.

He blinks. I blink. And like a thief in the night, he's gone. The only sign I have that he was here is the dirty towel beside the chair, my wet panties, and a racing heart.

"Tequila, please." I sit on the barstool in front of the now empty bar. It's five in the morning, and the club is now closed. The only ones that remain lingering behind is the staff.

Lin, the bartender, sets a shot of tequila in front of me, and I take it graciously, downing the amber liquor and welcoming the instant warmth. "I'm so fucking tired I could pass out right here," I groan, sliding the empty shot glass across the bar toward her.

"I feel you, girl. Tips are good, but fuck, I hate the weekends." I laugh, pull some money from my bag, and slide it across the bar toward her.

"I know, it's crazy here. But I'm going home now and passing the fuck out." I wave her goodbye and move to stand when Cassie comes into sight. She loops her arm with mine and practically drags me out of the club with a very dramatic groan.

"Let's hurry the fuck up before I fall asleep while driving." I roll my eyes at her and take her car keys.

"I'll drive." I throw my bag in the backseat and climb into the driver's seat and quickly start the engine.

"How were your VIP rooms tonight? I had two bachelor parties, and you know how those are." I nod because I do. I've never had a bachelor party in a VIP room before, but I have dealt with them on the main floor, and that is no fun. They always act like entitled pricks.

My mind is still stuck on the hazel-eyed man back inside room six who got himself off while watching me. Talk about an ego boost. He could've chosen another dancer tonight, but he chose me. I squeeze my thighs together at the image of him. My panties have been wet ever since I left the room.

"Earth to Tate! Talk to me. What happened tonight?" I look over at her, contemplating if I should tell her what happened or not. I wonder if she's ever had that experience before. Yes, I'd seen people touch themselves while I've performed, but never has it been a whole show like tonight. Hazel Eyes put on a show of his own. A show just for me.

Deciding to share, I start, "Tonight, in one of my rooms, this guy…" My words could use a pause, because I'm not a prude, but I don't want just to blurt out that I watched a guy come. He came on his hand then licked it. No rule states the clients can't pleasure themselves, so he isn't at risk of losing his membership. "He… he jerked off in the room." We look at each other, and instantly we both burst out in laughter.

"Lucky bitch! I haven't seen or had a dick in way too long! I'm a fucking virgin again," Cassie exhales dramatically.

"Me too! It's been way too damn long since I've been touched." Nine months, to be exact.

"You need to get a BOB or get laid."

"You're one to talk! You haven't been on a date in weeks, and I don't need a BOB." B.O.B. is battery operated boyfriend. A vibrator. I'm not against sex toys, but my fingers and the showerhead work just fine for me. For now, at least.

"Because I've been dating a bunch of losers, and I'm over it. At least I can make myself orgasm. These loser guys I've dated couldn't even do that much. I'm tired of teaching boys how to touch me and where my clit is," she says, reclining her seat back with a sigh. When Cassie and I first met, she was dating someone new every week. Now it's been at least two months since she's been out, and this is the longest I've ever known her to be without male attention. She's beautiful, and men have a way of gravitating naturally toward her.

Cassie shares her wild sex stories with me on the ride home, and the moment we step inside our apartment, she excuses herself to her bedroom. I hold back my laughter when I hear the faint buzz of her vibrator and her soft purrs. Silently giggling to myself, I strip out of my sweats that I'd changed into after work and go straight to the shower.

With my showerhead on the highest personal massage setting, I put it between my legs and let orgasm after orgasm rake through my body, all the while imagining hazel eyes and that magnificent pierced cock.

SEVEN

King

"**W**hat the fuck were you thinking?" Eli snaps, his fingers tangled in his hair as he aggressively pulls at the roots, his elbows resting on his desk.

"I wanted to see her." I shrug, while Rowen, who's sitting beside me, rolls his eyes, mumbling a "Dumbass" under his breath.

"Why? Why the fuck did you have to go there? We agreed to stay away!" Eli turns his attention toward his computer and types away, turning the monitor to face Rowen and me. On the monitor is the video recording from tonight at Sinners, in VIP room six. A grin spreads across my lips when I see my little butterfly appear on the screen, putting on a show just for me as I sit there, getting myself off. Fuck, she's a goddess. I haven't come that hard in a long fucking time. I wonder how hard I'd come inside of her tight little cunt. Better yet, I wonder if she'd let me go bare and fill her with my seed, then watch as she clenches and pushes it all out. Fuck. I'm getting hard just at the thought.

Rowen groans, turning the screen back around. "Fuck man, I don't want to watch you fuck yourself." I laugh and spread my legs, grabbing my crotch to adjust my growing dick.

"What were you doing there?" Eli asks, leaning back in his chair.

"What does it look like he's doing there?" Rowen mumbles with a shake of his head.

"I wanted to watch my butterfly dance. That's what I was doing there." She's been mine from the moment I saw that butterfly tattoo on the back of her left shoulder. She's mine, and I'm not going to let her fly away before I've had a chance to have my fun.

Eli shoots me a look that makes me roll my hazel-colored eyes, waving my hand through the air. "Save the speech. I'm not going to fuck up the plan. I just wanted to have a little bit of fun."

"It's happening tomorrow night. Rowen, set it up. And King, keep your fucking hands to yourself. I don't want to watch you getting off to her. You know what we have to do."

"That doesn't mean we can't have some fun in the meantime. And why the fuck were you watching her tonight?" I counter. Eli looks at me with a slow smirk spreading across his mouth.

This motherfucker. He wants to watch my butterfly just as much as I do, but that's okay. I don't mind sharing. Though I'm sure as fuck not going to be told what to do.

"Stop thinking with your dicks, both of you." Rowen stands from his seat, glaring at us. "Midnight tomorrow, room six, it's going down. Don't fuck it up, King." He scolds before walking out of the room. I stand, walk behind the desk, and stand next to where Eli's seated, watching the computer screen as he plays the footage from tonight at the club.

"Do you think Ro will be okay being near her?" he asks with a sigh, his shoulders slumping.

"He was near her Monday night when we all watched her dance."

"Yeah, and we had to leave because it was too much for him to be that close to her. I don't want to overwhelm him by having her around him."

"He'll be fine. She won't be here for long anyway, and then she won't be a problem anymore," I say, choosing not to give any further pushback. The truth is, I'm worried about Rowen being near my little butterfly. Oh well. If it ends up being a disaster, I hope I'll at least get to feel her warm body wrapped around me first.

We're only keeping her for a couple of days, and then we are to give her away. It would be easy. Or at least I hope.

Who am I kidding? I knew from the moment I set eyes on the raven-haired beauty that it wouldn't be easy to let her go.

Fuck. We were all going to be fucked.

I could already tell she could be the undoing of all three of us.

EIGHT

Rowen

There's no such thing as a coincidence.

It wasn't a coincidence that *she* ended up working at Sinners, and it wasn't a coincidence that we ended up in a VIP room with her Monday night. And in less than twenty-four hours, she'll be coming home with us. Sharing the same space as me… again.

She came back into my life after being warned not to, and she didn't even recognize me, but soon she will. And she'll regret ever stepping foot in this city again.

Our city.

I'd never forget those big blue eyes; how could she forget mine?

Her hair color may be different, but I knew it was her the moment I saw those eyes. Her eyes—as bright and clear as a turquoise ocean. One look was all it took, and I knew it was her. The universe fucked me over and put her back into my life. The girl who made me break every single promise that I ever made to her before I ruined her.

I ruined her and sent her running far away from me.

When we locked eyes on Monday night, her lips parted, and I

thought she recognized me, my eyes, but the spark of recognition never came. It pissed me the fuck off. I know I was being irrational and temperamental by thinking that after all these years, she'd miraculously recognize me. I'm a fool for thinking that would happen, but that didn't stop me from being angry about it.

I had to sit there with my brothers, watching the girl I ruined, dance around a fucking pole and live carefree. I hated the way her ocean eyes were able to calm the storm brewing in my mind and get me hard. She had no fucking right to have any effect over me, not after what I did to her. And my traitorous cock had no fucking right to get hard seeing her nearly naked, dancing around seductively.

I had to leave. Her presence was suffocating.

After I left the VIP room, I'd grabbed one of the dancers and took her to a backroom and fucked her, hoping to fuck the blue-eyed girl out of my mind.

That didn't work.

If anything, it's made my obsession worse. I've spent countless hours in Eli's office watching the security cams from Sinners, watching her as she dances around nearly naked for disgusting fucks who don't deserve her time. Even from a computer screen and miles away, she's calling to me like a siren… and little does she know, I'm going to soon answer that call.

I'd be a liar if I claim that her not recognizing me doesn't hurt.

But that's okay, because she soon will.

The ocean-eyed girl took something from me years ago that I'll never get back.

Her face haunts my dreams at night.

I see her face when I think of every fucked up and painful thing that has happened in my past.

Thirteen years ago, I ruined her, and she promised never to return home, yet here she is, acting as if she didn't make a promise to me. The game is on, hellion. You broke your promise, and now I'll keep mine.

Ready or not, here I come.

NINE

Tate

Time is going by painfully slow tonight.

Most nights seem to speed by, but this night is going so slow and feels as if it'll never end.

I've done four lap dances, two VIP rooms, and have been on stage twice, and it's still only half past eleven.

Fuck my life and my aching feet.

I wasn't supposed to work this weekend, but one of the dancers called me and asked me to cover for her because her kid had caught the flu. She's a single mom, so I agreed. Now here I am. Working my sixth day in a row when all I want is to desperately climb into bed and sleep for a week straight.

Don't get me wrong, I enjoy working. Dancing has always been an important part of my life and I enjoy my job, but sometimes I need a break. Do I plan to be a stripper forever? No. But until I figure out what I want to do, this is it. For the first time in my life, I have control over my future and the freedom that I've always longed for. I'm not worried about the future; I'm living in the present and enjoying every fucking second of it.

The money at Sinners is good, and since I'm not a lavish spender, I have built a comfortable savings account to survive for a couple of months. Having financial security is important to me. I've been at the lowest of lows and highest of highs, and I'll never go back to that. To the person I was before.

Cecelia found me a few minutes ago to tell me I had another VIP dance, and I've been taking my time walking across the club to the VIP rooms.

Tonight, my ass is a little more covered. I'm wearing a sheer red baby doll chemise that makes my already incredible tits look even better, and a matching red thong underneath. My stilettos are black, and I look like a sexy housewife that any man would be lucky to come home to and have his way with.

My VIP dance is in room six. The area I've been thinking about nonstop.

As I approach the room, the first thing I notice is that there's not a security guard standing in front. It's busy and we're short-staffed, so I don't stress too much about it. Security will be by soon, it'll be fine. Cecelia probably hasn't told them that there are clients in this room yet.

Knowing security will be here soon and that I have a panic button if needed, I walk inside the room, gasping when I discover the room is nearly pitch black. The music is already playing loudly and the only light is a faint soft yellow glow from the stage that illuminates the pole. An eerie feeling creeps down my spine and makes my skin crawl. The ominous feel of the room has me on edge.

With a deep breath to steady my nerves, I put one foot in front of the other until I reach the stage. I've been in this room dozens of times; I know my way around even in the dark with only a soft glow to guide me. The room is too dark to tell if anyone is here yet, so I can only assume I'm not alone.

Reaching the stage, I lift my foot ready to step onto the platform just as something is placed over my head, and I'm enclosed in complete darkness, the faint light of the stage now gone. My back is pressed against a hard warm body and a hand covers my mouth.

Fuck. Fuck. Fuck.

I kick my foot back, the pointed heel of my shoe stabbing into the shin of the person behind me. The man grunts, but doesn't release his grip from me. It only causes him to tighten his hand around my mouth. He's squeezing my jaw so tightly that I can't scream or bite. My heartbeat quickens as fear sets in. The music fades as the sound of my heartbeat becomes my sole focus.

He found me.

I scratch at the hands of the fucker that's manhandling me, only to have my arms jerked painfully behind my back. He holds my wrists together effortlessly with one hand. With my arms behind me, he eases his grip and slides his hand around my small waist, pressing me tightly against his chest so that my arms are pinned and there's no chance of moving.

My body is lifted from the ground, so I kick and continue kicking. I know I land a good few kicks, but he doesn't falter. He's carrying me, and when I feel the cold air hit my skin, my body goes rigid.

I can hear cars in the distance, so I know we're outside. Whoever the fuck just kidnapped me is silent. I hear heavy footsteps, but not a word is spoken.

What the actual fuck is going on here? This can't be happening. I can't be someone's prisoner... not again. Fear encompasses my nerves and my mind goes to those dark places, wondering who the fuck has taken me. What do they want with me?

Surely, they can't get very far, right? There must be someone outside witnessing this, or someone from the club has to notice that I'm gone... right?

Fear of the unknown has me shaking uncontrollably, and I'm all too aware of the fact I'm barely clothed.

Without being able to speak or see, my hearing is heightened. I hear a car door open and then I'm set down on my feet, but a rough calloused hand on my shoulder and the hand over my mouth prevents me from being able to run. "I'll remove my hand, but don't scream. Nod if you understand," a deep voice says against my ear, sending shivers down my spine and leaving goosebumps on my exposed flesh.

Quickly I nod, and just as he said, he removes his hand from my mouth. I don't move, just stand there shivering with god-knows-what over my head and stay completely still while my heart's beating rapidly in my chest. The hand that was on my mouth is now resting on my back, and I shift from his touch just as I'm shoved forward.

I fall with a squeal, and a second set of hands grabs me and pulls me toward another warm body, sitting me on a lap. A mans lap no doubt. My back is against his chest, and his hands are wrapped tightly around my waist, pinning my arms down to my sides. The door closes, and I jerk sideways when the car hurriedly speeds away.

I feel like my heart is galloping in my chest, and I'm hyperventilating, choking on my sobs.

Holy fuck. These fucks kidnapped me and are taking me away from the club.

"It's okay, my little butterfly," a second voice whispers in my ear, rough fingertips tracing over the butterfly tattoo on the back of my left shoulder. I still and tense in his grip, his hand flattening over my stomach as he holds me securely on his lap. I wriggle, hoping he'll loosen his grip on me or set me down on the seat.

No chance. Instead, his grip tightens, and a low growl leaves his throat that shoots fire straight to my traitorous core.

"Stop doing that, butterfly. Now's not the time." He raises his hips against my ass, and I can feel the bulge that's growing underneath me. This bastard is getting hard. I've been kidnapped and have a sack over my head, and this bastard is getting hard at my unfortunate situation.

Motherfucker. I will set myself free and claw his fucking eyes out. But first, I need to see. I need to take in my surroundings and know what I'm up against. I may be small, but I can fight.

The rest of the drive is quiet. I don't know how many men are in the car, but they keep silent and so do I.

I should be fighting, screaming, asking questions, but I don't do a damn thing. Instead of struggling and trying to break free like I should do, I sit perfectly still on a stranger's lap and fucking enjoy the feel of a warm body beneath me. Call me crazy, but I felt comfortable having his arms wrapped around me.

This man is my captor, and yet I'm not afraid. Yeah, I'm definitely fucked up. I make a mental note to call my therapist after I'm freed.

I don't know how long we drive for, but eventually we come to an unpaved road. I can hear snaps and pops underneath the tires as we drive over the rocks and whatever else we come across along the bumpy road. The car comes to a stop and the engine cuts out. "Are you scared, butterfly?" His voice makes me shiver, but I don't think I'm shivering in fear. In fact, it's for an entirely different reason. I'm unafraid as his fingertips lightly trail up and down my arms in slow and steady strokes.

I suck in a deep breath, willing my nerves to calm and shake my head. "No," I answer, unsure if I'm telling the truth or not.

I feel the rumble of his chest against my back when he lets out a silent chuckle. "You should be. We're going to have fun." There's a dark, sinister promise in his words, and again I don't know if I'm shivering with fear or excitement.

I'm shifted, and then the cold air touches my skin again. We're outside. But where?

The man, whose lap I'd been sitting on, carries me bridal style in his strong arms. On instinct, I wrap my arms around his neck.

"I'll kick your ass if you drop me," I warn when he begins walking, rocks crunching underneath his steps, and I can hear the footsteps of whoever else is with us. I realize there is at least one other man besides the one carrying me, but I wasn't certain exactly how many there were in total.

The man carrying me laughs beautifully. It was fucking music to my ears and was equal parts manly and sexy. And fuck me for squeezing my thighs together at the sound.

"Don't make promises you can't keep." His tone lacks malice. It's teasing, playful even. Instantly I relax in his grip. He isn't going to hurt me. I am not certain about the other man or men, but the one holding me isn't for sure, or so I hope.

He climbs a few stairs, then a door is unlocked by someone else and it creaks open. I'm aware of the presence of the person beside me, even if he doesn't speak.

What the fuck is wrong with me that I don't immediately ask questions or try to fight him off? I'm not as fragile as I may look. Sure, the one carrying me feels muscular, and I know he'd give me a run for my money, but I could at least hold my own for a while. Yes, I felt a very fucking strange sense of comfort in the car when he held me on his lap, but I've been lured into false senses of security before. No, this is different. I know that. I can feel it.

I'm battling with myself. Fight my kidnapper, or relish in the comfort of his arms and see where this leads and what he—what they—want from me. I choose option two. I can play the role of damsel in distress. I'll play nice to get the answers I want.

We climb more stairs and I listen carefully for background noise, seeking any indication of where I am and wondering if I'll hear any familiar voices. I can hear two sets of feet apart from the heavy steps of the macho man carrying me.

Okay, so I'm with at least three men. Great. Now how the hell am I going to get out of this, and what the fuck do they want?

Mystery guy number one sets me down on something plush. I spread my hands around me to get a feel of what I'm on.

It's a bed.

Oh, fuck no.

If they kidnapped me thinking they could get some pussy just because I'm a stripper, they're really fucking wrong. The thought pisses me off like never before.

"What the fuck do you want from me?!" I yell. I wasn't as angry as I should've been when they kidnapped me. I wasn't angry when we were in the car, but now that I'm on their fucking bed, I'm angry as all hell.

"Oh, so now she wants to speak and ask questions," mystery man number I-don't-know-who says, mocking me.

A hand brushes along my barely covered tits, and I freeze. My heart begins pounding in my chest and when the hand touches my skin again, I swat it away, blindly backing further onto the bed. The hand touches me again, this time grabbing onto my ankle and pulling me down to the edge of the bed.

"Get off me! Don't you fucking dare touch me!" I scream, kicking at the fucker who's trying to cop a feel. He grips onto my thighs and pins me down on the bed.

"Don't worry, I'm not going to touch you. I don't fuck without consent." It's the same guy from the car who carried me. I can tell by his voice. His hands trail up my thighs and to the thin elastic band of my thong. "When I take you, you'll be screaming for an entirely different reason." I can hear the smugness in his voice. Despite my attempts to keep my knees together, he manages to successfully remove my panties. He doesn't touch my exposed pussy that's likely flashing him, and at that, I relax a little.

The bag over my head is removed quickly, and I blink a few times to adjust to the light.

There, in front of me, stands three tall men, all dressed in black and wearing masks.

Holy shit.

I recognize those masks instantly. And the minute I meet their eyes, I know who they are. They're the group from the club that watched me. And the man holding my panties—I know he's the one that carried me. He's also the one that jerked off in front of me last night.

Holy fucking shit.

One by one, they remove their masks, and their faces come into full display.

A gasp escapes my parted lips as I take in the sight before me. Pulling my skimpy clothing down to cover myself, I press my knees together, not wanting to show them the effect they have on me.

They are pure sex on legs and the most attractive men I've ever seen in my life. Without their masks, I could see the tattoos that snake all the way up their necks.

Okay, Tate, snap out of it. Stop checking out these fuckers, they just kidnapped you!

Shaking my head, I clear my throat. "Why did you take me? What do you want from me?"

"I'm Eli, that's Rowen, and you're well acquainted by now, but that's King." Brown eyes points to the two men beside him. Eli—the one with brown eyes—looks like the angel of death in his black suit and perfectly slicked back hair. With his oval face and round eyes, he's absolutely fucking beautiful. Good God I am in trouble.

The green-eyed guy—Rowen—stands next to him with his hands in his pockets, his eyes pulled together in a scowl pointed directly at me, his jaw clenched so tightly he might break teeth. He seems like a prick, but he's still a perfect specimen of a man.

And the most charming of all—King aka hazel eyes—is now sitting beside me on the bed with a grin that makes me forget how to breathe. He's wearing black jeans, and a t-shirt, just like the previous night when he exposed himself to me. His hands are covered in tattoos, and instantly I wonder where those tattoos lead.

Actually, I'm wondering the same thing about all of them. I can see the tattoos on their necks and hands, and I'd like to trace them with my tongue.

Holy fuck, Tate, you need to stop. You've been kidnapped!

I shake my inner thoughts away. I'll discuss Stockholm Syndrome with my therapist once I escape these beautiful men. If I were wearing panties, they'd be noticeably soaked. I can only hope to keep my knees closed enough so they don't see my glistening core.

Finding my voice, I shake myself out of my mesmerized stupor. "Great, but that doesn't explain why I'm here. Let me go!" I hiss. King's fingers trace over my knee and slide up my thigh, and quickly I push his hand away, giving him a scowl that only causes him to chuckle.

He leans into me, taking a lock of my black hair, and twirls it around his fingers as he whispers, "I can smell your arousal." Carefully, he unties my mask that I was still wearing and allows it to fall from my face. A smile spreads on his delicious lips when he sees my full face.

"Why the fuck am I here?" I ask again, my eyes only on King.

"You'll find out soon," Eli answers, causing me to turn my attention away from the deep hazel orbs I was getting lost into. His chocolate eyes rake over my nearly exposed body, the same hunger in his eyes as King. Rowen is the only one that's not looking at me with lust, instead, I see hatred in his emerald eyes. I don't know why there's hatred, but it's plain as day. He's looking at me with a deadly stare as if he wants to cut me open and watch me bleed.

"Fuck that. Tell me now." I shove King's hand off me once again and stand, crossing my arms over my chest. Eli mocks my stance and stalks toward me until we're toe to toe. I have to tilt my head back to look at him even in heels. "Why the fuck did you kidnap me?"

The corners of his lips curl in an amused grin. He doesn't answer me, he only looks me over from head to toe once more and walks toward the door, Rowen following behind him. That's when I notice where exactly I am—in a very large and nice bedroom.

"You'll find some clothes in the closet and toiletries in the bathroom for you. There's not much, since you won't be here very long." Rowen exits the room without another glance back at me.

"What does that mean?" Fear shoots through my veins. I won't be here long… Does that mean they're going to let me go or kill me? My anxiety is at an all-time high and I need to know what their plan is. "What do you mean!" I yell, getting a chuckle from behind me.

"King, let's go," Eli snaps, walking toward the doorway. He stops and looks back at me with a slow smirk.

"Goodnight, butterfly." King smiles, smacking my ass on his way out. The door closes and I hear the click of a lock. I run toward it and grab the doorknob, knowing it won't budge.

Those bastards locked me in here.

What the actual fuck is going on? I have to get out of here.

TEN

King

My butterfly has been screaming and beating on the door for hours now. She's acting like a wild fucking animal, and I'd be lying if I said it didn't get my dick hard. I like hearing her fight against a situation she has no possible way of getting out of. The more she screams, the harder my dick gets. I'm tempted to march my ass right back upstairs to her room and really give her something to scream about. I wonder if she'd cry if I were to shove my dick down her throat.

I'm downstairs with Eli and Rowen, analyzing the looks on their faces when they hear her screams. Eli and I are both amused, while Rowen is angry. His jaw clenches each time she screams, and he's only getting angrier. It would normally be humorous to see him get so angry, but I know why he's angry, and I hate that for him. I hate that her mere presence is causing him extreme discomfort.

Eli and Rowen are my brothers, not by blood, but that's irrelevant. When one is distressed, we're all distressed. Even if it is slightly amusing.

"Are you going to be okay with her here?" Eli sits back in his chair, his eyes shifting between Rowen and the deck of cards in his hand that he's shuffling.

Rowen grits his jaw, avoiding eye contact with us both. "I have no choice. It'll only be for a few days, then we'll get rid of her." His elbows rest on the table, his large hands wrapped around the neck of the beer bottle he's currently gripping. I wonder if he's imagining it's Tate he's strangling.

My mind once again takes off fantasizing freely about the girl upstairs, and how it would feel to have my hands around her neck. I bet she'd bruise beautifully. My lips curl up in a smile at the thought. "A few days is plenty of time to have some fun before she leaves," I say casually, chuckling when their shocked eyes snap to me. I shrug, not feeling embarrassed at all.

Rowen rolls his eyes just as Eli and I share a secret grin of amusement.

"Go make her shut the fuck up then," Rowen snaps, earning laugher from both of us.

"Someone's tense and needs to get laid," Eli mumbles under his breath.

"I'd rather claw my eyes out than go anywhere near her with my dick." I watch Rowen closely, noticing his irritation with her here. I should be a good brother and stay away from her, but I won't. Not when her cries and pleas for us to let her go is calling to me like a siren. Her words beg for freedom—an escape; but her eyes blaze with something else entirely. I noticed it the moment I removed the bag from her head and stared into her ocean eyes.

My butterfly wants to play.

After adjusting my dick that is painfully hard and pressing against my jeans, I stand with a smile, making the decision to answer my girl's cries for help. "I'm going to see if my little butterfly would like to have a slumber party." I take two pieces of pizza from the box in the middle of the table and set them on a napkin, carrying them as I walk across our cabin and upstairs to the room we've locked her in. I'm a man on a mission and don't bother waiting to hear the nonsense that Eli or Rowen may spew out.

I remove the key from my pocket and unlock the door, allowing myself entrance.

Tate is sitting on the floor beside the bed, her head laying back on the bed while she stares at the ceiling. Her turquoise eyes snap to me the second I slam the door closed. Her scowl is cute, but it does nothing to me.

"Are you hungry, butterfly?" Walking across the room, I sit on the bed beside where her head was lying, and hold the pizza out toward her.

She looks at the pizza for two seconds before her stomach starts rumbling, betraying her hunger. "Stop calling me that. My name is Tate!" She wants to be angry, but with her growling stomach, she can't. Feeling amused, I hold the pizza under her nose so she can smell the deliciousness, and just like I expected, that gets me a reaction from her.

Tate snatches the napkin from my hand and stands, pacing the room while she shovels the pieces in her mouth. "What do you want from me? Why did you three take me?" I wait until she's finished eating before I respond. I don't want her to speak with her mouth full.

"Don't worry about it, you'll know soon. For now, you should wash yourself and go to sleep."

"Did you really just say don't worry about it? Are you fucking crazy? You kidnapped me! You bet your ass I'm going to fucking worry about it!" She aggressively throws her napkin into the trash bin beside the nightstand. Tate may hate us, but she sure as fuck swallowed down that pizza. I wonder if she can swallow my dick like that.

"You'll only be here for a few days, so for now, you don't need to know anything. You'll know when it's time." Her shoulders slump as she too easily admits her defeat. I like when she fights, but I also like that she's realizing there's no hope for her. She's temporarily ours, and I can't wait to see what'll happen over the next few days.

Tate sits beside me on the bed, her head hung between her shoulders. "Why did you come to the club last night?" My lips pull into a mischievous grin.

I work quickly to remove my boots, then climb up further onto the bed and lie back, putting my hands behind my head and crossing my ankles. "I wanted to see you again," I answer simply. Her head snaps up, her eyes shifting between me and the bed.

With a grin, I wave my arm, gesturing for her to lay beside me. She was hesitant for only a moment. With a roll of her ocean blue eyes, she climbs into the plush cloud-like mattress on the four-poster bed and lies beside me, mimicking my position.

"You could've kept your dick in your pants though."

I'm unable to contain the laughter that erupts from me at her comment. "You were glad I didn't," I call her out, and she doesn't deny it. She rolls her lips between her teeth, maintaining silence for the first time all night.

I continue pressing, wondering how far I can get. "I bet you were wet all night long after I left." I know she was. I saw the way her pussy glistened underneath the glowing stage lights when she spread herself for me to see. Her thin thong had pulled to the side, and I saw everything. After I came, I had to get the fuck out of there before I acted on my urges and claimed her right then and there.

She remains silent beside me, her breathing becoming heavier. No doubt she, too, is thinking back to our short time together. Good. I want her to think about me, to dream about me. "You should get some sleep," I say, straightening up.

"Sleep in a house with three strangers? Yeah, no thanks." Ah, so recommending sleep earns a reaction from her.

"Do you think we'd do something to you?"

"Fuck yeah I do. I don't fucking know you, and I'm not going to make myself vulnerable by sleeping here and—" Before she could finish her sentence, I shift quickly so I'm hovering over her, my arms on either side of her head.

Her legs automatically spread for me, a gasp escaping her parted lips as she stares up at me with wide eyes. I press my hips against hers knowing she can feel the permanent bulge that's been in my pants ever since I held her warm body on my lap in the car. She's not speaking now. All bark and no bite. I think I'd prefer it if she did bite; that would make this more interesting.

Taking hold of her hands, I pin them above her head, pressing myself directly against her bare core. The silk baby doll dress she's wearing barely covers her ass when she's standing, and now that she's lying, it covers even less. Her panties are still in my pocket, the only barrier between us is my jeans.

"Butterfly, I'd never do anything you don't want. Taking women against their will isn't really my thing. When I have you, and I will have you, it'll be because you want it and you asked for it. You'll be screaming my name in both pain and pleasure when it does happen." Her pupils dilate, and I suppress my laughter to her reaction.

"That'll never happen! I will never want you or the two other goons who kidnapped me!" she yells in my face, angry because her body is betraying her. I pull away from her enough so that I'm able to look down at her pretty pink cunt, smirking at the sight of her glistening lips. Her mouth may tell lies, but her body tells the truth.

I can smell her sweet arousal; it's the sweetest scent. My jaw aches, and my mouth waters for a taste of her. Dropping my head down to her, I brush my lips faintly against hers while I remove her panties from my pocket and use the material to wipe over her wet cunt.

Tate gasps, her hips jerking toward me. It takes every ounce of self-control I can fucking muster up to pull away from her. "Get some sleep," I grunt, dragging myself away from the bed where Tate is still panting, her beautiful chest rapidly rising and falling. I can see her pebbled nipples poking through the thin material of her skimpy lingerie. Balling my hands into fists at my sides, I can feel the wetness from her panties on my palm, and suddenly all I want to do is throw myself at her and fuck her until she can't breathe. As much as I want to, I know now isn't the time. So I stomp out of the room and slam the door behind me.

I don't ever want to fucking hear Eli tell me ever again that I don't have self-control.

With a scowl on my face, I barrel down the hall. My eyes lock with Eli's, who's just stepping out of his bedroom. He takes one look at me before he folds over laughing.

"Rowen! You owe me—he didn't get laid!" He wipes at the invisible tears under his eyes.

"Fuck off," I growl. Motherfuckers. They bet on me getting my dick wet. Those little bitches.

"What happened? She turn you down?" Fucking Eli. He doesn't always know when it's best to shut up and quit poking the bear.

"Don't worry about what happened, brother, she'll be screaming my name soon enough."

He shakes his head. "Just be careful, don't get attached to her. We're delivering her in three days." he warns, and I nod. Even though I feel like it's already too late for that. I knew there was something about her the moment our eyes met on Monday night.

Fuck that, I knew there was something different about her the minute I first laid eyes on her months ago. I watched her through a computer screen for months, and now, I have her in person. She's down the hall, within reach, and I have three days with her. Three days to do God only knows what.

I see the darkness within Tate. It calls to mine. All I want is to push her over the edge and bring her inner demons out to play. Such fucking fun we could have.

With a wide smile, I push past Eli and stomp down the hallway toward my bedroom. I waste no time removing my clothing and lying on my bed. With her panties tangled around my fingers, I bring the small piece of fabric to my nose and inhale her scent, groaning in sweet relief.

Holy fuck. She smells good.

Closing my eyes, I hold her panties in my left hand while I fist my meaty cock with my right and begin pumping up and down my length, inhaling her scent every so often.

With Tate's smell in my nostrils, the image of her wet pussy spread bare before me, and my fist pumping my aching cock, I barely last. I'm like a teenage boy who can't control his damn self.

I come, and I come hard.

The thick, creamy ropes of my cum shoot from my purple mushroom tip and lands over my stomach.

I'm too exhausted to move and too frustrated to do anything else. My dick is still painfully hard, and all I want to do is run into Tate's room and fuck her until she begs me to stop.

I lie there staring at the ceiling, tracing mindless circles in the drying cum on my stomach.

Three days. I have three days to ruin the girl down the hall.

ELEVEN

Tate

I lie in bed for what feels like hours after King left the room. I keep staring at the ceiling fan swirling around and around, and contemplate how I'm going to get the fuck out of here. I heard the door lock so I know it would be useless to try it. Screaming won't get me anywhere; I know that from experience. If someone really wants something, hearing "no" or "let me go" isn't going to change their mind.

I don't know these bastards that kidnapped me, nor what they want with me. At first, I thought it was *him*. I thought *he* found me, but quickly realized that's not the case.

I was careful. After I left the city, I'd never talked about it. I'd never told anyone about my history here, so *he* wouldn't know where to look for me here.

I'm safe. Well, I was.

I stare at the fan until my eyelids become heavy and I can't keep them open anymore. My body is still on fire, and I can feel my wetness between my legs. Fucking King. He had no right to come near me. Fuck him and fuck my body for reacting to him. Cassie was right; I should've found someone and got laid. I'm blaming my reaction to him on my lack of sex.

Speaking of Cassie, I truly hope she's realized I'm gone and is now out trying to find me. I don't know what these three macho men have planned for me, but I do know it won't be good.

Why do I feel like I've escaped one evil, only to be faced with an evil unlike any I've ever known?

Frustrated and exhausted, I eventually drag myself out of the bed and into the bathroom. It's simple—log walls with white fixtures. I slip off my baby doll dress, lock the door behind me, and step into the glass shower, not minding the cold water that sprays over me at first. The cold is exactly what I need to extinguish the flame that King started.

Showering in a house with three strangers isn't the smartest thing to do, but the shower is fucking magical on my aching muscles. Stupidly, I allow myself to relax underneath the waterfall.

By the time I finally step out of the shower, I'm relaxed and cleaned from head to toe.

And I may or may not have used the shower head to bring myself to orgasm once or twice, which was an even dumber thing to do. But my traitorous body had reacted to King earlier, and I'd been horny ever since.

I find some clothing in the closet after my shower, and color me surprised when they turn out to be my perfect size.

I don't even want to know how they knew what size bra and shoe size I wear.

Instead of overanalyzing the clothing situation, and instead of trying to break the bedroom window like I should've, I dress in a pair of red silk pajamas and climb on the cloud of a bed.

I am stupid to allow myself to be vulnerable by sleeping in their house. I should stay awake or at least keep one eye open, but I can't. I am too exhausted from working a week straight.

I fall asleep the second my head hits the pillow.

When I come to, I don't know what time it is, or what time I even went to sleep; all I know is I slept better than I have in months. The bed is incredible, and I make a mental note to tell Cassie that we must replace our mattresses and get whatever type of mattress this is. It's incredible.

God, I'm so ridiculous. I should be demanding answers to my questions, breaking open the window, or figuring out how to pick the lock, but because I've lost my mind, I'm not doing any of those things.

Instead, I'm resting in a bed, feeling more relaxed than ever.

Okay, so I'll sleep a little longer, and then I will get up and figure out how to fight my way out of here. I *am* getting out of here.

With a sigh, I stretch my stiff limbs and roll slowly onto my back. My left hand connects with something hard and warm beside me, and instantly, my eyes widen.

With a racing heart, I turn my head to see what I've touched, only to find a sleeping King beside me.

What the fuck?

He's here in my bed. Well, not my bed, but he's next to me in the bed I'm sleeping in.

What. The. Actual. Fuck!

I briefly wonder if this is his room and he had no choice but to sleep here. But I quickly turn that idea down because there are only items for me in here. I don't know why they have things for me, considering they've told me that I'll be leaving soon. I'd seen a good number of outfits and pajama sets in the closet last night—all brand new with expensive price tags on them.

Holding my breath, I turn on my side to face King, studying his perfect features. His light-colored beard, his long eyelashes fanned out on his cheeks, and his dirty blond hair is free of the bun I've only seen him wear, and his long locks are spread across the gray pillowcase. He's shirtless, and from what I can see, his entire torso is covered in tattoos. I'm nearly certain there's not a single blank piece of skin remaining on him. His nipples are pierced, and knowing what else is pierced brings tingles to my body. I can still feel his crotch pressing against my heated core from last night when he was on top of me.

My lips tingle with the phantom promise of the kiss from last night.

Fuck. I really am insane considering my feelings of lust toward him. The man that kidnapped me.

He's sleeping—he's vulnerable. I should be clawing his eyes out and demanding to be set free. I'm sure by now Cassie has realized I'm missing. Hopefully she'll come looking and someone will find me soon. I can only hope. That's when it hits me.

No one can come looking for me.

The police *cannot* become involved. They can't.

With an exhale, I squeeze my thighs tighter together as I continue studying King's perfect features, taking slow and steady breaths in an attempt to control my nerves.

"How long are you going to stare at me?" he rumbles in a raspy morning voice that shoots straight to my core. Holy shit. That's the hottest voice I've ever heard.

"Is this your room?" I ask, even though I already know the answer, but that's my way of asking why he slept in here.

"No. My room is down the hall."

"Is there something wrong with your bed?"

"No. My bed is fine," he replies, his full lips curling into a smile.

I roll my eyes. We're not getting anywhere. "Why did you sleep in here then?" His eyes open, and those intense hazel eyes lock with my turquoise ones and hold me captive.

Slowly, he extends his arm toward me and gently caresses my face, brushing my dark hair behind my ears and pushing my bangs out of the way. "Because you're in here. We may not have much time together, but I want to be near you during the time we do have." Holy shit. I wasn't expecting that answer. My lips part, an electrical wave shooting through me. I feel drawn to him, like I've never felt to anyone before. What the fuck is wrong with me?

This isn't going to end well for me, that's for sure.

I ask the lingering question that's been burning on my tongue, "Are you guys going to kill me?" holding my breath as soon as the words come out.

He continues stroking my hair, not missing a beat when I ask the question. His eyes hold mine, and I search for answers but find none. His eyes reveal nothing.

With a heavy sigh, he replies, "No, butterfly. We're not going to kill you." I know his answer is genuine, but that doesn't sooth the knot that's forming in my stomach.

"Then why did you kidnap me? There's going to be people looking for me."

King lets out a full belly laugh, completely shocking me. This fucker is actually laughing at me! My eyebrows pull together in a scowl.

"My little butterfly, we both know that's not true." His hand moves to my waist and quickly I'm rolled onto my back, and he's hovering over me, *again*, resuming our position from last night. He pins my arms above my head and leans down to me, placing a single kiss on my lips.

His lips are plump and totally fucking perfect. They're soft, and in an instant, my body ignites in a flame. I want to feel his lips skim over every inch of my heated skin.

My legs spread automatically and he lets go of my hands long enough to grab my legs and wrap them around his waist, his hips pushing against my sex so I can feel his cock already growing against me.

I'm wearing thin pajama shorts, with panties that I know are already wet. His calloused hands slide up my legs and inside of my shorts until he's grabbing handfuls of my ass, kneading my cheeks like dough while pulling my hips roughly against his. My toes curl, and fuck, I am fucking turned on and want him more than I ever wanted anything right now.

I need him like my next breath. I've completely lost my fucking mind.

Our lips move in perfect sync, my moan vibrating against his lips as he continues kneading my ass. I feel a phantom of his teasing finger sliding up to my pussy lips. We're so lost in each other, consumed by our lust, that I don't notice when the door opens.

A raspy clearing of a throat makes me freeze, my eyes snapping open to see King staring down at me with amusement. Craning my neck, I look around his large build to look toward the door.

Deep brown eyes stare back at me.

Eli shakes his head from where he stands in the doorway with his arms crossed over his chest. "Get up, breakfast is done." With a chuckle, he steps inside the room and picks up the t-shirt from the floor and throws it at King, who has already rolled off of me and is lying beside me with a very visible tent in his boxers.

"You're a fucking cockblocker," King groans, grabbing the t-shirt and quickly sitting up to pull it over his torso.

"Cover yourself, I don't want to see your dick," Eli grumbles with an eyeroll. King laughs and climbs out of bed, retrieving his sweatpants from the floor and pulling them on.

"Then you should've given me time to take care of it." He looks at me with a wink. "Rain check, I'll have to eat you later. Let's go, butterfly."

Before going downstairs, King and I stand side by side in the bathroom at the double vanity, brushing our teeth and washing our face. We're becoming very fucking domestic.

In the light of day, I'm able to take in my surroundings as he leads me downstairs. We're in a cabin, and I know if I look outside, I'll see that we are in the woods.

Great, we're at least an hour outside of town. Away from anyone. It's just the four of us.

Fuck. My. Life.

Even if I do have a chance to run away, I'd likely get lost. I've never been this far outside of the city. I don't know my way around. But I can't let that stop me. I must find a way to get out of here.

King must've sensed my distress, because he wraps an arm around my shoulders and leads me into the kitchen where Eli and Rowen are laughing about something. Rowen's laughter quickly dies down the moment I enter the room.

Okay, weird.

King pulls a chair out for me and I sit while he takes his seat right next to me. He takes an empty plate and loads it with food, then sets it down in front of me, placing a kiss on my temple.

Hmm. This is too weird.

"You two look awfully cozy." Rowen's cold emerald eyes meet mine from across the table. His eyes are such a vibrant bright green, and vaguely they look familiar. I'm positive that I've seen those rare glowing eyes somewhere. He's familiar, but my mind isn't the same anymore.

"You should've seen them a few minutes ago. Dry humping like horny teenagers," Eli adds, shoving a forkful of pancake into his mouth.

"It wouldn't have been dry humping had you not interrupted us!" King throws a piece of bacon across the table at Eli, the two of them erupting into laughter. Meanwhile, Rowen's cold eyes never leave mine. If he thinks he can make me uncomfortable or intimidate me, he's fucking wrong. I glare right fucking back at him. Bastard.

"So, is anyone going to tell me why you kidnapped me?" I cut in, asking them all, but only looking at Rowen.

"You are a means to an end," he states harshly. "Someone has taken something that belongs to us, so you'll be helping us get it back." My blood runs cold. His explanation is void of emotion, as if I am an inconvenience they have to deal with in order to get whatever it is that they really want.

I scoff. "You're going to trade me?" He nods. "But why me? What do I have to do with anything?" They can't be serious. They're going to trade me like some type of animal.

"Someone wants you. Can't imagine why, but they do. We have you, so we'll get what we want by giving you away." In my peripheral, I can see King and Eli staring at Rowen and I, they're eating silently.

"I don't understand. What are you trading me for? You were hired to kidnap me?"

"It doesn't matter what we're trading you for; that's our concern, not yours. We weren't hired exactly, but we saw the perfect opportunity and took it." King reaches underneath the table and places his hand on my thigh, squeezing it gently, as if he's trying to provide me comfort. Oddly enough, I appreciate the gesture.

They're not going to kill me, but that doesn't mean that whoever they're trading me to wouldn't. Who could possibly want me so badly? And why?

I have so many questions, but by the way Rowen's staring at me and grinding his molars, I know he's not in the mood to answer any more questions. I could push him, I should push him, but I choose to shut the fuck up for once.

"Eat your food before it gets cold," Eli says, pointing toward my plate. I take the glass bottle of syrup and pour it over my pancakes before cutting into them and shoving the warm fluffy goodness into my mouth. I may be angry, but I'm not going to let a perfectly good plate of food go to waste. I'll need my strength to escape these fuckers.

Without another word, Rowen stands abruptly from the table and leaves the room, leaving the three of us to finish breakfast ourselves. He's a strange one with clear anger issues. What the fuck is his problem with me?

I'm the one who should be angry... and I am... right?

TWELVE

Rowen

Tate.

She calls herself Tate. What a perfect fucking name.

I can't be around her. I thought I'd be able to, but I can't. She defied me by coming back to this city, and she doesn't even recognize me, which only adds to my anger.

Seeing her walk into the kitchen with a smile and King's arm around her shoulders, I wanted to fucking scream at them both. I wanted to hold her down and fuck her bloody until she remembered me. I searched her turquoise eyes hoping to find recognition in them, but again, I found nothing.

I found nothing within her to resemble the girl she once was. If it wasn't for her eyes, I would've second-guessed myself. Her eyes give her away. They're a direct portal to our past. She may not look the same, but one look into her eyes and I see everything that she's trying to hide.

Gone is the gentleness that I used to find in her eyes. And I know she's been through more things than I'm aware of, more than I can even fathom.

I don't want King and Eli to look at her the way they do. Especially King. That bastard will ruin her more than I ever have. I ruined her, and until she remembers me, I want my scars to be the only ones that ever mark her perfect creamy skin.

I had to remove myself from the kitchen during breakfast because I couldn't stand having her that close to me again and having her in my space. My need to get away from her is what brought me down to the basement gym to work out my frustrations.

My shirt is off and I'm pushing myself harder than ever, hitting the punching bag to release all my anger and annoyance. When Eli told me about her, I was on board with his plan all the way. It wasn't until later when I saw a photo of her that I became hesitant to go along with his plan. He and King know everything about my past, they know everything about her; they just didn't know who she was. It was a mere fucking coincidence that *she* turned out to be the very one that holds the key to us getting control of our city again.

I'm all in, and I can't turn back now. I never wanted any harm to come to her, but whatever happens is now out of my control. My brothers come first; I'd never turn my back on them.

The minute Tate stepped foot into our city, we became aware of it. We made sure she got a job where she did so we could easily keep an eye on her. She was a hot piece of ass that King and Eli wanted to sink their teeth into. But it wasn't until recently that we learned how useful she could actually be to us. They spent months watching her while I stayed away, only learning who she really is not long ago.

Sinners was the first business venture the three of us embarked on. Men love to see naked chicks, and we found they'd pay a hefty price in order to keep everything they do inside of our club discreet. And that's exactly what Sinners is. A discreet strip club where the identity of our clients and dancers are hidden, and for the right price, there's a dancer who is willing to do anything the client wants.

Except Tate. No matter the price, she has many limits.

She doesn't even get fully nude, and a lap dance and time in the VIP rooms is the furthest she'll go. Meanwhile, we have some dancers that'll spread their legs or drop to their knees for a high price.

After everything she has been through, I'm surprised she'd even be comfortable working in a strip club. But then again, she did always surprise me. And that's exactly what she's doing to me now. Her mere presence in my house is charming me and I can't control my feelings around her. We have a fucked-up history, and she acts as if she's unaffected, while I relive the guilt and nightmares every single night.

Thirteen years ago, I told her to run and never come back, and here she is. Back in the city that started it all, back to the place that holds our history. A history she seems not to remember. Or at least it's me she doesn't remember. And how could she fucking not? What we experienced together isn't something you can easily forget. It's not something you could *ever* forget.

You never forget your first love, or the first time you fuck.

As I hit the punching bag repeatedly, I'm picturing *his* face. The monster that's haunted my nightmares for years. I'm so wrapped up in my own head that I don't notice Eli entering the gym until he stands behind the black punching bag and holds it firmly in place for me, keeping it still while I deliver punch after punch. He allows me to punch the bag until my arms are sore and fall limp to my sides.

Eli steps away, walking across the room, "You okay, man?" he asks, adjusting the weight plates on the bench press. I grab my white towel and water bottle from the padded gym floor and wipe the sweat from my face, swinging the damp towel over my left shoulder, taking a long pull from the cold water bottle.

"Yeah, I'm good." I grunt, avoiding eye contact.

"Are you sure? You were hitting that bag pretty hard." I know that he's been worrying about me ever since he learned who Tate is. If this was happening to either him or King, I would worry too.

Eli and I have known each other for years. We met at a grocery store. I was sixteen at the time, and he was seventeen. I was caught stealing food, and he distracted the clerk and helped me get away. We were both living on the streets, him longer than me, and instantly, he took me under his wing and taught me how to survive. He was the brother I never had. Few months later, we met King, and the three of us have been inseparable ever since. They're the family I always craved.

I'd once thought that about her, but now when I look at her, all I feel is anger and disgust toward myself. She makes me hate myself.

"This is just proving to be harder than I thought, but I'll be fine. Where is she now?" I say, running my fingers through my sweat-soaked hair.

"She's upstairs with King. You know, if it's too hard having her here, we can make other arrangements until we make the exchange," he offers, and I roll my eyes at the thought of her with King. Not because I don't think King deserves her, hell, we've shared many times in the past, but I know how attached King can get, and the way he looks at her... I worry he's getting attached. They've been together less than twenty-four hours, and I can already tell they're just alike.

King is sensitive, and Tate is easy to love. He's bound to see her pure heart and that'll only complicate things. We cannot get attached and back out of our plan, no matter how many second thoughts I have.

"It's fine, she can stay here. King seems to be doing a good job so far keeping her occupied," I say with a shrug. Eli watches me silently. Clearly, he isn't buying what I am selling. "Are we fully prepared to make the exchange?" He nods, laying down on the padded bench underneath the bench press.

"Everything is set. We'll just have to keep her here a few more days, then we'll make the exchange. We'll have complete control over the city again." I chug the rest of my water, then toss the empty bottle into the trash on my way out of the gym. Even after a workout, I am still worked up and tense. I'll be tense for as long as she's in my space.

As I walk up the stairs toward the living room, laughter fills the air. *Her laughter.*

A sound I haven't heard in years. The jovial tone shoots straight to my groin, and my traitorous cock raises in salute at it, pointing out toward her as if it knew it's way home.

There, in the living room, Tate is perched on the couch, her black hair spread out as she has her head thrown back, eyes closed, and her hands are on her stomach. I missed what King said, but whatever he said made her laugh uncontrollably, and suddenly I feel resentment toward him for making her laugh the way he did.

I want to be the reason for that beautiful sound. I once had been the reason. But I'm also the reason she stopped laughing.

King's attention turns toward me, but mine stays on her. Tate straightens and looks at me with those eyes.

Clearing my throat, I put my scowl back into place. "I'm going into town. Do you need anything?" I stare at her when I speak, but we both know my question isn't for her.

King stands from the couch and walks toward me, shaking his head. "Nah, man, I'm good. I'm going to take Tate to see the grounds." I look at my brother. Thankfully, my dick is down now. I don't need to be getting hard by the sound of her voice or at the sight of her. No matter how fucking gorgeous she is. With a final look at her, I switch my attention back at King and nod. "I'm going to shower, then head out. Call if you need me to pick up anything." I give them my back as

I walk away.

"I don't think he likes me," Tate says in a whisper that was meant for King, but was loud enough for me to hear.

If only she'd remember me.

She's not wrong though; I don't like her, and I'm already fighting the urge to rip her open and watch her bleed the way she used to.

She's the reason I am the way I am. She's to blame for everything.

She ruined me just as much as I ruined her.

God, I want to ruin her all over again.

THIRTEEN

Tate

"**K**ing, stop! Get off me!" I squeal, tears streaming down my cheeks. My stomach muscles are clenched and aching. "I'm serious! Get away!" I'm laughing so hard that tears are blurring my vision.

King had discovered I'm rather ticklish and has been torturing me ever since. After breakfast, we were sitting in the living room and I'd complained about my aching feet, so he took it upon himself to massage them, and that's when he found out they were my weak spot. I was way too fucking ticklish there and the bastard is now holding me down and tickling my damn feet. I'm going to kill him; he better sleep with one eye open tonight.

After Eli and Rowen left, I went upstairs to get ready for the day, King followed me, and that's where we are now. I'm lying on my stomach on the floor, while he's straddling my waist, holding my legs firmly down with one hand while he tickles my feet with the other hand.

Holy fuck it feels good to laugh.

"I'm going to pee myself! Please, stop!" I beg, attempting to kick him, but he's too strong and doesn't even budge.

King chuckles and rolls off me, pulling my body on top of his. I straddle his waist and smile down at him. His hand raises and with a subtle pace, he brushes my hair out of my face while he stares up at me with a smile and a look in his eyes that I can't quite put my finger on. Whatever the look is, it provides me comfort.

My laughter fades and my tears dry as I stare down at him, aware of our position and the fact I can feel his bulge, and I'm sure he can feel my wet panties. Neither of us make any move to take things further, and for that, I'm thankful.

"Why are you trading me? What are you getting in return? Who are you giving me to? I deserve to know. You're playing with my life." I ask all the questions that have been lingering on the tip of my tongue ever since Rowen told me over breakfast that they were trading me like I was some fucking pawn, but it doesn't make sense to me. I inhale a deep breath and hold it in, honestly not expecting him to answer.

"The Westside Disciples. They've been making an unwelcome appearance in our city lately. We're giving you to them, in exchange for them leaving our city." His answer takes me by surprise and leaves me with further questions.

"I don't get it. A gang? Why would they want me?"

"I don't know, but they do. And we have you, so it's an even exchange." I shake my head and attempt to climb off him, only to have him grab my hips and pull me back to him.

"It's not an even exchange! You're giving them my life!" I slap his hands away, and this time, he lets me go and allows me to climb off his hard body. I scramble away and stand quickly to my feet, crossing my arms over my chest, and pace back and forth across the room. "Why would they want me? I'm not involved in any gang activity." I pause, turning to face him when he stands too, his height towering over me. He's a giant, at least six foot five. I look like a child compared to him, and I probably look ridiculous with my neck craned to scowl up at him. "What do you mean by your city?" I ask, my arms falling to my sides. King shoves his hands into the pockets of his sweats as he looks down at me, looking at me like a predator who's sizing up his prey.

Realization hits me like a slap in the face. "You, Eli, and Rowen… you're the Triad," I whisper more to myself than to him, his expression darkening as he stares me down, void of all emotion. His silence is all the validation I need.

I've heard stories about the Triad ever since I arrived. They're ruthless gangsters that control this city. They protect those that need protection, and handle those that cause havoc. They have every cop and politician in the city on their payroll, and they've been suspected of a long list of crimes, but there's no evidence. Even if there was, the officials they keep in their pockets would bury it. They control this city and everyone in it.

Rumor has it that Eli has connections to a gang in Wales where he was apparently born. But of course, there's no proof. Everything I know about the Triad came from Cassie and other dancers at the club.

My lips part at the realization that I'm in the presence of the Triad. I wrap my arms around myself protectively and take a cautious step backward, away from King, which only causes a laugh to rip from his chest. "Don't act scared, my little butterfly. It doesn't suit you when we both know that you're not." He steps forward and I instantly take another backward until I'm backed against the wall. He pins me back, his hands on either side of my head.

"Tell me why the disciples, or whoever they are, would want me."

"You know enough already," he says in a husky whisper, his nose running along my jaw as he inhales my scent. "You smell like vanilla

123

and sin. I wonder if you'll taste as good as you smell." I gasp, shoving at his muscular chest. He doesn't even budge an inch. Of course I'm no match for him.

"You're lying. You don't know why they want me. You knew where I was, so you just decided to take me without any questions and trade me for control of the city because they're starting to take over." I'm feeling confident as I stand to my full five foot five height. "You don't know anything. That sounds like a bad business decision to me." He stiffens, and I know I'm right. A laugh slips past my lips at the fact I am able to catch something that he clearly hasn't thought about.

King raises his hand, and on instinct I flinch, my hands covering my face as I press myself further against the wall.

"Butterfly…" His eyebrows pull together, the look in his hazel eyes sad and nearly painful to look at. "Did you think I was going to hit you?" I stare at him, but don't speak. With a racing heart, I shove at his chest, and again, he doesn't move. His fingertips trail along my jawline and trace over my lips. "Who hurt you, pretty girl?" He seals his lips over mine at that, and suddenly I'm weak in the knees and melting into him. I don't realize I am crying until I taste the saltiness in our kiss.

Right there, I climb King's rock-hard body like a damn tree and wrap my legs around his waist, my arms around his neck. His large hands hold me up by my ass as our tongues fight each other for dominance over the kiss. He carries me across the bedroom toward the bathroom and deposits me down on the counter. Our lips part long enough for him to remove our t-shirts, then we're back to feasting each other in a frenzy kiss. Our teeth clatter, the kiss is bruising, and oh God, it is truly fucking perfection. Fire scorches my core as my body is awakened.

King's hands slide down my body to the pajama shorts I'm wearing. He grips them firmly and pulls them down my legs roughly, along with my panties. My bare ass is on the cold tile of the vanity, my nipples hard, and my pussy wet and aching with need. He sucks my tongue into his mouth while his fingers slip between us and finds my cunt.

Parting my folds, he roughly shoves two thick fingers inside me without warning, causing me to cry out.

"Fuck, butterfly, you're so fucking wet. Is this all for me?" The smug bastard smirks and all I can do is nod breathlessly. "Tell me what you want," he growls against my lips.

I should stop this. We have no fucking business doing this right now or ever. I'm not thinking straight, this is purely my body's reactions instead of my brain. This man has kidnapped me, I'm practically being held hostage, and here I am…being an easy hoe, ready to spread my legs for him. This isn't me; this is not something that I would ever do. I'm not this type of person, yet here the fuck I am.

Trying not to overthink it, I push down his sweats and boxer briefs, watching in awe as his massive cock springs free, the metal in the tip staring at me suggestively. I watch him with a smirk, salivating at the sight. Leaning closer to him, I wrap my hand around his length and pump him from root to tip. "I want you to fuck me. Make me forget everything except your name as I scream it at the top of my lungs." I surprise myself with my words. I've never been sexually confident before.

King growls, his fingers sliding into my hair and gripping it painfully. Yanking my head back, his lips kiss over my exposed neck, nipping and sucking over my delicate skin, all while he continues to thrust and curl his fingers inside of my pussy, hitting a spot that hasn't been touched in far too long.

Our lips reconnect and like the greedy thief he is, he steals all the air from my lungs. "I'll feast on your sweet cunt later. Right now, I need to be buried so deep inside you, I forget where I end and you begin." He removes his fingers from my pussy and sucks them inside of his mouth.

Holy fuck, that was the hottest thing I'd ever seen. God, I'm so needy for this man.

His eyes hold mine and I watch him suck clean the fingers that were just inside of my pussy, groaning when he dips them in my cream and takes another taste.

King grips my hips roughly, pulling me to the edge of the counter, lines himself up with my wet entrance, and in one painful thrust, he fills me to the brim. I cry out, my legs wrapping around his waist. The burn of the stretch is a welcomed, delicious pain.

He pulls out and thrusts back into me, fully seating himself. His massive cock stretches me and touches my cervix, the feeling equal parts pleasure and pain.

With his hands on my hips, King fucks me with everything he has. The piercing in his cock drags over my G-spot repeatedly and sends a delicious wave of euphoria though my body. I lean forward and flick my tongue over both of his nipple rings, sucking one nipple into my mouth. He throws his head back and groans, his hand disappears between our bodies, and his thumb finds my clit. He rubs my sensitive pearl in a circular motion, bringing me closer to my edge.

"Fuck butterfly, you're so fucking tight." He pants, leaning toward me until our foreheads press against each other. My pussy clenches around him with a vise grip. It's been months since I've had anything other than my fingers or a showerhead. I'd forgotten how incredible it feels to be pounded into another galaxy by a cock. "Scream my name. Scream my fucking name!" he roars, sweat beading at his hairline.

"King! Oh God, King!" I yell his name, our lips fusing together again like magnets. "Harder! Fuck, King. Harder!" I need more. I need the pain.

He pulls out long enough to remove me from the counter and turns me around so I'm facing the mirror. With a hand on my back, he pushes me forward and props one of my legs on the counter so that I'm open even further for him. With a smirk on his lips, he feeds his cock back into my greedy pussy and fucks me without mercy.

One hand rests on my hip while the other rubs up the length of my leg until he reaches my center and finds my clit. He pinches my sensitive bud of nerves, rolling it around between his thumb and index finger. He plays me like a violin. My lips part as I scream his name over and over again like a mantra, white-knuckling the counter all while watching our reflection in the mirror.

His large, tattooed body behind my small frame, his mouth sucking my neck, one hand rubbing my tit and the other between my legs rubbing my clit furiously. We're a fucking sight to look at. I have to stand on my tiptoes in order to reach him due to our height difference, and the ache in my calf is worth it.

Every thrust sends me closer and closer toward an orgasm that I know is going to be earth-shattering. I'm already dripping, I can feel my wetness on my thighs and the way our skin sticks together.

"Come for me, butterfly. Come right fucking now," he demands with a growl, and right on cue, I explode around his throbbing cock, just as he stills and fills me with his warm cum.

I cry in pure ecstasy, my body going limp in his arms as he continues rubbing my oversensitive clit. My pussy milks him for everything he has to give me, my body jerking in sync with his cock while he rubs me through my orgasm.

King rests his forehead on my shoulder, his strong arms holding me securely and keeping me upright. I stare breathlessly at myself in the mirror.

With his cock still hard and inside of me, he carries us to the glass walk-in shower and steps inside.

Only once the warm water is spraying down our naked bodies does he drop me on my still wobbly legs. "Stay still, I need to taste you now." He pushes my back against the tile wall, my back arching when it touches the cold tile.

With a chuckle, King kisses down my body until he reaches my core. He buries his face in my pussy and inhales deeply. My hands find his head, and I free his silk locks from the hair tie, letting my fingers rake through his wet hair.

Taking my right leg, King wraps it around his shoulder and latches his mouth onto my pussy. He sucks and slurps every part of me so roughly it's as if he's trying to suck my soul from my body.

The sight of him between my legs is the hottest fucking thing. Our cum is still dripping down my legs, but that doesn't stop him from eating me like he's a starving man at a buffet.

"Oh God, King! Don't stop. Right there. Yes!" His velvet tongue flicks over my clit, once, twice, then he's sealing his plump lips over my bud. He sucks it into his mouth, and I temporarily go blind from the pleasure. Two thick fingers push inside of me, and in no time, I'm seeing stars and floating away to another galaxy, high on King-induced pleasure.

King stands, his arms wrapping around me to hold me upright. A smirk spreads across his lips, and I lean forward and lick over his beard and his lips that are glistening with both of our releases. He pushes me back against the wall again, his fingers tangling in my hair, our lips coming together and our tongues massaging against each other.

He tastes like the perfect mix of both me and him. Holy fuck, this man is intoxicating. If I don't get out of here right now, I'll be in neck-deep trouble.

Somehow, we managed to shower, despite the fact we couldn't keep our hands off each other. After eating me out, King fucked me again against the shower wall and didn't stop until my voice was hoarse from screaming his name and I had no more orgasms left to give.

I was right about King; he was covered from head to toe in tattoos. The only tattoo-free parts of him are his face and cock.

I've seen the tattoos on the other two guys' necks and arms, and I wonder if they're fully covered like King.

After our shower, he kissed me, then went to his bedroom to get dressed while I stayed in mine. In the closet, I found jeans, a long sleeve t-shirt, and knee-high flat boots. The outfit was a perfect fit and totally my style. Again, I don't want to know how they knew my size.

I've just finished twisting my hair into a French braid when King returns to my room wearing a knowing grin that screams he'd just been laid, and I know I'm wearing a matching one. Part of me can't believe I'd been so easy. I met him last night, and here I am, already jumping on his dick the first chance I got. I'd never been that type of woman, but apparently for King, I am. The other part of me is perfectly content with my decision. They are trading me off to a rival gang and I am likely to end up dead, so why not enjoy some dick before I go? Not only did I have a stranger's cock inside of me, but he was bare, and I let him come in me. What is wrong with me?

King caresses my cheek as he looks down at me with soft eyes. "What are you thinking about?" I look up at him and give him a soft smile.

"Nothing important."

"No regrets, right?" I quickly shake my head and lean up to wrap my arms around his neck.

"None, I promise." He dips his head and pecks my lips with a chaste kiss.

"Come on. I want to have some fun with you. Eli and Rowen will be out all day, so it's just us." He takes my hand, intertwining our fingers together, and leads me downstairs and outside into the crisp fall air.

Stepping outside confirmed my suspicion. We're in a cabin in the middle of the woods. We're secluded, no other cabins in sight, and I know we're quite far away from town. "No one is around to hear you scream." His warm breath tickles the back of my neck. I turn around to face him, crossing my arms over my chest.

"You can't scare me, so stop trying." He watches me with an amused grin.

"You're different." He leads me away from the cabin and further into the woods.

"Different from who?"

"From any other girl I've known."

"Don't compare me to anyone else." I scold, narrowing my blue eyes at him.

He stops in his tracks and turns to face me with a laugh. "It's a good thing, butterfly. There's fire within you."

"Why do you call me butterfly?"

"For the same reason you have a tattoo of a butterfly on your shoulder." He smiles and gives me his back when he turns around to walk further into the woods. He stunned me with his response. No one knows the meaning behind my tattoo, but he figured it out instantly.

I chose a butterfly because that's how I see myself. I was once trapped inside of my cocoon, and then I was reborn and given wings to be free and be who I really am. I've evolved just like a butterfly.

I'm reborn and free.

I can't explain my instant connection to King, and I know he feels it too, but doesn't want to. I don't want to either.

Somehow, I feel like we're more alike than I'd like to admit.

In a few days I'll be gone, most likely dead for real this time.

No, fuck that. I'm not going to become a coward now. I didn't survive many shitty things in my life just to end up dying at the hands of some gangsters. Nope, not today, not happening. The Triad wants to hand me over to the Westside Disciples, but that's sure as fuck not going to happen. I'll make certain of it.

I'll go along with King and the rest of them for now. But they better watch their backs because I'm not going down without a fight.

Twigs and leaves snap and crunch underneath our boots. King walks three steps ahead of me, and I rather enjoy the view. His ass looks phenomenal in his jeans. He's wearing his hair down, his light locks curtaining around his broad shoulders. The ache between my legs with each step is the only telling sign of what King and I had done only a few short hours ago.

It's been so long since I've been fucked, and I can still feel him between my legs. As if he can tell what I'm thinking, he turns around and looks at me with a knowing smirk. "I can feel you staring at my ass." I look up at him, a slow smirk spreading across my plump lips, and I shrug my shoulders in response.

"What do you expect? It's a nice ass." He chuckles, reaching his hand out toward me. I place my hand in his and allow him to lead me further into the woods. "Is this the part where you kill me and leave my body to be eaten by the animals?" King throws his head back and lets out a full belly laugh. His laughter is becoming my new favorite sound. It's so deep and carefree, causing an unfamiliar and unexpected warmth to flood my body each time I hear it.

"God, you really do have death on your mind."

"What do you expect?" I throw my hands up dramatically. "You do know it's likely that I'm going to die soon, right? Just let me go, tell Eli and Rowen that you lost me. I have done nothing to deserve this." His laughter ceases and his hazel eyes drill into my blue eyes. He lunges toward me, his hand wraps around my neck as he slams me back against a tree, knocking the air from my lungs.

"That's not how this works, butterfly. We may have fucked, but make no mistake about where my loyalty lies. I'd never choose a piece of pussy over my brothers. Our deal to trade you for control over the city borders was a group decision. That's not going to change just because of your sweet pussy. No matter how fucking good it is." His gritted words send a shiver straight down my spine.

Okay, perhaps I read the situation wrong.

Since I like playing with fire, I run my hand down his chest and cup his dick through his jeans, earning a low growl from him. "We'll see about that." I give him the sweetest smile I possibly can, and peck the corner of his mouth, ducking underneath his arms and walking away from him. I'm not dumb; I know the only reason I was able to walk away was because he allowed me to.

One second I am walking away from him, the next second he's picking me up and throwing me over his shoulder, holding onto the back of my thighs. His perfect round ass is in my face, so I smack it, only to earn a spank of my own in return. "Hey! That hurt! Put me down!" I protest weakly, wiggling against his grip, which only results in him tightening his grip on my legs to keep me secure. His open palm connects with my ass again, and I groan, the sensation going straight to my core.

"Behave. I want to show you something and we're almost there." With a huff, I wrap my arms around his waist from upside down as he continues walking, holding onto me as if I weigh nothing.

We come to a stop, and King bends down to set me back onto my feet. King turns me around after holding me for a moment so I can function properly, my back to his chest, with his arms wrapped around my waist securely. A wide grin spreads across my lips seeing the quads in front of us. He dips his head and kisses my cheek. "Wait here." He walks in the direction of the large brown shed, unlocks the door, and disappears inside.

Barely a minute later, he returns with a helmet and a red gas can. He tosses me the helmet while he fills one of the quads with gas, and once he's finished, he brings it to life and climbs on. I waste no time in pulling the helmet over my head and climbing on the four-wheeler behind him and wrapping my arms around his waist.

King revs the engine a couple of times then speeds off. My grip around him tightens and uncontrollable laughter escapes me as he speeds further into the woods, dodging trees and anything else in our way. It's the most fun I've had in a very long time.

And that's how our day was spent.

Just the two of us venturing further into the woods. We even took turns driving. Though I drove slower than he did, it was still incredible. We even stopped a few times to make out like horny teenagers, and he may or may not have fingered me into an orgasm right there on top of the four-wheeler.

It was the perfect way to spend the day before I get plunged deeper into danger, and unknowingly come one day closer to my death.

FOURTEEN

Eli

"**W**here is she?" Malakai asks for the third time, his patience growing thinner and thinner with each passing minute. It's humorous to me. I don't answer to him, and it would be wise for him to get that through his thick skull.

Rowen and I are sitting down with Malakai, the leader of the Westside Disciples. King stayed behind to babysit Tate, so it's just Rowen and I this time.

Typically, we'd handle business together, but we couldn't risk leaving Tate alone, and King was against the idea of tying her to her bed and leaving her there all day.

Poor bastard is already becoming pussy whipped.

"She's safe, for now." I clear my throat, my hands going to my black silk tie and loosening it. "You'll get her, and in exchange, you leave the city. You already know you're on our turf, and we don't need any more bloodshed." Unless we're the ones causing the bloodshed of course. But the Triad would never harm innocents, and since the Westside Disciples decided to be foolish and sell their whack product in our city, they've been harming innocents which started a war. A war that needs to end now.

We'd usually never make a deal; we'd solve the feud in death and eliminate our enemies. Only this time, it's not that simple. So, for now, our only hope that they'll crawl back into their hole, is that we make a deal.

Tate in return for them leaving.

We'd already made a deal with Marco, Malakai's brother and second-in-command. But before we turn her over, we wanted to meet with Malakai. Knowing the shady bastard he is, I wouldn't put it past him to back out on a deal that Marco made.

"Marco already agreed, but we all know that your word is final," I say, watching as he sits back in his seat, sipping from his bottle of beer. As a show of good faith, Rowen and I came into their run-down bar on the outskirts of the city to have a meeting.

"So, do we have a deal? The girl in exchange for you staying the fuck out of our city?" Malakai looks over his shoulder to where Marco stands, and they both share a silent nod.

"Alright, yeah, we got a deal. What you discussed previously with Marco still stands. Wednesday night you deliver her to us, and we'll stop selling in the city."

"In the Triad's city," I correct.

He nods. "Your city." I extend my hand out toward him and we shake on our deal.

"I am curious though, what do you want with her?" He sits back and looks at me with a smug grin.

King was the one that brought it to my attention that there's one question we haven't asked. Why does a rival gang want a nobody stripper? She's nothing special. I'd been so focused on getting the fuckers and their product out of our city that I didn't care to learn the reasons behind their sudden interest in Tate. That was foolish on my part.

"Thanks for coming by, we'll meet again Wednesday at ten. You can show yourself out." I study his face for a moment, then nod, and stand to my feet. I knew he wouldn't answer my question, but I had to ask anyways.

It wasn't uncommon for Rowen, King, and I to use people to get what we wanted, but there was something about this situation with Tate that left me with too many questions, questions that I shouldn't care about the answers to. She's supposed to be a means to an end, but now I'm wondering if she may be worth more than I'd originally thought.

I know the reason for that is because of Rowen. It's because of his past with her that makes me wonder why she's so important to the Westside Disciples. Based on what Rowen's told me, she disappeared thirteen years ago without a trace after he made her leave the city, and out of the blue, she reappeared nine months ago.

We've looked into her reappearance, and even her life after leaving the city, but found nothing. This girl is a mystery, and the more I think about it, the more I'm beginning to have questions of my own, and I'm on the crust of doubting myself and our plan.

Rowen has said before that he's tried to find her over the years, but there was no trace of her. It was as if she never existed prior to arriving nine months ago.

She has no family, and there's no reason for her to return to this city of all places.

Our city.

I see the turmoil in Rowen's eyes whenever I look at him, and because he's my brother, I worry about him. He puts on a brave face, but I know how much she's triggering him. Her presence is causing him to relive events he shouldn't have to.

Wednesday can't get here soon enough. Then we will be rid of her, and Rowen can go back to being himself. I'm hoping we can get all the answers we need by Wednesday, otherwise, the deal may be off.

"Something feels weird," Rowen says once we're in the car, and I drive us toward the freeway.

"What does?" I glance over at him.

"Malakai. I'm willing to bet my life that he doesn't even know who she is. She's been living here for nine months, yet he had no clue who she was, and now suddenly he wants her." He's right. It is a little strange.

"You think there's someone else pulling the strings."

"I do. I think there's someone else who wants her, and either that person is promising Malakai something for her, or he's trying to trade her for something, just like we are." He appears deep in thought before continuing on, "I'm going to ask around and see what I can find out before Wednesday."

"Regardless of what you find out, is that going to change anything?"

"No, we're still getting rid of her, but we can't have loose ends. Not knowing anything about her is a loose end that we can't afford."

"If you don't like the answer to your questions, are you going to be okay with walking away and leaving her with them?" It's a fair question, but he remains tight-lipped.

He has too much anger and guilt over the past. I don't think it's a good idea that he asks around and gets the answers to his questions. If he learns something he doesn't like, I know he will not be okay with handing Tate over to the enemy, regardless of what he says. He may act hostile toward her, but he doesn't want to see any harm come to her.

At least not from the hands of others.

Rowen acts like he hates her, but it's himself that he hates. He hates what she makes him feel.

We stop by Luigi's Pizza to pick up dinner on the way home. When we arrive back at the cabin, Rowen takes the boxes of pizza and wings inside, while I carry the cases of beer.

The moment he catches sight of Tate, he visibly tenses. I hate that for him.

And I am not the only one that notices the tense air either.

We carry the food into the kitchen. He grabs some paper plates while I open the boxes on the counter.

King walks in with an arm wrapped around Tate's shoulders and hands her a plate from the stack. She gives a polite smile in return.

She reaches for a piece of the supreme pizza, only for Rowen to be a dick as he grabs the piece she was reaching for quicker than she could.

With a scowl, she tries again with grabbing a different piece, only for him to snatch it from her yet again.

King and I share a look with raised brows.

"You're our fucking prisoner, you can eat the scraps after we're done," Rowen snaps. "King should've tied you up like the animal you are," he spits, shocking us all into silence.

Rowen's acting like a child. He continues grabbing food quicker than she can. I expect her to back down after his outburst, but she surprises us all.

She grabs a buffalo chicken wing from King's plate and throws it across at Rowen, the sauce smearing across his cheek. His eyes snaps to her, and fuck, if looks could kill, she'd drop dead right now at our feet.

"What the hell is your problem?" she demands, licking the buffalo sauce from her fingers then props her hands on her hips. "You're acting like a damn child." With a huff, she picks her plate up again and fills it with food. Rowen's fuming now; the fucker is damn near red, and either Tate doesn't notice or she simply doesn't care.

His fists clench, and before she can see it coming, he throws a piece of pizza right at her face. It hits her left check before it falls to the floor with a splat. The marinara sauce leaves red splotches of oil and sauce on her face.

Slamming her plate down on the counter, Tate stomps toward him until they are toe to toe. It's funny seeing someone of her size getting in Rowen's face. She barely reaches his shoulder and has to tip her head back to look at him.

Rowen stares her down, his brows pulled together in a deep V, his fists balled at his sides, and his jaw noticeably twitching. Tate is only adding fuel to the fire.

She's like a chihuahua fighting against a tiger.

Rowen attempts to speak but then decides against it. With a snarl, he stomps out of the kitchen.

"Yeah, you better run!" she yells after him, throwing her hands up with a huff of frustration. "You big fucking baby!"

I'm certain my eyes are wide, and my jaw has dropped to the floor. Rowen has never walked away when he's been angry. Between the three of us, he's the one with the worst anger issues. His uncontrolled anger has even scared me a time or two before. She challenged him, and he walked away.

He walked away.

Interesting.

Pussy whipped King goes to Tate's rescue and wipes the pizza sauce off her face, and all I can do is stand back and laugh at their exchange and her stupidity. She's flagging down a bull, not knowing what could've happened. "You shouldn't push him like that." Her ocean eyes snaps to me and shoots daggers.

"He started it," she mumbles under her breath.

"Keep pushing him and see what happens," I warn.

"I'll be fine. He won't hurt me, and King wouldn't let it happen anyways." She's confident in her words, but King and I know otherwise. If Rowen comes after her, there would be nothing we could do to stop him. He could easily kill her in a fit of rage, and we'd turn a blind eye to it. As much as King may like her and want to keep her alive, when it comes to Rowen, there's no stopping him.

It's kill or be killed.

We stand by each other before any piece of pussy.

FIFTEEN

Tate

It's Monday night.

Come Wednesday, the guys will be handing me off to the Westside Disciples.

I don't know what they want with me or why they're so interested in having me that they're willing to give up control over the part of the city where they sell their drugs, but they're doing it. Rowen can't wait to be rid of me, King is dreading it, and Eli is neutral.

Rowen has spent all day avoiding me like a plague after our kitchen incident last night.

King has been stuck to me like a lost puppy, and honestly, I'm enjoying it way too much. There's an undeniable connection between us. I feel drawn to him, and I've been secretly hoping that he'll choose to pursue our connection and not trade me like a fucking sack of potatoes.

I'm angry. So fucking angry.

I can't allow them to turn me over to the Westside Disciples where who knows what the fuck they'll do to me.

My time here is coming to an end. I have to get out, and I have to get out now.

I'm in the bedroom I've been staying in, sitting on the window bench staring out into the darkness of the night when I hear the bedroom door open.

"Hey," I breathe out with a sigh, not bothering to turn around. I'd just assumed it was King since he's been in my room every chance he gets. I am never alone since I've been here, and I'm not complaining.

"King went out for a while." A gruff voice comes from behind me as I continue staring out the window until Eli's reflection shines into view behind me. I watch him as he sits on my bed and leans forward to rest his elbows on his knees. I turn around to face him, pulling my knees to my chest and wrapping my arms around them.

"I hope you know that my blood will be on your hands," I say, and he just stares at me with a stoic expression.

"Wouldn't be the first time I've had blood on my hands, and it definitely won't be the last time either." He stands, staring me down for a moment before advancing on me.

I back away from him with a gasp, his hand finding my throat as he pins me back against the window. I stare at him with wide eyes, full of fear. This is the first time he's touched me, and the first time I've been alone with him. Unease churns inside my stomach. I'm afraid of him.

Eli leans in closer to me, his nose running along my jaw and up to my hair as he inhales my scent. "Hmm." He hums against my hair, pulling back until our noses touch.

His grip on my throat isn't tight, but I'm not confident that he's not going to strangle the life out of me.

Eli lingers for another moment, then in a flash, pulls away from me. "I wanted to know what it is about you that has King so fucking whipped." He looks me over, as if he's contemplating his next words, his deep chocolate eyes staring deep into my blue eyes. His gaze is so deep and intense I feel as if he's staring into my soul and peeling all my secrets. "I see nothing special about you."

His words hurt, even though they shouldn't.

I watch carefully as Eli squats down in front of me, his eyebrows pulling together as he stares at me. He's beginning to make me uncomfortable; I don't know what it is that he's seeing, but he's trying to figure me out.

"How many men have hurt you?" he asks in a low voice, our eyes never once straying from each other. His words take me by surprise and completely fucking shock the hell out of me.

How did he know I've been hurt before? Was I really that obvious by the way I crawled away from his touch?

I don't speak. He studies me carefully, like I'm an ant under a microscope. He's not looking at me with pity, instead, he's looking at me with bewilderment.

We remain in a silent stare off until he pulls himself away from me and exits my room. I stay frozen on the bench, my hand going to my neck to rub it slowly.

He didn't grab me hard enough to leave a mark or even actually hurt me, just enough to rattle me and allow me to feel a brief moment of fear. Really, it was the look in his eyes that scared me. I've seen that look before—the look of your inner demons battling to break through. I would know that look, it's the same one I see every time I look in the mirror.

What the fuck is going on with these guys? I need to get the fuck out of here and fast. I'm not going to stick around and let them hurt me or trade me off.

Fuck that and fuck them.

I'd have to wait until morning when I'm allowed outside, and then I would run. They haven't locked me in the room since the first night, but they kept the cabin doors sealed so there's no way for me to go outside without their supervision. I'd need a key to unlock the front door. And I know just the place to get it.

I'll convince King to let me outside and then I'll escape him. Sure, he's the largest of the three and could probably crush me, but I didn't escape death only to face it again. The woman I once was is now long gone.

He broke me, but they are quickly reminding me who the fuck I am.

The woman I have become no longer sits around and lets her life be controlled by the hands of a man. That weak woman died *that* night.

When King comes to my room, I pretend to be asleep.

The bed shifts with his weight as he lies behind me and pulls me close to him. I stay perfectly still and keep my eyes closed, waiting for his breathing to even out.

I'm hoping I'll be able to take his keys once he's asleep and unlock the front door and set myself free.

After several minutes, I still don't feel him properly asleep when suddenly, his deep voice rumbles. "I know you're awake. Tell me, butterfly, what's going on inside that beautiful head of yours?" I sigh, open my eyes and stare into the darkness of the room.

So much for taking his keys. Guess I really will have to wait until tomorrow when he lets me go outside.

I ask a question that'll allow me to get to know the man beside me a little better. Maybe I can learn his weak spots and use them against him. "Tell me something about yourself. About your childhood." He noticeably stills behind me and lets out a heated breath.

"Why?" he asks calmly, stroking my hair gently.

"Because I don't know you and I've spread my legs so quickly for you, and I don't want you to think that I'm easy. And who knows what'll happen come Wednesday, so I deserve to know the man that's sending me to get either gang-raped or murdered. Or both." My words are full of malice, and I mean every single thing I say.

I didn't have harsh feelings toward him at first, but now as we get closer to my uncertain future, I sure as fuck do.

With a heavy sigh, King's grip around my waist tightens. "There's something between us, so don't pretend there's not. We both know you're not easy either, you haven't been with anyone in a while." How the fuck does he know that?

I get the feeling he's known me a lot longer than I've known him.

"As for my childhood, it's not something I'd like to reminisce about. Never knew my dad, and my mom died of cancer when I was thirteen. I lived with my aunt for a few years. She fucking hated me, but liked the checks she got for taking me in. Every penny was shot in her veins or snorted up her nose. Eventually, I ran away and did what I had to do to survive and support myself. One day, I met Eli and Rowen, and the rest is history." I wasn't expecting him to actually answer my question, but now that he has, it has my heart racing.

I turn onto my left side to face him.

My eyes have now adjusted to the darkness, and I stare up at his hazel eyes. I wasn't going to give him sympathy or tell him I was sorry, after all, I wasn't the one responsible for his fucked-up life.

I had a fucked-up life too. But I don't want or need sympathy.

"Sounds like we were dealt some pretty shitty cards in life," I say, earning a chuckle from him.

He leans in and kisses my forehead. "Yeah, butterfly, we were." We stare at each other in silence for a few minutes.

"It was nice knowing you, King." I sit up on my knees, giving him a devious smirk. "You might as well fuck me while you can." I push him onto his back, climbing on top of him so I'm straddling him, and with agility, I remove my shirt, leaving myself naked. I was only wearing his t-shirt, so once it was removed, I become fully nude.

King doesn't need to be told twice to fuck me.

His hands slide up my bare chest, cupping my tits, his lips attacking mine. Our eager hands work together to remove him of his clothing.

I am already wet and ready for him.

With his hands on my hips in a rough and bruising grip, I slide my core along his rock-hard erection while our tongues dance together. I grind myself over his length repeatedly until he can't take it anymore.

King lifts me and sinks me slowly down the length of his cock, a groan leaving our lips in unison.

I've never had sex that feels this good before.

I will miss this feeling.

With his thumb circling my clit, his cock pounds into me like a racehorse.

As I near my orgasm, he stills his thrusts and yanks my body up until I am straddling his face. I cry out at the loss of his cock but recover soon enough once I realize what his intention is.

Securing his head between my thighs, I cover his face with my cunt. I rock my hips against his mouth and grab his hair, taking exactly what I need from him.

His skilled tongue works my pussy like no other. I am fucking putty in his hands. He knows exactly where to lick and where to touch to bring me to orgasm.

My release is so fucking close I can feel it. King sucks my clit like a delicious lollipop while his fingers curl inside of me, hitting against the spot that causes my vision to blur.

My body jerks, warmth filling my being, and before I know it, my orgasm floods me with a heart-stopping intensity.

King quickly pulls his fingers out of me, and I feel a gush of wetness squirt out of me, causing me to scream my release.

I'd never squirt before. I wasn't even aware I was capable of doing it. But holy fuck it is the most amazing experience.

King clearly doesn't mind drowning in my pussy juice. The dirty fucker devours it with his mouth and continues sucking my pussy until I am crying through another orgasm.

He grabs my hips and pulls me down his body, turning me until I am straddling him again. "Get back on my dick, baby." His beard glistens with my juices, and when he kisses me, I feel the wetness on my face.

I turn around so my back is facing him and glide down his now throbbing shaft. My pussy is sensitive in the best way possible. Leaning forward, I rest my hands on his thighs while he grabs a hold of my hips and fucks me from the bottom.

Moving one hand over my ass, he wets his thumb with my juices, then presses it against my puckered hole. My muscles tense at the intrusion as he shoves a thumb inside of my ass.

"It's okay, baby. Loosen up." I do exactly that. I relax my body, and he slowly pumps his thumb in and out of my ass while he fucks me raw.

King fucks me into countless orgasms.

I had a plan, but the second I had his dick, that plan went out the door, and all I wanted was to accept the endless orgasms, which he happily delivered.

SIXTEEN

Rowen

heard them.

All night long, I heard Tate and King fucking in the next room.

The walls aren't thin, but she was loud.

The sound of his grunts and groans and the headboard hitting the wall brought back memories I didn't want in my head. The sound of her brought back memories. I was aware they'd already fucked before, but I didn't need to hear it.

By what I assumed was round two, I stormed out of my bedroom and went down to the gym.

I knew King could last a while, and they had already been going for well over an hour. I wasn't about to stick around and listen to any more rounds.

Inside the gym, I put on my gloves and let my anger out on the punching bag. We are so close. So fucking close to getting rid of her, and my uncertainty is starting to take over and get the best of me.

Ever since King told us about her flinching, and Eli told us about the haunted look in her eyes when he grabbed her, I couldn't stop thinking about her, even more than I already was.

I kept thinking about her face every single time she was underneath me and how those ocean eyes would stare at me like I was her fucking savior instead of the one tormenting her.

She promised she'd never come back, yet here she is, under the same roof as me, getting fucked by my brother. I don't care that she's fucking King. I just don't want to hear it. Not when I so easily remember how sweet she tastes and how tight and warm her pussy feels being wrapped around my cock. I shouldn't be having these thoughts, and I fucking hate myself for remembering.

I remember, and she doesn't, and that angers me even further.

Though I'm beginning to get the feeling that she is jolted to her past with me when she looks at me. I've caught her staring at me with her brows pulled together in a deep V and a dark look in her beautiful orbs. I'm not certain, because she hasn't said anything, and she immediately looks away when I catch her staring.

I want her to remember, and then I want her to run. Fast and far away from me.

And this time, never fucking look back.

I want her out of my head.

I don't know how long I've been in the gym, but by the time I remove the thin gloves, I can see that my knuckles are bleeding, and when I walk upstairs from the basement, the sun is beginning to come to life and paint the sky with a dusting of dawn.

The aroma of coffee fills my nostrils, and I know Eli is awake. He's always been an early riser, not this early, but I know it's not King. He's not a morning person, and after hearing him and Tate going at it, I know he won't be awake before noon at least.

I walk into the kitchen, expecting to find Eli, but stop in my tracks when I see her sitting on the barstool in the kitchen, her knees up to her chest and her back facing me.

Selfishly, I take a moment to watch her movements as she brings the coffee mug to her lips and sips it.

She's wearing only King's black t-shirt; her toned bronze legs are on full display and begging to be looked at.

Walking further into the kitchen, I make my presence known but don't look toward her even when I feel her eyes on me. Instead, I busy myself with getting an empty mug from the cabinet and filling it with coffee from the fresh pot she prepared.

"Morning," she mumbles from behind me.

I look over my shoulder at her, watching how her lips pucker as she blows into her steaming mug of coffee. Coffee that I already know is full of creamer and tastes like pure sugar.

Tate has always liked a smidge of coffee with her creamer. I used to tease her about just drinking the creamer instead of putting coffee in it since it's purely creamer anyways. She's always made her coffee that way, then she will heat it up until it's nearly boiling because *it tastes better hot, and the creamer cools it down*. I don't know how she doesn't have a mouthful of cavities from the sweetness of her coffee.

A small ghost of a grin tugs at my lips at the memories I have of her. The few good memories that aren't tainted with her cries and blood.

"Morning," I respond, opening the fridge to pull out some ingredients for breakfast. "You hungry?" I hold up the carton of eggs and she nods.

"So, tomorrow you get rid of me. Are you happy?" Her tone is cold and distant.

I don't dare look at her.

I keep my hands focused on the task at hand, making her favorite breakfast, banana French toast with bacon crumbles and syrup mixed in the egg batter.

"I hope you're a good cook, since that is the very least you could do for me." She's trying to get a reaction; too bad I'm not going to take the bait.

"Be grateful I'm even doing this much for you."

"You're playing with my fucking life, you do know that, right? Have you stopped to think why these thugs might want me? What they'll do to me?" She's scared. She puts on a tough act, but she's scared.

Good, she should be.

"You seem like you've been through worse. I'm sure you can take it." Fuck. Did I really just say that? That was low. The color drains from her face and a frown finds her perfectly plump pouty lips.

"Fuck you, Rowen." I can't help but smirk at the sound of my name coming from her lips.

"No thanks, you probably still have King's cum in your loose pussy. Didn't realize what a whore you'd become." My words hit her like a slap in the face, and I feel like fucking shit for saying them, but I want her to feel as low and badly as I do. I want her to suffer right alongside me.

I don't see the punch coming.

One minute we are in a stare off, and the next minute I am cupping my bloody nose. "Go to hell," she spits, turning on her heel and storming out.

Fuck, that hurt. "I'm already there," I whisper to myself, turning the sink on to begin cleaning myself up.

I'd just gotten my nose to quit bleeding when Eli walks into the kitchen and instantly bursts into laughter, seeing the bloody napkins and my already undoubtedly bruised nose.

I flip him off and throw the napkins into the trash and wash my hands.

"What the hell happened to you? Let me guess, a little raven-haired stripper with a nice ass?" He grabs a mug and fills it with coffee, still laughing at my expense. "What did you do?"

"Fuck off. Why do you assume I did something?" He shoots me a knowing look and I sigh. "I said something pretty fucked up and she punched me."

"Sounds like you deserved it then." I did.

I instantly regretted my words as soon as I said them.

I don't think she's a whore. I just knew that word would trigger her. She hated it every single time he'd call her that.

"I'm not a whore!" Turquoise eyes full of tears stared straight into my own, my heart aching as he forced me to say things to her that I knew weren't true, things I hated saying because I knew how much it affected her.

"I'm not a whore!" she cried.

"That's good, keep telling her, boy!"

"Y–y–yes, y–y–ou are. You're my whore!" I choked on my words, struggling to tell her the vile things he wanted me to.

"Louder!" he roared.

"You're a dirty whore!" I yelled and she sobbed harder.

"Whose whore is she?"

"She's my whore! She's my dirty little whore!" I couldn't hear the zip of his pants over her sobs, but I knew what he was doing the moment I looked over at him. Bile rose in my throat seeing his expression darken as he looked at her naked, shivering body.

"Ro? You okay?" I snap out of my thoughts at the sound of Eli's voice. He places a hand on my shoulder and squeezes, offering me comfort.

I nod vacantly, but he knows me better than that, though, thankfully he doesn't push me.

"Talk to me if you need someone, please, brother." I nod again, unable to speak. "Good. So, anyways, I was thinking about the whole Westside situation. And you're right, there's got to be more to it than them just wanting a pretty piece of ass." I already know that. There's no reason why the Westside Disciples would want Tate, unless they'd also be trading her just like we are.

But trading her for what? What do they want from her?

"We already know this; it doesn't make any sense, though." I finish cooking and fix us both a plate, handing him his and making my way toward the table while he follows.

"I checked into it though. Before two weeks ago, they didn't know what she looked like or who she was. We've been watching her since the moment she stepped foot into our city, and she's never met or had any run-ins with any WD members, or their associates." I can tell there's more, so I urge him to continue when he pauses. "Ro, they know her by her real name." My eyes almost bulge out of their sockets.

Nine months ago, when Tate got off the bus into our city, we knew about it instantly. The Triad knows of every single person who decides to take up residence in our city. No one slips under our radar.

King and Eli were instantly interested, meanwhile, I couldn't care less about her. That's because I didn't know who she was. I avoided her, as I do most women, when she interviewed for Sinners, a club we own. Of course they made sure she got the job—it only made it easier to keep tabs on her.

I never bothered looking at their new fascination, I never do, but I should have. Now I'm regretting that I didn't, right from the beginning.

"Who here would know who she really is, want her for some reason, and have affiliation with WD?" Eli's question hangs heavy in the air between us.

Fuck.

"We can't give her to them until we know all the facts. We're going in blind, it's not smart." Am I saying this because I genuinely believe it and care for her well-being? Or because I want to be selfish and keep her?

"I agree. Not when we can't see the bigger picture and the motives behind their reasons for wanting her." I'd tried to separate my personal feelings from the situation, but I should've known that would be impossible to do when it comes to her. Had it been anyone else, I would've been able to turn them over without any hesitation or questions, but it's her. It's Tate.

The girl I failed to protect all those years ago.

I guess part of me is looking at this as my second chance, and by protecting her now, maybe I wouldn't feel so guilty for not protecting her then when she needed me to the most. Perhaps I could learn to hate myself a little less by making up for things in my past.

"You do know that by not delivering her, our deal will be off, right? The disciples will continue to sell in our city." I say, shaking my head.

"Let's go to the meeting tomorrow. Surely there's something else Malakai wants besides Tate, and maybe, just maybe, we'll be able to get it out of him and find out why he really wants her." I highly doubt that. Malakai is smart; he'd never allow anyone else to know his reasoning behind the shit he does. But I nod, because Eli is standing beside me, wanting to keep Tate a little while longer despite the fact it would be problematic for us.

"Okay, but she can't go home or back to the club. She can't be seen in public at all. They know what she looks like now and they'll come after her if she's at home unprotected. For now, she stays with us until we find out the reasoning behind them wanting her. Let's not tell her yet, and I'll tell King when he gets up."

"He might be asleep for a while; they were fucking like jackrabbits last night." I roll my eyes, taking a sip of my coffee.

"I don't know how the fuck you slept through that last night." He chuckles, giving me a wink.

"I didn't, I jerked off instead. She's nice and loud; King's a lucky bastard." Eli stands up from his seat with a laugh when I flip him off. "I'm going to win her over, maybe get my dick wet too." I couldn't tell if he meant it or not. Wouldn't surprise me though, he never cared before about sticking his dick in the same hole King and I stuck ours. It isn't uncommon for us to share women, but he'd only be sharing a pussy with King, not me.

Realization hits me as I clean up the dishes from breakfast.

She isn't going anywhere. She's staying with us for as long as we need, in our space, under our protection.

Yes, I want to protect her, but I don't want to be close to her again. I can't be close to her for a longer period of time.

Fuck. This won't be as easy as I thought, and perhaps, I should've thought this through further before I jumped the gun and suggested it.

I'm battling too much with myself, going back and forth, uncertain of what to do and how to feel.

All I know is I might be fucked.

All logical thoughts fly out the door the moment she appears in my space.

Thirteen years later, and I'm still weak when it comes to her.

"Are you fucking serious?" I groan, closing my eyes and counting to ten in an attempt to ease some of my anger.

"Sorry, brother, I need King today." Eli grips my shoulder and squeezes hard. He'd just informed me that he and King are going into the city, and I have to stay behind to babysit.

We couldn't risk leaving Tate alone.

There's nowhere for her to run to, and no one knows where our cabin is located, but we still can't risk leaving her alone.

With an exasperated sigh, I grab a bottle of water from the fridge and walk into the living room where Tate and King are both lip-locked, swapping spit.

"We'll be back, butterfly. Be good for Rowen," King says, and her head turns toward me, her eyes narrowing.

She's in a pair of leggings that does delicious things for her peachy ass, and a long sleeve sweater. It's a little chilly—Eli did good with picking out the clothing for her. On her small feet, she's wearing Chuck Taylor converse. This is the most relaxed she's looked since she's been here.

Do I want her to be relaxed and comfortable in my space? That's yet to be decided.

"Do I have to stay here with him?" she whines, rolling her eyes.

"Trust me, princess. I'm not fond of being stuck here with you either. I'd rather shoot myself in the foot than be stuck babysitting your ass."

"Can I be the one to shoot you?"

"Alright, children, that's enough. We're leaving, so please behave. We'll be back later," Eli comments, slipping his jacket on and leaving without another word.

King kisses her goodbye, then he leaves as well.

We face each other for several minutes even after we hear Eli's car leave the driveway.

With a slow smirk, I turn away from her and find purchase in my beloved gym to let out my frustrations.

SEVENTEEN

Tate

The door is unlocked.

Rowen forgot to lock the door after King and Eli left.

The fucking door is unlocked! I repeat, *the fucking door is unlocked!*

After they left, Rowen went down downstairs into the gym and played his music so loud that I can hear it from the living room where I've been sitting.

I was trying to concentrate on watching the TV, but the door kept calling my name, so I got up and checked the doorknob, sending a silent prayer that it would be unlocked.

My prayers were instantly answered because it is unlocked!

The doorknob turns, and with a deep breath, I jerk it open, suddenly triggering obnoxious beeping, but it blends in with Rowen's loud music.

Fuck. I didn't think about them having an alarm set, no wonder why he didn't lock the door. They set the alarm. Of course, they did.

I instantly take off running down the stairs and away from the cabin.

There's no telling how long it would take for them to realize that the alarm has been triggered and find me missing. Now's my chance to escape, and I'm fucking taking it. I'm not staying behind and letting these fuckers trade me like some type of toy. Fuck that.

Learning that I would be alone with Rowen today was a nice surprise. All day I was anxious to make a move toward my freedom, and look how easy it turned out to be!

I don't know where the fuck I'm going. I'd been blinded when they brought me here and I've only been allowed outside a couple of times.

An idea pops into my head, and I run toward the shed where King had the quads parked.

My lungs are on fire, my legs are aching, but I don't stop running until I reach the shed, and the moment I do, a smile spreads across my lips.

There, in front of me, is King's black four-wheeler with the fucking key in it!

Jackpot! Today is my lucky day.

I waste no time climbing on and twisting the key to turn it on, pulling the helmet on my head.

Safety first.

I'd never driven one before, not until King showed me how. I hope there's enough gas to get me the fuck out of here, or at least as far away as possible. I know it's not likely that I'll be able to drive this thing all the way into the city an hour away.

I can't go home. I'm certain they know where I live.

Fuck, I have to get out of the city all together.

Speeding through the woods, I race and turn to dodge everything that's in my way. I'm giving it as much speed as I can, driving back in the direction of the house. I know from my drive with King that the area behind their cabin leads to nothing. If I want to make it toward the road, I have to go down the driveway, the same way that Eli and King had taken.

Fuck, what if they see me? It's not likely, but it's possible. I'm sure they're far enough away by now, but what if they're not? It's a risk I have to take, and I'm too high on adrenaline right now.

My only focus is to get the fuck out of here and fast.

I'm keeping my eyes on the lookout as I come closer to the cabin and speed past it. I look behind me to make sure that Rowen is still inside. The door is opened as I left it and I don't see him anywhere. With a smirk, I turn my focus back toward the driveway, speeding further and further away from the house.

I can see the road ahead of me. I'm close, so fucking close to getting to the road and one step closer to my freedom.

Perhaps I spoke too soon because I'm just about to reach the road when I see Eli's black Range Rover flying straight toward me. My heart begins beating so rapidly in my chest that I can hear it pounding. I can no longer hear the roar of the four-wheeler; I can only hear my heart.

Fuck. I am so close.

I'm determined to make it out of here. The pathway to the road is narrow, only big enough for one car. I don't slow down, I keep driving straight toward Eli, hoping he'll realize that I'm not slowing down, and he will eventually get the fuck out of my way. But somehow, I doubt that he would stop and get out of my way.

They're not going to let me go.

He hasn't stopped. The car is coming right toward me, not slowing down either.

We're getting closer and closer to hitting each other head-on. My palms are sweaty, and if one of us doesn't give up, we're going to crash into each other.

Fuck. I won't make it. I'm the one to finally give up.

I hit the break and come to a sudden stop with a jolt. I've been so focused on the car in front of me that I never realized someone was following behind me.

Rowen.

His strong arms rip the helmet off my head, and he picks me up and tosses me over his shoulder, carrying me back toward the cabin. He doesn't have a shirt on and I can feel the sweat that's pouring down his back.

I slap and scratch his back, his grip on my thighs only tightening in response. He's huffing and puffing, clearly out of breath from running to catch me.

Well, that was a failed attempt at an escape.

He carries me all the way to their house and straight up the stairs, neither of us saying a single word to each other.

Once we reach my bedroom, he throws me on my bed and walks out, slamming the door behind him and then I hear the click of the lock.

My heart is still racing, and I know this isn't the last time I try to get away from them. I may have failed today, but you know what they say.

If at first you don't succeed, try and try again.

And that's exactly what I'm going to do.

EIGHTEEN

Eli

Tate tried to escape.

She tried to fucking escape.

King and I had only been gone twenty minutes when he received the notification on his phone that the cabin alarm was triggered. He pulled up the cameras and replayed the video from when motion was detected, and there on the screen, plain as day, we watched Tate run out of the house.

We have cameras all around the house and hidden in the woods. She ran out of our cabin and straight toward the shed where our four-wheelers are located. We keep them nearby for times that we need to venture further into the woods. They're not often used.

We usually keep them in the front, but since we haven't needed them lately, they've been in the back shed. They needed a few repairs and that's why we'd taken them back there.

Immediately, I flipped my car around and sped back toward the cabin. I'd turned down the driveway just as she was nearing the road, and for a second there, I didn't think she was going to stop.

We were playing a dangerous game, but I wasn't going to crash into her. At least I don't think I was going to.

She was in survival mode. She doesn't know that we decided not to hand her over, so I really couldn't blame her for being worried and trying to escape.

She tried and failed and had her little fun, and this once, we'll let it go. But if she thinks she can try that again, she'll be sorry.

Rowen locked her in her room, and that's where she'll stay until we're ready for her. Even King wasn't interested in paying her a nightly visit.

It's Wednesday night and we're on our way to our meeting location with the Westside Disciples.

Rowen and I brought King up to speed with our new plan, and no surprise there, he was perfectly content with going along with it. He's willing to do anything necessary to protect Tate, even after her attempt to escape.

The poor bastard is already smitten with her, and I knew that from the moment he laid his eyes on her months ago.

He's had a weird obsession with her that's only grown since they've officially met in person, and she's been staying with us. Staying unwillingly, I might add.

Of the three of us, King is the one that's the most sensitive. He hates hard and loves even harder. Though it does take a lot for him to hate a person.

He may be a cold-blooded killer, but he's sensitive with his heart. That's why it doesn't surprise me that he and Tate have been so close the last few days.

As long as she doesn't shift our dynamic, I don't see an issue with it. Not yet at least.

I already know that she's the one who's fully capable of ruining us.

She could be the end of us, and that thought terrifies me. We've never allowed a woman to come between us, and I don't want to start now.

Shaking myself from my thoughts, I turn my attention to Rowen who's engaged in an intense stare off with Tate. They've been scowling at each other, starting from the moment she was let out of her room.

We brought backup with us tonight, Nico and Vlad, just in case the Westside Disciples decide to be stupid, and we'd need either backup or to get away quickly. They don't always come with us, but they have our backs when we need them.

We haven't yet told Tate that she's staying with us. Rowen wanted to keep her thinking she was being traded, so that's the story we are sticking with. For now, at least.

I nudge him in the shoulder to get his attention, and with a sigh, he turns around.

We're sitting in the backseat while King and Tate are sitting in the third row. She'd said something snarky to Rowen, and he'd turned around to shoot daggers at her. They're acting like damn children, and I was ready to kick both of their asses on the side of the road.

They're on my last fucking nerve right now.

"Focus, brother, keep your head clear," I say, only loud enough for him to hear, and he nods.

Forty minutes later, the car comes to a stop at the abandoned warehouse on the border of the Triad's city and the Westside Disciples' city, the location we agreed on to meet. From what I can see, we are the first ones here.

Instantly, my guard is up, and I keep watch outside the windows, as do the others. I don't like this one bit. It's dark, vacant, and right now, we're sitting ducks.

Where the fuck are the Disciples?

As if they can hear my question, a car pulls into the parking lot a few feet away from us and skids to a stop. I recognize the car and nod toward the guys.

Rowen and I get out first, same time as Malakai.

I turn to Tate. "Stay put," I warn.

"Nico, sit with her," I say, just as King's big ass struggles to get out of the tiny third row in our SUV.

Nico replaces my seat in the back and Vlad stays behind the wheel.

"Where's the girl?" Malakai stands in front of his car with his arms crossed over his chest and Marco beside him.

"I'd love to give her to you, but I have a few questions first." I stand in the middle as always, King to my left and Rowen to my right.

Malakai scoffs. "I don't have to answer a god damn thing. We made a deal, now hand her over."

"You see, what's interesting to me is that there's no connection between you two. What reason could you possibly have for wanting her?" I've been looking into it for a few days. Trying to find any possible connection between the two, but there was absolutely nothing.

Whoever wants her doesn't know what she looks like now or what name she goes by. I know for a fact that Malakai isn't aware of her current appearance and name change.

They've seen one photo of her. I'm not sure how old the photo is, but she looks completely fucking different, like a damn plastic Barbie doll. The woman they were expecting and the woman sitting in my SUV right now are two completely different people.

A night and day difference.

Pop. Pop. Pop.

It happened so fast. One second, all five of us are standing and talking, the next second we're all ducking for cover and have our guns drawn that we always have on us.

The sound of bullets hitting metal followed by yells can be heard. Nico and Vlad are at our sides, and while I don't appreciate the fact they left Tate alone, I do appreciate that they are quick to jump to our aid to assist us when shit's going sideways.

"It's a fucking ambush!" King roars, jumping up from the side of the SUV where we had taken cover and begin popping off shots of his own. I, too, jump up to cover him and that's when I see Malakai and Marco both laying on the ground with a bullet between their eyes. Holy shit.

What the fuck?!

We are shooting blindly, not knowing who or where the bullets are coming from, only knowing that they keep coming.

Nico goes down with a thud and a groan.

"Cover me!" I yell, running from my spot over toward Nico who's holding his chest as blood oozes out of his wound and covers his hand. I rip my jacket off and apply pressure against his chest.

We all make it out alive, that's the deal. Nico has a family, he is family, and he's not dying on my watch.

The bullets are continuing to fly around me. I watch my back while also trying to stop the bleeding from Nico's chest. My sole attention is on him when I hear a scream pierce the air, my head instantly snapping up and going to find the source and cause of the scream.

My eyes land on Rowen—at the blood staining his white shirt and Tate's wide frightened eyes.

"Rowen!"

The next seconds go by in slow motion.

Vlad runs toward me to take over caring for Nico, urging me to go to Rowen.

King is standing his ground, shooting back, and in the distance, I can see faceless figures moving in closer toward us.

Rowen drops to the ground, limply dropping his gun at his side. I can only watch him for a second; I need to assist King now that these faceless fucks are coming in closer and circling us.

Vlad hauls Nico to the front seat of the SUV and starts it before coming toward me to cover King so I can go check on Rowen.

There on the ground beside him is Tate. She's kneeling beside him and is shirtless, using her own cloth to apply pressure to his bullet wound. I kneel across from her, my hands covering her small bloody hands.

Rowen groans out in pain, his eyes finding mine. "Don't die on me, brother. You stay with me, do you hear me?" I demand, and his lips curl up into a small grin.

Tate raises her head, her eyes widening as she looks over my head.

I hear it before I see it.

The single gunshot followed by a grunt and a thud.

Holy fuck.

Tate just shot someone with zero hesitation.

The gunshots stop, and I am assuming whoever Tate shot was the last one standing.

In an instant, Vlad and King are loading Rowen into the car and Vlad's driving us back home.

Everything's happening so fucking fast, my mind can't catch up.

King is on the phone with the doctor, telling him to meet us at our penthouse. Our cabin is too far, and both Nico and Rowen need a doctor immediately and our penthouse is much closer.

I have Rowen's head on my lap and Tate sits at the other end continuing to hold her shirt against his bleeding bullet wound.

He's been shot in the chest, and she isn't letting her grip slack even when King and I have both tried to take over. Her eyebrows are pulled together, her and Rowen staring at each other so intensely it doesn't feel right to interrupt. They're having a moment, as weird of a moment as it may be.

"You can't die." Her whispered words linger in the air for too long.

We're five minutes from the penthouse when his breathing becomes shallow and ragged. Despite her applying pressure to his wound, blood is still oozing out and covering her hands.

"Stay with me, brother!" I yell, and King perks up from the backseat.

Rowen's breathing is too fucking shallow for my liking. I can't lose one of my brothers. I can't. I won't let it fucking happen!

With a smile, I watch as Rowen lifts a bloody hand to Tate's cheek and caresses it gently. "Lee, my angel," he whispers before his hand falls and silence fills the car.

NINETEEN

Tate

Lee.

He called me Lee.

No one has called me by my real name in months.

No one in my new life knows who I am, or at least that's what I thought.

How does Rowen know who I am? I thought I'd done a good enough job of covering my tracks and hiding my real identity.

As far as I'm concerned, Lee is dead. She died nine months ago at the hands of her abusive husband.

I'm in the living room of their penthouse, standing in front of the floor-to-ceiling window staring out at the city down below me. My mind is in a million other places and I'm mentally miles away from everything that's going on around me. I'm lost inside my own head, only to be pulled out when King wraps his jacket around my shoulders and turns me to face him.

I'm shirtless, only wearing a red lace bra, and I still have Rowen's blood on my hands and streaks on my cheek. It's starting to crack and itch now, but I can't wash it off. Not yet, not when I don't know if he's going to live or die.

"You should go take a shower. You can use mine. First door on the right upstairs." He wraps his arms around me and pulls me into a hug, kissing the top of my head. "He's going to be okay, butterfly. The doctor is with him, go shower and then we'll talk."

As soon as we got to the penthouse, Rowen and Nico were both taken to another floor, where they were going to meet with their doctor.

Vlad brought me inside of the penthouse, then he left to go to one of the lower floors where the rest of them were. I don't know how long I've been standing here, but the mention of a hot shower does sound incredible.

If he'll be okay, I'll wash the blood off... but if he's not, then I want his blood on me.

Silently I pull away from King's touch and take the stairs two at a time making my way toward King's bedroom.

In the bathroom, I take the rest of my clothing off and set them inside of the small trash can beside the toilet.

I don't want to be reminded of anything from tonight.

With hands that won't quit shaking, I open the frosted glass shower door, reach my hand in and turn the water on, waiting until it gets hot before I step inside. I take the washcloth and some of King's bodywash and begin washing myself, scrubbing Rowen's blood off my skin, watching as the pink water circles the drain.

I'm scrubbing my skin for the third time when King steps behind me in the shower and wraps his arms around my waist from behind.

"Why did he call me Lee?" I blurt, needing to know what they know about me. He turns me to face him and studies my face for a minute. He dips his head and crushes our lips together. I place my hands on his muscular chest, shoving him away from me.

He narrows his eyes at me. "You know why." I don't.

"So, you three get to know all this shit and I get to be kept in the dark?" I roll my eyes and throw the wet washcloth at his face.

"You know exactly why he called you by your real name, Lee. I put some clothes on my bed for you." He turns his back to me and begins washing himself, a clear sign that he's done talking.

Why the fuck is he acting mysterious?

Obviously, if I knew why Rowen had called me Lee, I wouldn't be fucking asking.

Instantly, chills shoot down my spine and the only thing that comes to mind is Sebastian.

Is he behind this? Is he the reason why a gang I've never heard of suddenly wants me? Did he find me?

In the back of my mind, I know he's innocent. He's not here, and he's not the reason those Westside fucks want me.

They're dead now, so I wonder what that means for me. I'm hoping they'll let me go and I can resume my life, but I know that's not likely. I know they'll never let me go.

And I'm aware of the fact that Rowen knowing who I am has nothing to do with Sebastian.

Unable to be around King any further, I open the door and step out of the shower, taking a towel and wrapping it around my body. I walk into the bedroom, and just like he said, he'd laid out clothes on his bed for me. There's a black t-shirt and a pair of sweatpants that I assume belongs to either Rowen or Eli because they are a little too small to belong to King. They're all massive in size, but King's legs are bigger than Eli and Rowen. He has massive thick thunder thighs.

I quickly dress myself, cinching the drawstrings on the sweatpants as tight as they'll go, and roll them up at the ankles so they're not too long. I pull on the black socks that were beside the clothes and walk back into the bathroom to brush my hair with King's hairbrush.

When I walk downstairs to the living room, Eli has just entered and he stares at me with a dark but sad look in his eyes.

I gulp, my heart dropping to my stomach at the sight of him. "Is… is he okay?" He holds my gaze for a moment before he nods, and I let out a breath I didn't know I'd been holding.

Like a sad little boy, Eli walks right toward me. I hold my arms out for him and he steps into my embrace, lowering his head on my shoulder. He's allowing himself to be vulnerable around me.

"Doc says he'll be fine. I'm going to grab a shower and go sit with him for a while. He's still unconscious, but if you wait, we can go down together." He raises his head, his fingertips trailing along my heart-shaped face slowly before he brushes my hair behind my ears. "Wait for me." He presses a faint kiss to my lips, then turns toward the stairs.

Twenty minutes later, Eli returns downstairs. I am sitting in the living room, anxiously waiting for him. He holds his hand out toward me and I take it, and he leads us toward the elevator. We stop at the floor directly below us.

"We own this entire building. A lot of our staff lives here, but we turned this apartment specifically into our own little operating room for the staff on our payroll. With our line of work, going to the hospital isn't an option," he explains, unlocking the door and leading me inside of a dimly lit apartment that smells of disinfectant and copper.

My grip on his hand becomes tighter as he leads me down the hallway and opens the door to one of the bedrooms.

"Doc will return him home once he's well enough and doesn't need to be monitored. Until then, he'll stay here with Doc and a nurse," Eli says.

Wow, they really did think of everything. I can't speak, so I nod, letting go of his hand and walking into the bedroom toward Rowen.

Hesitantly, I sit in the chair beside the bed, and Eli sits on the arm of the chair stroking my back gently.

"He can't stand being in the same room as me, the only time we've spoken is when we've fought, and yet I was worried he was going to die." I scoff, leaning my head against Eli's side.

"I was worried he was going to die too. I don't know what I'd do if I lost him or King, these fuckers are my only family." He sighs and picks me up as if I weigh nothing. He slides down into the chair and holds me on his lap.

"Why does he hate me so much?"

"That's his story to tell." My eyebrows crease in confusion, and I turn my attention back to him.

"What the fuck does that mean?"

"It means exactly what I said. His reason for keeping you at arm's length and being a dick is his reason, and his reason only to tell."

"He called me Lee," I gripe with a whisper, searching his eyes, hoping to find any piece of an answer.

"I know, and you'll get your chance to talk to him." He turns me around so my back is against his chest as he wraps his arms around my waist.

We sit there for hours, the only noise around us coming from the beeping from the monitors that Rowen is attached to.

His large body makes the small twin bed even smaller. I'd laugh if now were the time for that.

I can't help but feel like this is all my fault. It is my fault.

Rowen was shot because of me.

I don't remember falling asleep, but when I come to, I'm on the chair alone.

The sun is up, and it's only Rowen and I in the room. He's still asleep, so like a creeper, I watch him. I stare at his flawless face.

Carefully I lean forward and take his hand, my fingertips tracing over the intricate tattoos that cover both of his arms.

I'm mindlessly tracing over the ink on his right inner forearm when I feel the raised skin underneath the ink.

With confusion, I carefully turn his arm toward me to examine it.

Scars.

He has scars inside both of his arms, scars that I instantly recognize because I've traced them before. I've traced them hundreds of times with my fingers and my tongue.

I sit back in the chair with a gasp, letting go of his arm as if he'd burned me. I cup my hands together over my mouth, my eyes wide and full of shock.

I'm a fucking idiot.

Rowen's intense emerald eyes slowly flutter open and connect with mine. Several minutes pass by with us staring at each other before he finally speaks, "You weren't supposed to come back. Why did you come back?" he whispers in a groggy voice, and instantly, I know exactly what he's talking about.

A single tear rolls down my cheek as I stare at him in silence.

How could I not have seen it sooner? How could I not recognize him?

Those eyes, everything about him is the same.

Yeah, he's older now than when I saw him last, but he's not someone anyone could ever forget.

It's been thirteen years since the night I last saw him, but he still looks the same, only older. And looking at him now, I can finally see it.

"Why didn't you say anything?" I whisper, allowing my tears to fall and stain my cheeks.

"I told you not to come back. You never did know how to listen," he says with a small but pained grin.

Instantly, memories of the first time we met flood my mind.

"This will be your room, sweetie. Go ahead and unpack your bags, then wash up and come downstairs for lunch," the woman said with a smile, giving me a tight hug. I waited until she left my new bedroom before I sat down on the bed beside my suitcase and let out a sigh. I pulled out my notebook from my backpack and wrote her name down.

Andrea—foster mother number four.

This was my fourth foster home in two years.

My dad decided to decorate the walls of our tiny apartment with his brains right in front of me, and since then, I've been in foster care.

Andrea seemed to be nicer than all the others. I hoped that she would always be nice and willing to keep me.

I was ten now, and the older I got, the more I become unwanted. No one wanted to adopt older kids. Everyone wanted babies.

I was sitting on my new bed when the door creaked open, and a green-eyed boy entered. He looked older than me, but his eyes were kind and I thought we could become friends. It would be nice to have a friend for a change. I was never at the other homes long enough to have a friend, neither were the other kids.

"Hi, I'm Rowen. How old are you?" he said with a smile as he walked further into my room. "You're new here?" I nodded.

"I'm Lee and I'm ten. How long have you lived here?" He didn't look like Andrea, so I assumed she wasn't his real mother, and he, too, must be a foster

kid like me.

He sat down on the floor in front of me. "Two weeks. There are no other kids, it's just us here. I'm thirteen, but I guess we could be friends."

"What does it matter how old I am?"

"Because I don't want a baby as a friend," he deadpanned.

I rolled my eyes. "Well, you didn't have a friend at all before me. So, you're welcome," I said, crossing my arms across my chest.

He laughed and pulled out a granola bar from his pocket and opened it, breaking it in half and holding half out toward me.

"Make sure that you sneak some food at dinner for later. We only get one meal a day, so take what you can get. This house is hell, but I'll protect you." His honest words sent shivers down my spine.

Andrea seemed nice enough, but I knew by now that looks could be deceiving. My other foster parents seemed nice too, and then they became mean.

My mom looked nice when she was alive, but drugs made her mean. My daddy was nice too, until mom died.

I missed my parents. They had problems, but they wanted me sometimes. Isn't being wanted sometimes better than never being wanted?

Looking into Rowen's kind but rare green eyes, I knew he was telling the truth.

Rowen would protect me, and he'd be my very first friend.

Tears roll freely down my cheeks. Rowen catches them with the pads of his thumbs as he cups my face in his hands. "Why did you come back here, Lee?"

"Don't call me that. Lee's dead," I whisper. He nods weakly in understanding.

His question is valid. I, too, had questioned it myself many times over the last few months why I came here instead of running anywhere else.

I grew up in this city, and there's nothing good to remember here.

Thirteen years ago, I witnessed Rowen commit his first murder, and I promised him I'd run and never return to this city.

I'd run away from the hell, only to plunge deeper when I met Sebastian. I escaped his dollhouse of hell, and here I am again.

Right back where my life started.

Right back in the presence of the man who owns all of my firsts.

What a full fucking circle I completed.

"I don't know why I came back," I answer honestly. "Why didn't you tell me who you were?"

He takes my hand and traces over my palm with a sigh. "I'd thought that you would've recognized me. When you didn't, I didn't want to say anything. Seeing you again has brought back a lot of memories for me. Bad memories. You're fucking with my head too much." I nod in understanding, because being here again has brought back memories for me too. "Why did you come back here? What happened?" he asks. I inhale, shaking my head as I stare into his remorseful eyes.

Eyes that hold many years of apologies that I don't want to hear. I never wanted to hear a single apology from him.

Rowen saved me, even though I know he'll never see it that way.

"When you're doing better, we'll talk, and I'll tell you why I'm here. For now, you need to rest." I lean up and press a small kiss to his cheek that he flinches away from. It bothers me, but I don't show it.

Rowen had inner demons that I knew would take time to heal from. And it would start with him forgiving himself, which I know is easier said than done.

His eyes close and I stand up from the chair and walk toward the door, stealing one last glance at him. I send a silent prayer to anyone listening that he'd be okay and heal quickly.

When I return to the penthouse, Eli's sitting in the living room nursing a glass of scotch. I walk into the kitchen, grab a bottle of beer from the fridge and pop the cap on my way back to the living room. I sit on the couch beside him with a sigh.

"So, you remember Ro?" He breaks our silence first after a few minutes.

I nod. "Yeah. Yeah, I do. I don't know how I didn't recognize him at first."

"It's been a while, he's uglier now so I don't blame you," he jokes, nudging me in the shoulder playfully to lighten the mood.

"D–do you know… about our history?" His eyes snaps to mine, and he holds my gaze. He reaches over and takes my hand in his, giving it a gentle squeeze.

"I know about Rowen's past, yes. He's told me all of his secrets, and if you ever want to, you can tell me yours too."

"Why should I? Your plan to get rid of me failed, so how long until you try again?"

"Tate, we both know you're not going anywhere. You're ours, and all four of us know it." His words send chills down my spine, but somehow, I knew what he was saying was true.

I feel like I was meant to cross paths with them from day one. I could've freaked out, screamed, or fought that day when they took me from the club, but I didn't because from the moment King had wrapped his arms around me, I felt comforted and whole. I couldn't explain it then, but now seeing Rowen again and knowing who he is, I can't help but wonder if it was fate bringing me back to him.

I'd thought I was too young at the time to know what love was, but that wasn't true.

I've loved Rowen since I was ten years old, and now he's back in my life.

For how long, I don't know.

Only time will tell.

TWENTY

Eli

Tate has spent every waking moment downstairs with Rowen.

Doc says he's going to make a full recovery and is already starting to recover well. He woke up the next day after being shot—that was three days ago. And she's been by his side ever since. The only time she leaves is when he's asleep. She comes upstairs to shower and eat, then she's with him again. Not that I mind, I'm glad that they're spending time together, and after all these years, he's taking a step in the right direction toward healing and learning to forgive himself for the abuse they both had to endure as children.

They're both victims and had to experience things that no child should ever have to experience. For years, I've watched Rowen struggle and battle himself for things that happened in their past. I've helped him through the nightmares. I can only hope that he'll forgive himself as much as she seems to have forgiven him.

Tate is bringing out feelings in all three of us. Feelings that I'm not sure how to process. For the second time in my life, I feel alive, like the ice wall I built around my heart is beginning to thaw. All it takes is a simple glance from her to feel whole.

It's the strangest feeling really. I barely even know her, yet there's something about her that has me so easily gravitating toward her. Seeing Tate with my brothers and how easily they cling to her makes me want to become a better man and experience the same treatment they receive. I'm jealous of them.

Love makes you weak.

Women are only to be used for one thing.

I can hear my father's words playing on repeat in my head. Hearing his gravelly voice so clearly sends a shiver down my spine.

I'd be a fool to allow myself to be weak again and fall for another woman. I know what happens when you let your guard down and allow a woman to become your weakness.

"She's a weakness and any woman who makes you weak must be eliminated."

"Do it, son. Pull the trigger and eliminate the distraction."

My father's voice has been playing on repeat in my mind more often these days. I should be listening and staying away from Tate the temptress. I know I should, but instead, I'm looking for any way to put a smile on her face.

I'm standing in one of the once empty rooms in the basement with a boyish grin spread across my face as I put the finishing touches on the studio.

King had told me about Tate and her love of ballet and that she used to be a dancer. That's where I got the idea to turn one of our empty rooms into a studio for her. I had to pay triple the regular cost to have it finished so quickly, but it was worth every single penny.

Two of the walls are painted a light cotton candy pink, and the other two walls are covered with floor-to-ceiling mirrors with a ballet barre mounted along them. The wooden maple floors are newly polished, and in the corner of the room is a media station so she'll be able to turn music on while she dances. The room is perfect, and I can't wait to see the smile it'll bring to her face.

She's so beautiful when she smiles, and I'm like a giddy boy waiting to see her smile and know that I'm the reason for it.

When I enter Ro's makeshift hospital room, I see he's asleep and Tate's small body is curled up uncomfortably in the chair beside his bed. It's seven and already dark out, and once again she's been down here all day.

Walking toward her, I gently brush my fingertips along her smooth cheek. She wakes with a start, her hand gripping mine firmly, her eyes flying open and landing on me.

"It's okay, it's just me." I kneel in front of her, watching as she rubs the sleep from her eyes and slowly sits up. "Come with me. I have something to show you." I take her small hand in mine and stand, pulling her up with me.

She's silent as I lead her out of the room and down to the basement. The only time she makes a noise is the soft yawns that she lets out. I know she's exhausted, and the bags underneath her eyes are the telltale indicators as well. She sleeps in that uncomfortable chair in Rowen's room, and I know she likely isn't getting much sleep in it.

"Where are you taking me?" she finally asks as we approach the basement.

"I have something to show you. Close your eyes." She rolls her blue eyes before she decides to obey and closes them.

"Keep them closed until I tell you to open." She nods, and I lead her through the basement gym and into the area that I turned into her studio. With a bright smile on my face, I turn on the lights and lead her into the middle of the room. "Open your eyes," I say, suddenly nervous about her reaction.

Tate's eyes open slowly, and I watch as they widen and she takes in the sight of the studio. Her studio. "Oh my God," she gasps, covering her mouth with her hands, walking in circles around the room. "Oh my God, Eli." Her hands are shaking, her eyes are becoming glossy. "You… you did this… for me?" She sucks in a gasp of air as the first tear falls down her smooth cheek.

I nod, watching the soft rise and fall of her perfect chest. I walk to the storage shelf and pick up the shoe box, walking back toward her and extending the box. She looks at me through her thick wet eyelashes for a moment before she takes the shoe box with shaky hands and opens it, carefully taking out the brand-new pointe ballet shoes.

"Why did you do this, Eli?" she asks, hugging the shoes to her chest.

That was a great question, why did I do it? I didn't have to do it, especially when she is a nobody.

She's nothing to me.

Liar.

I've known her for less than a week, yet here I am, going out of my way to do something kind for her.

You're becoming weak. You're allowing some piece of pussy to control your feelings.

I shake away the voice in my head, not wanting it to be right. I'm doing something nice for someone that means a lot to my brother. That's it.

At least, I hope.

"Consider it a thank you for saving mine and Ro's life. You shot one of the guys that ambushed us when I didn't see him approaching."

She studies my face for a silent moment. "Thank you, thank you so much. No one has ever done anything like this for me before." She wipes her tears away and rewards me with the smile that I was waiting for.

The simple smile that curls on her lips is enough to brighten anyone's day.

"Enjoy it. I'll leave you alone if you want to dance for a little bit." She nods, giving me another smile before we say our silent goodbyes and I leave her to test her new studio.

She deserves it... but I'm not yet sure why I feel that way.

TWENTY-ONE

Tate

The crowd erupts into a cheer of applause as I complete my final performance of the night. The heavy red velvet curtain comes down from the ceiling, closing off myself and the rest of the dancers from the audience. I'm breathless and sore, sweat lining my body.

I can still hear the audience clapping from backstage and a wave of relief comes over me at the sound.

They're clapping for me.

They're cheering for me.

I've been with Ciel Ballet for a year now and have been the lead in every single recital. Tonight, the performance was of Romeo and Juliet, and of course I played Juliet. I was given the role without even having to audition for it.

I never have to audition.

Most of the other dancers here don't like me. They've been here longer than me, yet they think I get special treatment. In a way, I guess I do.

For me, dancing is as easy as breathing.

Yes, I put in a lot of work, but I swear in another life I was a ballerina, *and that's why it's so easy for me now. The other girls spent their entire life in ballet classes and preparing to move to pointe and become the dancers they are today. I've only had a year of professional dance lessons.*

Three months was all it took for me to graduate to pointe, and by the time I reached six months with the company, I was preparing for my first solo recital. Willa says I was born to be a ballerina.

Thanks to her, I get to do what I love every day. Getting to dance and do something I've wanted to do since I was a child makes it all worth it. It makes all of the things that go on at home worth it.

Backstage, the other dancers mingle and talk amongst themselves. I have my own dressing room, and since they don't talk much to me, I slip past them and go up the stairs that lead to my dressing room.

The moment I step inside, an eerie feeling comes over me when I see the vase containing two dozen white roses on my vanity table.

Always two dozen, and always white roses.

Gulping, I grab my sweater that's hanging on the back of the door and pull it over my arms, suddenly feeling too exposed. I don't have to read the card to know who the roses are from.

They're from him. *They're always from him, always waiting for me in my dressing room after my performance. I get a lot of flowers after my performances, but he's the only one who gives me white roses.*

White because white symbolizes purity.

I find it funny, considering he knows that I'm not pure.

I'm standing in front of my vanity staring at the flowers when the door creaks open. I don't need to look up to know who it is, I feel it in the air the moment he enters my space. My skin prickles, a shiver runs down my spine, and my stomach ties in knots.

He stands behind me, his fingertips trailing over the exposed skin on the back of my neck, his touch burning. "My little bird, you danced beautifully tonight, as always." He turns me to face him, his eyes as dark as the devil's.

"I thought you were away on business." I'm disappointed he's here. It's been nine days since I last saw him, and he said he was going to be away on business and would miss my recital tonight. He's not supposed to be here.

He studies my face carefully, his bushy black eyebrows pulling together in a deep V. "Little bird, are you not happy to see me?"

"Of course, I'm happy to see you. I just didn't expect you so soon." Lie. I'm not happy to see him.

With his next breath, he crushes his lips against mine, stealing a kiss I didn't want to give. I wonder if he can taste the lies on my tongue. "Get changed. We have a long night ahead of us."

The music stops and I stumble, falling to my knees as I'm pulled out of a memory and back into reality. I roll onto my back, taking slow deep breaths to calm my erratically beating heart. I remind myself that it's just a memory and I'm not with him anymore.

He's dead, and I'm free from him.

Sitting up, I raise my right hand to trace over the scars on the back of my neck and on my left shoulder that are hidden beneath my butterfly tattoo. The scars that he left on me.

I'm safe, I'm alive, I'm free.

I repeat the words in my head until I believe it and I'm able to get back on my feet. That's enough dancing for now; it's beginning to trigger memories I'd prefer to keep buried for as long as possible.

Eli gave me this studio three days ago, and I've split my time between being here and being with Rowen who's been sleeping his days away. I'm not complaining, it's good for him, he needs it.

I'm not sure why Eli converted this room into a studio for me. I'm assuming this means that I'll be their permanent prisoner if he's changing part of his living space for me. And honestly, I don't know how I feel about it. The whole situation is fucked up.

I'm fucked up.

I should be trying to escape again, fight them, anything to get away. Yet, I'm not. I'm not doing any of the things I know I should be doing. Instead, I'm wearing ballet slippers that I haven't been able to wear in way too long, and I'm enjoying the feel of freedom.

Only, I'm not free.

I'm being held captive by three men and allowing the lines to become blurred.

I'm still lost in thought when King enters the studio. I don't notice him right away. Not until he wraps his arms around me from behind and rests his chin on my shoulder. "What are you doing here?" I snap, attempting to pull away, but he doesn't allow it. He tightens his grip around my waist.

"I came to watch you dance, and to convince you to come and have dinner with me." Dinner? I hadn't realized it was that late already.

"No, I'm not dancing for you." I attempt to pull away again, and this time he lets me go.

"What's going on, butterfly?" I turn to face him, a frown creasing my lips.

"Nothing. I guess between dancing again and knowing who Rowen is, it's just bringing up too many memories from my past," I explain with a sigh.

He nods, then turns me so I'm facing the mirror and he's behind me again. "Let me help you relax." His voice is low and sultry in my ear, his fingertips trailing up and down my bare arms, leaving goosebumps in their wake.

My eyes are glued to our reflection in the mirror, carefully watching every part of me that he touches. He nudges my head to the side, and

I comply, watching as his lips connect with my delicate skin and he sucks the sweaty flesh into his mouth, his velvet tongue circling my flesh.

He's sucking and kissing my neck while his fingers trail down to my waist. He pushes my small spandex shorts down my legs, growling when he sees that I'm not wearing panties.

"Mmm, easy access," he mumbles against my skin, pulling away long enough to remove the thin tank top I'm wearing. He hums in appreciation, taking one of my nipples between his thumb and forefinger, rolling the pebbled bud around. "Keep your eyes on the mirror, baby. I want you to see how beautiful you look when you come," he whispers, nibbling on my earlobe and biting down gently.

My body is on fire and desperate for his touch. Slowly, his right hand trails down my body and he parts my folds, dipping his fingers into my wetness. I keep my eyes focused on our reflection in the mirror, watching his fingers as they circle my clit.

"King, I want you," I mumble breathlessly, seeing how my pussy glistens with my wetness.

"Your wish is my command." He kisses my shoulder, pulling his hands away from my body long enough to undress himself. He grips my hips firmly, lines himself up with my entrance, and with one painful thrust, he's spreading me in the most delicious way, filling me to the brim with his cock.

I cry out in pleasure, my head falling back on to his shoulder, my eyes closing and mouth opening. "Keep your eyes open, butterfly. Watch yourself." I obey, my eyes practically glued to the sight of us in the mirror, watching as his cock disappears into my body over and over again, inch by delicious inch.

Our groans and pants are mixing together, our bodies both becoming hot, pressed against each other. His left hand is gripping and tugging on my nipples while his right hand is between my legs rubbing my clit. "Harder, King, fuck me harder," I pant breathlessly.

He growls, shoves me against the mirror, and grips my hips firmly with his calloused hands while he thrusts into me, hitting the spot within me that only he can reach. I raise my right leg and spread it out on the ballet barre, spreading myself even wider for him.

My breath is fogging up the mirror and I'm struggling to keep my eyes on him. The pleasure coursing through my body is too much, my orgasm is on the verge of exploding and soaking his cock.

"Fuck, butterfly. Your pretty pussy feels so good wrapped around my cock," he grunts, each thrust sending me further against the mirror. "You need to come, now!" His right hand finds my clit, he traces quick circles over it, sending me closer and closer to my orgasm.

I'm climbing higher and higher. And when the barbell in his cock drags over the spot deep within, I come with a scream, drowning his cock with my pussy juice at the same time he roars his release and shoots his warm seed deep inside of me.

"Fuck yeah, that's it, baby, just like that," he praises, catching my tired body as I fall limply in his arms.

He kisses the side of my head, both of us collapsing to the floor. "Spread your legs, baby. I'm ready to eat." He lays me on my back and suctions his mouth over my pussy, sucking my clit until he sends me screaming into another orgasm.

TWENTY-TWO

Rowen

"You stupid little shit! Get your fucking ass in here." The angry fat man was holding Lee's blonde hair in his fist, swinging her around the room like a ragdoll. "Get in here and do what you're supposed to do, or else I'll have to do it!" he spat, and without hesitation, I walked the rest of the way into the basement, further into his studio where he stood with her. The musty smell of mold and sweat instantly made me gag.

If I didn't obey him, then he'd touch her, and I hated when his meaty hands were on Lee's fragile prepubescent body. Her pale skin was still covered in purple, green, and black bruises from the latest punishment she endured for refusing his advances when he tried to touch her body and she fought him off.

Tonight, she didn't get to say no.

Usually, whenever she fought him and said no, he'd hit her, but tonight that wasn't going to happen.

If she said no tonight, she wouldn't just get hit, instead, he'd open his toolbox and use one of the tools on her that he always threatened her with, or worse, instead of hitting her, he'd touch her private areas himself.

I'd rip his fat ass to shreds if he ever touched Lee.

I was the one raping Lee every night, not Greg—our foster father. It was *me that did his dirty work, and when I disobeyed, my punishment was worse than hers. But it was a punishment I'd gladly take if it meant she'd be okay for the night.*

Lee always begged me to not disobey. She said she'd rather it be me who hurt her instead of him. She could barely handle me, and I knew if he was the one to do it, then she'd be split in half. She was so tiny and malnourished. Her bones protruded from her skin.

Andrea, our foster mother, was at work, which meant it was time for Greg to complete his "work" as he called it.

Every time, I hated myself for hurting her, but she was always there to reassure me that it was okay and I was doing her a favor.

No matter how my angel tried to justify it, I was raping her.

And Lee was an angel. She was sent to me to help me through the days, even though I knew how selfish it was to think that she was meant for me when I was the devil who'd been hurting her.

Greg hit her, but I invaded her body.

I hated myself. I hated myself even more when my body betrayed me and I derived pleasure in what we were doing, and the pleasure would build until I'd come inside of her.

Every time that I'd pull out of her body, my dick would be covered in her blood.

Greg would leave us alone in the studio afterward, and she would curl up in my arms and assure me everything was fine.

How could she think that? How could she not blame me when I was hurting her? And my dick was covered in the evidence of her pain. She was twelve now; we'd been doing this nearly every night for two years, and not once had she ever blamed me or been afraid of me.

I hated myself to the point that I began cutting. I needed a release for my pain, and I found the way to get that release was by taking a razor to my arms. My left forearm was still wrapped in a white bandage from my most recent date with my razor.

"Get the fuck over here!" Greg yelled, shoving me in the back and pushing me toward the twin bed with the white sheets in the middle of the studio.

Lee was already on the bed, her knees to her chest and her hands covering her malnourished naked body. Even with sneaking her food, she was still extremely small and sickly pale. Bile rose in the back of my throat just seeing her and that scared look in her eyes.

The sick fuck—Greg—recorded us and sold his homemade kiddie porn on the internet to his pervert friends. I vowed one day to hunt all his friends down and kill those sick worthless fuckers.

Tonight was different than other nights.

Lee had a miscarriage two weeks ago, and since that happened, I hadn't been able to see her.

Greg had kept her locked in the basement and convinced Andrea that she'd snuck out and that's how she got pregnant. They locked her away for "her own good" as they said. And now I was seeing her for the first time in two weeks. I didn't exactly know what happened, all I knew was that Lee woke up in the middle of the night bleeding and Andrea took her to the hospital.

I didn't see Lee when they returned, but I overhead Andrea and Greg talking about the miscarriage after they came back from the hospital.

Lee was pregnant. I got her pregnant.

I promised to protect her, and I failed. I was ruining the beautiful angel that was sent to me.

I must protect her. I didn't know how, but I knew that I needed to protect her from this life with Greg.

I loved her, I always had, even despite hating myself for hurting her, I loved her. We both needed to get away, and it had to happen sooner rather than later.

While Greg was setting up the camera and getting it adjusted, I was sitting on the bed holding Lee in my arms and stroking her silky blonde hair that always smelled like honey and vanilla.

"I'm sorry about the baby," I whispered in her ear. Her head jerked up and her sad blue eyes stared into mine.

"I didn't know I was pregnant," she whispered, tears rolling down her pale cheeks that I quickly wiped away.

"This shouldn't be happening. I'm so sorry, Lee. I promise, I will get you out of here." She wrapped her arms around my neck and shook her head.

"I will never leave without you, Rowen." Before either of us could say anything else, the spotlight was on us, and Greg was already filming. We knew what that meant, so she laid back while I undressed myself.

I kept my eyes closed while I assaulted her; I couldn't stand to look in her eyes and see the pain and discomfort I was causing her, especially after having a miscarriage. She was still bleeding and raw.

Once we were finished, as usual, Greg took the white sheets off the bed containing her blood and folded them, placing them in a secure bag in order to ship them to one of the men on his pedophile website that liked to have souvenirs.

When he left the studio, I laid down and held Lee's cold, shaking body in my arms while she cried.

"I'm so sorry, Lee. I'm so sorry for hurting you and doing this to you." She looked up at me with her teary eyes.

"Stop apologizing, Rowen. I want it to be you, I wouldn't want him to be the one touching me. And you didn't hurt me."

"Then why are you crying if I didn't hurt you?" She kissed my cheek and cuddled back into my arms, never giving me an answer to why she was crying. Instead, she removed the bandage from my arm to inspect the damage I'd done with my razor. Her pale blue lips parted with a gasp once she realized what I'd carved into my arm. There, on the middle of my left forearm, was her name carved deep into my skin.

The feel of a warm body and movement beside me wake me from my dreams. Only this time, I'm not waking from my nightmares in a panic.

It's been two weeks since I got shot and Tate hasn't left my side since.

We haven't spoken any further about our past, as that's been a heavy topic we've been avoiding, instead, we've been focusing on the present. And honestly, we don't even talk much, but when we do, it's simple and meaningless.

It's almost as if we don't know how to be around each other again when we're avoiding such a heavy conversation.

Since Doc cleared me to return to the penthouse and sleep in my own bed, she's been sleeping with me every night.

I know it's driving King crazy not having her there to keep his bed and his dick warm, but I appreciate that she's here taking care of me.

Speaking of King, the bed shifts before I hear his voice whispering something inaudible into Tate's ear, which causes her to giggle, and that instantly turns into a low groan.

"Stop, he could wake up. Hands to yourself." She giggles again.

"Come on, I can be quick. I miss you," he whispers, and now it's my turn to groan, only this time in frustration.

"Too late, I'm already awake. And don't you two dare think about having sex in my bed with me in it," I grumble, rubbing my eyes and slowly opening them.

"You can join," King says with all seriousness in his tone.

"He just got shot, leave him alone. Go make us breakfast," she scolds him.

"I didn't hear a denial to my offer of a threesome. I'll make you breakfast if you take a shower with me. Just because Ro is suffering, doesn't mean I have to." King is nothing if not persistent. Tate scoffs, then pulls him to her and plants a long, lingering kiss on his lips. My chest aches with jealousy.

With hearts in his eyes and a tent in his pants, King leaves my room, and suddenly I can't help but laugh.

"You've got him so pussy whipped," I say. She sits up on her knees and looks down at me, shrugging off my words.

"How are you feeling?" she asks with concern in her voice. Doc says I'm out of the woods, but need to take it easy for a few more weeks. She asks me the same question every morning and my answer is always the same.

"I'm fine. I'm feeling a lot better," I answer, but she doesn't seem convinced.

She's been giving me five-star treatment the last two weeks. Anything that I've needed she's been right there to help me with or do for me.

"Let's go get breakfast." I sit up, and she's right by my side to help me stand, even though I'm not in any pain.

I think in her mind that by helping me, it's also helping her, so I don't complain even though I no longer require any help.

With my arm around her shoulders, we walk downstairs toward the kitchen where King stands in front of the stove cooking breakfast.

Eli's sitting on the barstool in front of the island and the moment he sees Tate, his face lights up and he holds his arms out for her.

Odd.

Day by day, she's getting them more and more wrapped around her little finger. King is already head over heels for her, and I see Eli getting closer and closer to the point of no return with her. He adores her, and now it's only a matter of time until he too gets in her bed.

I'm not judging; I think it's just my jealousy speaking. I'm jealous because I loved her first and I want her to be the same way with me as she is with the two of them, but I can't let go of the past. I can't stop hating myself for everything that I did to her. She doesn't hold it against me—she didn't then, and she doesn't now.

But I do. I haven't gotten over it even if she has.

Tate has always been forgiving and has always looked on the brighter side of any situation, no matter how fucked up the situation may be.

"So, we have a lead as to who shot you. Obviously, it wasn't WD since Malakai and Marco are both dead," Eli says as he stands and moves to the dining table as King carries over the plates of food. "Vlad checked up on a couple of the guys that were shot, and only one of them has gang affiliation."

"Wait, so you're saying that they weren't working together?" I ask, lowering myself into my seat and filling my plate with food.

He shakes his head. "Nope. I think someone hired them to take us out. The Disciples are falling apart since Malakai's death, but King and I are going to talk to his cousin to find out everything Malakai wasn't telling us. We know they weren't the ones that wanted Tate, and I'm guessing whoever does is the one who assembled the team to ambush us," Eli continues speaking, and I watch as Tate's eyes widen.

"No, this can't be about me. Who the fuck would be so interested in me that they drafted a crew to ambush you guys?" She shakes her head, shoveling bacon and pancakes into her mouth.

"I don't know, but we're going to find out. So, I think it's time that you tell us why you returned to the city," King speaks up with a raised eyebrow.

"My past has nothing to do with any of this. There's no one looking for me, and no one who would even care enough to go through all this trouble," Tate defends, rolling her eyes.

"I think you're wrong. Whoever wants you, doesn't know that you changed your appearance and name. They know you as Lee, and that's what Malakai knew you as too. Lee with blonde hair," I say, reaching over to take a lock of her black hair in my fingers.

Her eyes are ready to burst out of her head with the assumption. "You need to help us, Tate. We'll keep you safe, but to do that, we have to know who's so interested in you," King adds. She sits back in her chair with a sigh. I can practically see her mind racing and realize that there are things she isn't telling us.

Hence the fact she's back here.

I knew that Eli had been looking into the ambush. The three of us were aware that the Westside Disciples were using Tate to trade, just like we had planned to do at first. But what we didn't know was what they were getting out of it.

Are they trading her for money? Drugs? Or something else entirely?

We're in the dark about what they were hoping to gain. All we know for certain is that there is someone in the background pulling the strings.

As for who that person is, only she can help us find the answer.

"Come on, Tate. Talk to us. Tell me why you came back here," I say, taking her hand in mind. Her eyes meet mine and slowly she nods with a small sigh.

TWENTY-THREE

Tate

I sit there at the table, speechless.

They want me to tell them about my past and my reason for coming back to the city.

They think somehow it could be connected, but I'm not so sure. I know there's no way Sebastian is connected to this.

If he knew where I was, or that I was still alive, he'd come for me himself and not hire someone else to do his dirty work. He's always been very hands-on when it comes to me, so there's no way he'd suddenly stop now.

No, he's not behind this. This…I know for a fact.

However, with hesitation, I agree to narrate my past to them.

I agree to tell them the story of how I killed myself.

Eli is cleaning up breakfast since King cooked, and the rest of us are sitting in the living room, waiting for him to join us before I tear myself open and share the hell that I escaped from.

I'm standing, pacing the room, when Eli joins us in the living room and sits beside Rowen on the couch. King is sitting in the recliner, all with their eyes on me.

"Go ahead, butterfly. Tell us why you came back to the city," King says, giving me a reassuring smile.

I hate being vulnerable.

Rowen was shot because someone out there, other than them, is trying to kidnap me, so I have no choice. I must share the reason I returned.

With a sigh and a deep breath, I turn to face them. "I came back to the city because…" I pause, trying to sort out a way inside of my head how to approach this conversation. "I'm married," I blurt, and they all look at me in surprise. They weren't expecting for me to drop that type of bombshell.

"You have a husband?" King gives me a sinister look that makes me shudder. I have to look away from his cold hazel stare.

"Yes… I've been married for five years."

"What the actual fuck!" he roars, causing me to jerk in a flinch that doesn't go unnoticed. I hold his gaze, and in an instant, his eyes soften and realization sets in. He's beginning to piece two and two together and understand why I flinch the way I do sometimes.

"Shut up, King, let her talk. We need to hear everything." Rowen urges me to continue even though I saw that he, too, was surprised by my revelation of being married.

"My husband was an abusive bastard. He was so charming during the time we dated and got engaged, but the second we said our vows, everything changed. It started with snippy insults from him, then a few months into our marriage, it became physical. I had to quit doing everything I loved that he didn't approve of. I had to quit dancing, I couldn't see my friends, I couldn't even go to the store without him needing to know every small detail. He controlled everything about me. How I dressed, what I ate, where I went, what perfume I used.

When I say everything, I mean everything, even right down to my nail polish." I inhale deeply to look down at my freshly painted red nails. "I once got my nails painted a color he didn't like, so he broke two of my fingers." I can't make eye contact with them as I speak because I know I'd see sympathy on their faces and that's the last thing I want from them. Instead, I look down at my left hand and trace over my crooked pinky that I still can't straighten all the way.

"Did you ever try to leave?" Eli asks, but I don't look at him.

"Once. I was pregnant and didn't want my baby being raised around his abuse. I tried to leave but didn't make it very far. He found me and forced me back home." My voice is clogged with emotion. Slowly I spread my hand out across my flat stomach.

"What happened to your baby?" Rowen's the one to speak this time. I torture myself by looking up at him and meeting his eyes.

His usually green eyes are nearly black, his jaw tightly clenched. He's angry, and when I look at Eli and King, they share similar looks. They are fuming in anger. I can't blame them. I was angry too.

"He was angry at me for trying to leave and didn't want kids yet, so he beat the baby out of me." The first tear rolls down my cheek, and quickly I wipe it away, not wanting to cry in front of them or at all.

I've let Sebastian have enough of my tears, and I refuse to cry anymore over things he did. "He beat me so badly I had a miscarriage. The trauma was so intense that I'll never be able to have children." I walk toward the fireplace and sit down on the floor beside it. Leaning back against the wall, I bring my knees to my chest. "I dealt with his shit for five years. One day, I couldn't take it anymore. I knew he was going to kill me, so I let him. So to speak…" I lose myself in the memory of that night in our bedroom, and with a deep breath, I tell the guys my entire story of what happened nine months ago on Lee's last night alive.

"You stupid fucking whore! You always make me angry!" Sebastian yelled, saliva spraying my face as he screamed at me. We were nose to nose as he pinned my back against the wall by his grip on my throat.

My eyelids had become too heavy to keep open, my arms were too tired to continue fighting him. My fingertips were bloody. I could feel his skin underneath my nails from all the places I scratched him.

I succumbed to letting my eyes close as darkness took over. With my eyelids closed, I willed my pulse to slow using the exercises I'd been practicing over the last few weeks in preparation for that moment. And just like I anticipated, he loosened his grip on my throat, allowing me to fall to the floor with a soft thud.

I didn't react; I kept my eyes closed and held my breath. This plan required perfect execution. I knew there was a possibility I'd actually die, but it was something I was willing to toy with. And that's exactly what I was doing. I heard his footsteps as he walked toward the bed, and only seconds later he was collapsing onto it.

Exactly as planned.

On hands and knees, I crawled over toward him, placed my hands on his back, shaking him to see how deep in a drug-induced sleep he was.

It probably wasn't a smart idea to triple the dose of sleeping pills and put it in alcohol instead of water, but I didn't care.

Maybe he would die right along with me.

With my back against the bed, I gasped for air, only allowing myself a minute or two to breathe cherished air into my lungs before I had jumped up and sprung into action, carrying out the escape plan I'd been planning for far too long.

The first step was to cut my nails.

I used a nail clipper to carefully cut the nails that I'd been growing out for this exact reason.

His DNA was under my nails.

A few nail clippings were carefully placed around the toilet and thrown around in our bedroom and the rest were flushed. With quick steps, I had exited our room and hurried into the guest room, went inside the closet, and removed the blood bags that I'd hidden in there inside a minifridge.

Setting the blood bags on the bed, I dragged the minifridge back into the bedroom and restocked it with the water bottles I'd taken out when I began withdrawing and collecting my own blood.

I've seen Gone Girl and if she could do it, so could I, regardless of that story being fictional.

I'd spent three months planning this. I needed it to be foolproof.

Back in our bedroom, I had to work quickly. I needed to be long gone before he ever woke.

No time was wasted in carefully opening the blood bags and splattering it around the walls. I'd watched enough crime shows and listened to crime podcasts to know what to do and how to make it appear that I was dead.

I'd even grabbed the lamp from the bedside table and put blood on it to make it appear as if he'd killed me with blunt force trauma. I wore gloves to be careful that my fingerprints wouldn't be fresh anywhere they shouldn't be.

Taking Seb's hand, I wrapped it around the lamp to get his fingerprints on the murder weapon.

Once my work was complete, a smile curled on my lips. I stood back to admire my handiwork.

My blood was splattered on our headboard and walls, the lamp with his fingerprints had been ripped from the wall and was dropped on my side of the bed. A pool of blood was on my pillow and the sheets, my bloody hair that I'd ripped from my scalp was on my pillowcase and the bottom of the lamp.

Our room looked like the perfect crime scene, and I knew without a doubt that it would be believable.

The bloody bedroom, and the photos that Delilah would provide to the police once she learned I was missing, was the final piece needed for Sebastian to be charged with murder. Or at least have his reputation ruined.

I also knew without a doubt that the law enforcement in his family would have no problem covering up their perfect golden boy. In this town, he was a golden boy, a perfect saint, and now everyone would see him for the abusive son of a bitch he really was. I could settle for a ruined reputation if he doesn't go to jail.

A rush of excitement came over me just thinking about all the things the press would say about him.

I'd spent months documenting his abuse. Pictures, journal entries, video recordings. Soon, the entire town would see in full color the abuse he inflicted on me.

As much as I wanted, I couldn't stand there any longer. I had to get out and go.

My final move was to roll up the rug on our floor after dripping blood on the carpet. The rug was heavy, but I was high on adrenaline and so close, so fucking close to the finish line to stop now or get tired.

I'd dripped a few drops of blood on my way to the garage from the most recent vile of blood that I collected this morning. I stuffed the rug into the trunk of his car, ensuring there was enough hair and blood to make it appear as if my body had been wrapped in the rug and he'd transported me somewhere to dispose me of.

The last step was to take my backpack and duffel back from the garage storage closet. The bags and clothes inside were all brand new, bought in cash. Not only would I have new clothing, different from anything I'd ever been allowed to wear, but I also had a stack of cash that would be enough to get me where I needed to be and to set me up with an apartment and hold me over until I found a job.

My plan had been well thought out. Still, I couldn't help being a little paranoid.

After putting on black sweatpants and a black hoodie, I combed my fingers through my blonde hair, brushing it into a low ponytail and placed a black ball cap on my head. With the cap pulled down low to cover my face, I yanked up my hood to conceal my identity further.

With my bags on my shoulders, I slipped out of the garage side door and ran like a track star, away from that house. Away from the hell I'd been living in for far too long.

At the end of the driveway, I stopped and turned back around to steal one last glance at the house that held my blood, tears, and all my pain. With my middle fingers in the air, I smiled to myself before turning and running into the darkness of the night.

Today was the day I died, just not by the hands of my husband, and not in the way I expected.

I knew it was only a matter of time before he went too far and killed me.

Three months ago, I came to realize the only way out of this life and this marriage was by death. I came to terms with the fact I'd have to die in order to escape him. To be free. I made the decision that I'd rather kill myself than have him do it.

I wanted to live and be free, I'd been trapped in this life for far too long.

I'd escaped Greg and his hell, only to run into the arms of someone equally as sinister.

Living this life had been hard. I was dealt a shitty hand, and I'd looked for an escape long before I'd even met Seb.

In a way, killing myself wasn't only a fuck you to Seb, it was a fuck you to everyone in my life.

To my parents for being pieces of shit, to all my foster parents for not wanting me, to Greg who stole the remainder of my innocence that existed, and to me for being so fucking weak and for allowing life to fuck me over and spit on me.

Today was the day I used death to set myself free.

Today, Lee Spencer-Riley died, and Tate Dawson was born.

"After I left that house, I went to a truck stop, colored and trimmed my hair. I kept my head down so no one would recognize me, and took a bus here. I'd never told Sebastian about my past... so he doesn't know that this is where I'm from, therefore, he would never know to look for me here, if he even does know that I'm still alive." I exhale heavily. A weight being lifted from my shoulders.

I've told them everything that happened that night to lead me here. I don't know why I came here of all places, especially since this place was once hell for me, but coming back here for some reason felt right. I was pulled here by invisible strings.

Three sets of eyes stare at me with their jaws dropped and their eyes wide. Clearly, they weren't expecting all that I had to say.

"Butterfly." King was the first to break the silence.

"Hellion." Eli was next.

"Tate Dawson." Rowen repeated my new name over and over, his eyes softening as he looked at me. "You chose that name because of me." Eli and King look at him in confusion, then look at me for either confirmation or an explanation, but I'm too focused on Rowen.

After a few pounding heartbeats and deep breaths, I nod.

"Can someone fill us in here?" Eli spoke up.

"When our foster father would force us to... and record us... afterward when we were alone, we hated calling each other by our names because of how he would pleasure himself while moaning our names. Tate and Dawson were our aliases that we chose for each other. Something we came up with from some silly TV show we had once seen. When she'd call me Dawson and I'd call her Tate, we'd pretend that we were in our own little world and Greg didn't exist." Tears stream down my cheeks and drop onto my lap, but even as my eyes become glossy and my vision blurry, I don't look away from Rowen.

I keep holding his gaze, staring deep into the eyes that provides me comfort and safety nearly every day for three years.

The others are silent, allowing the two of us to have this moment.

Rowen drops to his knees and comes toward me. Immediately I crawl toward him and then lunge at him. He wraps my legs around his waist and holds me tightly in his arms, just as I bury my face in the crook of his neck and let the tears rake through my body.

Even on his knees he's still tall, so he's able to hold me wrapped around him perfectly. One hand wraps around my waist while the other hand is in my hair at the back of my head.

I am clinging so tightly to him that there isn't an inch of space between our bodies. I hold on to his warmth and his comfort. There in his arms, I feel him mending all my broken pieces, making me whole again. Now I am beginning to wonder if subconsciously, he's the reason I returned to our hometown.

If he was the one pulling me here.

In his arms is exactly where I needed to be.

My eyes open when I feel more arms around me. I can't help but giggle seeing Eli and King who join us on the floor and have turned our moment into a group hug.

"I'll allow this, if you keep your dick in your pants, King," Rowen scolds, earning a groan from King. I unwrap myself from his body and kneel in front of him, King to my right and Eli to my left, and all their hands on me.

"Hate to ruin the moment, but we still need to figure out who wants Tate. She's not safe until we know who's behind this. All that's certain is that they're willing to kill to get her." I sigh, sitting back on my heels. Eli is right, there's still a threat out there. An unknown threat.

"I'll look into Sebastian and see if he has anything to do with this. I know you don't think so, but after all you told us, better to be safe than sorry." Eli takes my hands and kisses my knuckles before standing to his feet.

"I have to go into the office for a few hours, and then tonight I'll meet you guys back at the cabin."

"We're going back to the cabin?" I ask, and he nods.

"It's safer there. It's off the grid and no one knows that it exists. Until I have answers, that's where it's safest for you. Vlad will be here soon to take you and Ro." My eyebrows pull together in a scowl, and I glance over at King.

"You're not coming with?" He shakes his head, grips the back of my neck and pulls me toward him, crushing his lips against mine in a bruising kiss that's toe-curling.

"I've got some shit to do, I'll meet you there later." With a smirk and another quick kiss, he stands and disappears up the stairs with Eli.

Rowen stands too, offering his hand out to me and I take it with a smile. He closes the distance between us and brushes my hair behind my ears. "My little angel. I'm so sorry for everything that bastard put you through." Instantly, I place my index finger against his lips and shake my head.

"Stop apologizing, it's not your fault. You didn't make me marry him and you didn't make him hit me." I can see the storm brewing in his emerald eyes and the guilt that he has over something he shouldn't feel guilty about.

"I can't help but think if I would've protected you better, then you never would've ended up with him. I promised to protect you the first day we met, all I ever did was fail."

"Do you really think that you failed at protecting me?"

"Yes, I do. Look at what happened with Greg. I didn't protect you from him, then you ended up married to someone who abused you. You went from one abusive situation to the next."

"Stop! You're not going to wallow in a self-pity party. You protected me! Nothing that has ever happened has been your fault. You saved me from Greg, and you're saving me now." I can tell he doesn't believe me, so I take a deep breath and continue, "That night, Greg came into my room... he was going to rape me, and you stopped him. You were a victim too. He forced you to have sex with me."

"Rape you. He forced me to rape you," he snaps, looking at me in disgust and stepping away from me. I am not letting him get off that easily, so I take a step closer toward him.

"He was going to rape me, and you stopped him. He forced us both to have sex. And if you want to say that you raped me, then fine, but I raped you too because I was also equally involved." I sigh, taking his hands in mine. "Did it hurt? Yes. Was I scared? Yes. Was I happy it was you and not him? Yes, a thousand times yes. I was so grateful that you stepped in and did those things to me instead of him."

"Those things should've never fucking happened, Tate! I failed you!" he roars, backing further away from me.

"None of those things should've happened, but they fucking did! I don't blame you. You kept me safe from him, and you saved me from him." I can hear footsteps in the background but pay no mind to it.

"Everything okay?" King wraps his arms around me from behind, kissing my cheek, and I nod.

"I'm fine, but Rowen is being a fucking baby." With a frown, I look over my shoulder back at King, and when I turn back around, Rowen has already stormed off, and I hang my head in defeat.

It's been thirteen years, and I had no idea he still blamed himself for everything that happened all those years ago.

I'm aware it's probably fucked up to think he did me a favor, but I honestly believe he did.

"Give him time. He blames himself for everything that happened to you," Eli says from where he's standing on the stairs. He came right toward me and presses a kiss to my forehead. "We're leaving, we'll be back later." I stay silent, watching him and King walk to the elevator and disappear when the metal doors close.

Give him time? Fuck that.

We were both victims to our foster father's obsession with kiddie porn and needing to record us for his and his perverted friends' pleasure.

I was ten years old when Rowen saved me from Greg attempting to rape me. He'd heard my screams and came into my bedroom, and that's when Greg forced him to have sex with me instead. We were young and virgins. We were both victims of that sick fuck, not just me.

It was either Greg or Rowen, and in my young mind, it was a no-brainer.

Was I ready to have sex at that age? Fuck no.

Was I glad it was Rowen? Yes. I've never once regretted my choice to have Rowen instead of Greg.

I wish Rowen could see himself the way I see him as my savior.

If I don't blame him, he shouldn't blame himself either.

He's not getting off that easily.

With a deep breath, I decide to confront him.

TWENTY-FOUR

Rowen

've just taken off my shirt to prepare for a shower when my bedroom door flies open and smacks against the wall, likely putting a dent in it from the force.

Tate stands in the doorframe with a determined look on her face and her fists balled at her sides.

Fuck, she's a woman on a mission.

I allow myself to appreciate her beauty for two seconds before I look away from her with a defeated sigh.

"You killed him to save me, yet you still don't think that you protected me." I look everywhere but at her. "Rowen! You killed for me!" Her voice booms, and finally, I let my eyes connect with hers. My lips curl down in a frown as I become wrapped up in the memory of the last time I saw Lee… thirteen years ago.

"No! Stop! Please!" Lee was screaming, begging him to stop hitting her. I knew he was whipping her with the belt because I could hear it whooshing in the air before it snapped against her skin, causing her to cry out even

louder.

Lee's caseworker came over today.

Greg and Andrea were trying to adopt her, and when her caseworker, Millie, told her what she thought was great news, Lee freaked out.

Andrea convinced her it was no big deal, and Millie believed her and left.

Greg immediately dragged her into her bedroom and locked the door.

I begged Andrea to make him open the door, but she said that she must be punished, then left to work, leaving us behind to face the wrath of Greg.

Lee knows not to disobey or do anything that would upset Greg, though I couldn't blame her for being angry that they're likely going to adopt her. She'd been trying to escape ever since she learned how bad this house truly was. We've both been trying to leave. Which is impossible to do, because we're always locked inside.

I was beating on the door yelling for Greg to unlock it and hit me instead, but he just yelled for me to go away then he would hit her again.

I had never heard Lee scream and cry so loud before.

Every time she screamed, it tore me apart.

Lee was thirteen now, and I was sixteen. We had been together in this house for three years, and every day that passed, I realized that no one would ever come to save us.

No one cared about us.

My caseworker had stopped coming a year ago, and her caseworker only visited once a month and believed that Andrea and Greg were saints for caring for two teenagers.

I kept promising her I'd protect her, and I continued to fail day after day. All I did was deliver her one broken promise after another.

Her screams were ripping me apart from the inside, just as my anger was increasing by the minute.

I'm pretty sure I had an out-of-body experience or blacked out for a moment because one second I was listening to her screams, the next second I was breaking the door down, yelling for him to leave her alone.

"Get out of here, boy! This doesn't concern you," he spat, raising the hand that held the belt in the air. I had grabbed his wrist, preventing him from swinging it at her again.

"That's enough! Get the fuck away from her!" I roared, rage flowing through my veins.

Lee was on the floor in a fetal position, her body bright red with welts from the belt, and from underneath her white t-shirt, I could see the crimson stains.

This was the last time this motherfucker made her bleed.

It's now or never, he must be stopped.

Lee's terrified turquoise eyes looked up at me and held my gaze.

Lost in her eyes, the only thing I could focus on was her scared but beautiful eyes.

I hadn't even realized what I was doing until I'd felt the warm liquid cover my hand and Greg collapsed to the ground.

My heart was pounding in my chest. I was certain if I looked down, I'd be able to witness it beat out of my chest.

Her eyes had widened as she stood slowly on shaky legs.

Greg's fat lifeless body was a mutilated bloody mess, and I could feel the blood splatters on my face and see it cover my hands.

What the fuck had I just done?

I'd been too consumed by my rage to realize what I'd done.

An overwhelming feeling of calmness had came over me.

I wasn't afraid of the fact I'd just killed someone.

I'd done it to protect Lee, the girl I loved.

"We have to get out of here." She was oddly as calm as I was after just witnessing me murder someone. She walked toward me, her eyes never straying away from the blood on my hands. Slowly, she took my hands in

hers, and I swear I witnessed her pupils dilate at the sight of the blood on my hands.

"You have to go. Run! And don't ever come back here," I said, pulling away from her touch. I killed someone. I was a monster. I was too much of a monster to touch an angel.

Lee's bright eyes finally looked up to mine as her eyebrows pulled together.

"Not without you," she said through gritted teeth.

Carefully, I took her porcelain face in my hands, smearing the blood from my hands on her perfect skin.

She gasped, pressing her body against mine, her arms wrapping around my neck.

"I love you, Lee. And I promise, one day, in another lifetime, we will be together. But right now, you need to run. Leave this city and don't ever come back." I pressed my lips against hers and sealed the promise that I fully intended to keep with a kiss.

I didn't know when or how, but one day, she would come back to me.

She was meant to be mine.

Every inch of her is sealed into my memory, she's someone I would never forget. With a final kiss, Lee did exactly as I said. She left the house that was our own personal hell for the last three years.

"Rowen?" Her sweet voice pulls me away from my stupor.

Like a hungry animal, I lunge at her, pressing her back against the wall and coming nose to nose with her.

"You liked watching me kill him," I accuse, not needing a response because I already know.

I can still feel the way she'd pressed her body against mine and the way her breathing had hitched.

My left hand wraps around her throat, not in an aggressive way that could cut off her breathing, but in a way that lets her know who's in control. My right hand grips her small waist in a bruising grip.

She's a temptress.

She's already claimed King, is seconds away from claiming Eli, if he let her that is, and now my own control around her is slipping fast.

Fuck.

I don't have any control around her anymore.

Not when she looks the way she does that causes my heart to beat right the fuck out of my chest.

I lower my head and crush my lips against hers, taking her perfect plump lips in a delicious kiss that awakens every feeling in my body and makes me hyper aware of how perfect she feels against me.

She presses her body against mine and climbs me like a damn tree. I help her up, taking her legs and wrapping them around my waist, my hands gripping her ass and kneading it in the thin silk sleep shorts that she's wearing.

"Do you remember how easily I took his life? His blood on my hands, on your face, your lips." I carry her toward my bed, throwing her small body on it. She bounces before settling right in the middle on her back.

Climbing onto the bed and on top of her carefully, I take her perfect face in my large hands, my thumbs stroking her soft cheeks.

"You looked so beautiful with blood on your face." Her breathing hitches. She raises her hips against mine to rub her core against the growing bulge in my sweats. "I bet if I touch your pussy right now, it'll be wet just from thinking about his death and blood." Her only response is a moan, her hips circling me as she rubs herself against me at a quicker pace.

Holy fuck, I am going to burst in my pants like a horny teenager if she keeps doing that.

She knows what the fuck she wants and is taking it.

"I knew then that you were turned on, and I know it now." I press a kiss to her lips, trailing my lips down to her neck.

Her face is flushed, she's close to an orgasm, but I am not going to allow it. Not yet.

I pull away from her, rip the t-shirt from her body and yank down her thin shorts and panties.

Sitting back on my heels, I let my eyes wander over her delicious creamy skin.

She is perfect, and as close to heaven as I can ever fucking get. If I'm not careful, I could lose myself in her.

Would that be so wrong?

Tate squeezes her thighs together, her chest rising and falling rapidly in anticipation of what's to come.

"Spread those thighs for me, let me see just how fucking wet you are," I growl. She obeys like the good girl she is and spreads her thighs for me, revealing her bare pink pussy that's glistening with her wetness.

Fuck.

My cock twitches in my pants at the smell of her sweet arousal.

"Don't ever hide yourself from me." I place my hands on her shoulders, pushing her flat on her back, tracing my rough fingers over her smooth skin. Taking her nipples in my hands, I flick and pinch both perfectly pink pebbles, eliciting a sweet moan from her lips that goes straight to my engorged cock.

"I killed him for you because I would do anything to protect you. There isn't a single thing that I'm not willing to do to protect you."

Her blue eyes narrow at me, "Then why were you going to give me away to a gang?" I don't answer her. Instead, I lower myself to her and crush my lips against hers, stealing her breath.

Tate's hands trail over my already bare chest, taking cover at the hem of my sweatpants. She pushes them down along with my briefs, her small hands working anxiously to free my cock.

"You saved me, and yes, it turned me on so fucking much to watch that. To know that you cared so much for me that you were willing to kill," she whispers against my lips.

I groan in pure fucking pleasure as she holds my cock in both hands while she slides her wet pussy up and down my shaft.

I need to be inside of her right fucking now. I've never needed anything more than the way I need to be inside of her. I don't even need air as much as I need her.

Shifting slightly, I reach over to my nightstand and take out the black and gold pocketknife that I keep inside. Coming back to her, I hold it in front of her face, watching her eyes widen and a mischief smirk spreads on her lips. I open the knife to reveal the shiny steel blade.

"What are you going to do with that?" She's so out of breath and trying desperately to continue rubbing against me or squeeze her thighs together to provide her some type of relief, but failing miserably.

I kick off my bottoms and move myself to sit back on my heels between her spread thighs, my cock standing proudly and pointing right at her as if it knows its way home.

"I told you, Tate, I will do anything for you. Absolutely fucking anything. You wear the invisible scars every day of what that bastard did to you. And now it's my turn to be scarred by you."

She's breathless underneath me. "Rowen." The way my name rolls off her plump red lips is enough to get me to the point of being so hard it's fucking painful.

"I'm going to bleed for you, just like you bled because of me." With lust darkening her eyes, she reaches up and grips my right hand that's holding the knife. She takes me completely by surprise when she removes it from my hand and presses the blade against her flat stomach but doesn't apply enough pressure to cut herself.

I watch frozen as Tate trails the knife over her creamy skin below her left breast, pressing deeper and dragging until beautiful crimson blood tips to the surface. The sweetest moan I've ever heard leaves her lips, her eyes never leaving my face.

While her blood flows down her stomach, I take the blade from her hand and press it against her left nipple, dragging it across slowly until I see a small bead of crimson.

Licking my lips, I lower my head and wrap my lips around her bleeding nipple, flicking my tongue over the peak, sucking the blood out of her.

The moment the first taste of her sweet blood hits my tongue, something snaps within me.

I'm suddenly a man starved and fucking desperate for more of her taste.

Forcing myself away from her, I trail the blade down the length of her body and press it against her clit, causing her to whimper at the contact.

Her eyes are fixated on the blade, but she doesn't look afraid. She appears to be focused and needy for more.

Pulling back from her, I lick the knife, relishing the taste of her.

With my eyes on hers, I press the blade against my chest, slicing open the skin of my left pec. I made her bleed multiple times, and now I want to bleed for her. I want her to make me bleed.

Her ocean eyes are glued to the drops of blood that's now running down the left side of my chest. Tate groans and licks her pouty pink lips. The cut isn't deep enough to cause any damage, but it does bleed a lot.

She surprises me by sitting up and licking the blood from my chest. Holy fuck.

That's the hottest thing I've ever seen.

With her lips painted red, she gives me a devilish smirk before she lies back flat on the bed and spreads her thighs even further, exposing herself completely to me.

"You're playing a dangerous game, angel. Once I take you, there's no going back. You'll be mine forever, and you'll never be able to get away."

"I'm yours forever, Rowen. No more running. With you, I'm home. Now do your worst." Her legs wrap around my waist once again. I follow her lead and lower my head, licking the blood from her chest.

I suck her open wound into my mouth, causing her to cry out once my tongue licks her ruined flesh.

With a gasp, she grabs my head and brings my lips to hers for a passionate kiss that's full of self-forgiveness and new beginnings.

The kiss says everything we aren't able to say.

I align my cock with her entrance, and with one thrust, I am filling and stretching her tight, warm, wet pussy. A groan vibrates against our kiss, and I am not sure which one of us it's from. The feeling is so fucking incredible. I keep pushing until I am fully seated inside of her taut body.

After all these years, there's a promise I'm able to keep.

We'd found our way back to each other.

My blood is dripping on her. She looks so fucking beautiful with the crimson marring her creamy clear skin.

I grip her hips and fuck her with full force, not holding anything back.

Our sex is rough, and messy, and so us. And I wouldn't have it any other way, and I know she wouldn't either.

We bled for each other; we're connected forever.

The sight of her writhing beneath me is all that I need to keep pounding into her pussy, getting her closer and closer to the edge of seeing stars.

Tate pulls me down to her once again and connects our lips. Our teeth clank together, the kiss sloppy and wet, but it's hot, and the lingering taste of blood on her tongue drives me crazy.

Each time I push into her, I bottom out and hit her G-spot that sucks me in further. I know I am hitting it by the way her soft tissues clenches around me, and her legs begin to shake.

She bites down on my bottom lip so hard that the coppery taste of blood fills my mouth.

Her nails dig into my skin and rake down my back. I roar out at the slight sting, knowing that she's drawing blood. She looks at me with hooded eyes. My little vixen knows what she's doing and wants to play.

In return, I dig my own nails into the skin of her lustful hips, drawing blood of my own. We are becoming a bloody mess and I fucking love it.

I love seeing blood on her skin because of me. Because she wants to bleed for me, and vice versa. My little angel is turned on by blood, and I have every intention of fully exploiting the newfound kink.

"Oh God, I'm going to come!" she cries in pleasure, and I pick up my pace and pound into her so hard that my headboard hits against the wall and my balls slap against her in a delicious symphony.

"Not God, just Rowen." I smirk, taking the knife from the bed beside her head and pressing it against her throat. She surprises me by tilting her head back to expose her neck to me even further. Meanwhile, my right hand slips between us and I begin rubbing her slippery clit.

The sound of skin-on-skin slapping together and the wetness of her warm pussy fills the room. Perspiration adorns my skin and drops of sweat drips down on her which she licks from her lips.

"Rowen! Fuck! Fuck! Yes!" Her legs shake, her back arches, and her eyes temporarily cross.

Her pussy squeezes my throbbing cock like a vise, and two pumps later, I am following her lead and exploding my seed deep inside of her cunt that's still going through an orgasm. We ride out our climax at a slow pace until both of us calm down from the intensity.

At some point during our climax, the blade had nicked her neck and she bled, but not badly enough to harm her.

She looks up at me with tears in her eyes. "Never let me go, Rowen. Please." I wipe her tears away, roll over on my back and pull her into my arms. "Shh, baby, don't cry. I'm not going anywhere." I place my fingers under her chin and tilt her head up so that her eyes meet mine. "I'm not going anywhere, and neither are you. I just got you back, and I'm never letting you go again. I should've run with you all those years ago, and I'm sorry I didn't, but I have you now." I press a chaste kiss to her lips, and she nods with a small but sad smile. There's something else brewing in her mind. "What's wrong, baby? Talk to me."

"Well… you know that I slept with King, right?" Her cheeks turn crimson, and I can't help but chuckle at her embarrassment. Especially now.

"Yeah, I'm aware. And sooner rather than later, you're going to end up fucking Eli too." I state matter-of-factly, without malice or any type of jealousy.

"Does that bother you?"

"No. We all want you, you want us, and there's nothing wrong with that. Does it bother you?" She thinks for a moment before shaking her head.

"Maybe it should… but it doesn't. I'm not embarrassed to admit that I want all of you."

"Hmm… are you sure about that?" With a smirk, I roll her over onto her back and kiss the crimson that tints her cheeks and highlights her neck. I kiss down the delicate skin of her neck, licking up the blood. A low moan hums through her throat as I bite down on her skin.

In the next breath, I am returning home and burying myself inside of her incredible cunt yet again.

After fucking Tate into my mattress again and once in the shower, we clean our wounds and bandage them. We'd went downstairs and had lunch, and now we're sitting in the living room, cuddled up on the couch watching a movie.

Well, she's watching a movie and I am enjoying her warmth.

But now by hearing her heavy breathing, I know she's asleep.

I look down at her small body that's tucked under my arm, studying her face.

Her dark eyelashes are so long that they fan across her cheeks when her eyes are closed. Her black hair is pulled into a ballet bun on top of her head and her bangs are brushed back to reveal her heart-shaped face.

She looks the same as she did all those years ago. She's grown into her features and her body, and she's a walking-talking-breathing temptress.

Tate is more than beautiful, gorgeous, or hot.

Her ethereal beauty is unearthly like.

There's not a right word to describe her beauty.

She doesn't even have to try; she's just naturally a drop dead stunner.

A goddess who has the power to stop men in their tracks and bring them to their knees. And when she opens her mouth and speaks, it only further adds to her beauty. She's always had a smartass mouth and I'm happy to see that hasn't changed.

I'm too focused on studying her sleeping face that I don't notice right away when the elevator doors ping open.

Hearing footsteps, I tear my attention from her and look up to notice that Eli and King are back home. Eli nods at me and points toward the hallway where his office is, and I know what that means.

He wants to talk.

Careful not to wake Tate, I slide out from under her and lay her back on the couch, covering her with the blanket before following King and Eli down the hallway and into Eli's office.

Closing the door behind me, I take a seat beside King in front of Eli's large cherry oak desk, both of them giving me skeptical looks as they eye the bandage that's on my chest, and I know they see the red scratches down my back when I'd turned to close the door.

"Either you and Tate fought, or you made up." Eli raises an eyebrow, sitting back in his chair.

King laughs and shakes his head, slapping me on the shoulder. "Our brother here got some of that sweet pussy today. I'll admit, she's never scratched me like that before and I'm a little jealous."

"Maybe you didn't fuck her good enough." I chuckle, punching him playfully in the arm.

"She creamed on my dick three times in a row the other night. I'm fully satisfying her. So, what's with the bandage?"

"We bled for each other." They both nod in understanding. Like me, they too have their own kinks that may be weird to others. We're close and comfortable enough with each other that we've shared our sex stories, plus we've shared women before so we each know what the other is interested in.

King and I share the same fascination with blood, and Eli's kink is cum. Many times, he's urged King and I to finish all over a woman's stomach or back so he can lick it off them.

Fuck, I can't wait for the day that I can get my brothers and my girl into bed at the same time. It'll be pure fucking magic to watch Eli lap my cum out of Tate's pussy while King fucks him.

The thought instantly brings my dick to life and I have to adjust myself in my sweats.

"Moving on. What did you find out today?"

"Vlad caught one of the guys who ambushed us. He thought they were all dead, turns out this fucker faked it until we left." Eli speaks up, filling me on what's been going on. We agreed that Tate shouldn't stay alone, so one of us will always need to stay home with her, which means one of us will be delayed on receiving information.

"He's on his way to the cabin now so we can interrogate him. We need to find out who hired him and why they want Tate."

King sits back eagerly in his chair and cracks his knuckles. Eli and I always do the interrogation when someone is brought to us in our workshop. After we get the information we need, King then gets to step in and have his fun. And when it comes to having fun, King is a sick bastard that enjoys inflicting pain.

I'm positive that the fucker gets off on it.

"I'm going to go see my butterfly. Call me when it's my turn to play," King singsongs as he gets up from the chair and exits the office, leaving Eli and I alone to discuss the rest of the events from today.

"We both know that Tate doesn't believe her husband could be the one behind this, but I don't want to rule anything out. I have our security team looking into him. Soon we'll know everything there is to know about him and his whereabouts. Also, they're gathering every article online about her disappearance."

"Regardless of if he's behind this or not, I want to get my hands around his neck and kill the fucker for laying a hand on her head."

"Agreed. I don't think he's behind it though from what she's told us. From the brief research I did, he's just a doctor who liked to beat the fuck out of his wife. I haven't been able to find any connection between him and any gangs. But security will find everything we need to know. Both gang and mercenary affiliation will be checked too. No stone will be left unturned."

My anger is building, and I am becoming frustrated with the fact there's nothing I can do. I scrub my hands over my face with a groan. "Yeah, okay. We'll wait and see what they can find out." I am so fucking angry and rightfully so.

"We'll figure this out, brother, she's ours now, and we're going to keep her safe. No one will get to her." I know that to be true. As long as I'm still breathing, she will be safe.

As long as any one of us is still breathing. She's connected to us in ways that aren't completely understood.

She was born to be mine. And sixteen years ago, she came into my life for a reason. She was meant to be mine from the moment I laid eyes on her.

I can only hope that Eli's fondness toward her will continue to grow. Knowing him, he doesn't allow himself to get close to women. He doesn't trust them.

Perhaps Eli is another one I'll have to protect Tate from.

TWENTY-FIVE

King

Three days ago, Vlad brought in one of the men who was involved in the ambush against us to my workshop.

Eli and Rowen have been interrogating him and trying to get answers as to who hired him to attack us and take Tate, and so far, he's been mute. He hasn't said a single thing, no matter the tactics they've implemented.

Since they can't get him to talk, now it's my turn to try.

My ways to get someone to talk usually work when the person who needs interrogated isn't cooperating.

It's nine at night and Tate is sitting in the living room painting her nails and watching an episode of *Gilmore Girls*. She loves that show, and watches it nearly every day. She can even fucking quote it, and if I wasn't so smitten with her, I'd find it annoying.

It's not safe for her to be in public, so Eli had bought her a bunch of girly shit the other day while we were in the city.

He went overboard buying her nail stuff and makeup that she doesn't even need. But it's nice to have a girl around to spoil. He also bought her some more clothes, which she has yet to wear since she's always wearing one of our shirts and panties. Not that I'm complaining, I actually prefer her to walk around naked.

I am listening to her quote something that Lorelai says as she sticks her hand inside of the UV light that Eli got her for the gel polish.

I only know what it is because she'd rolled her eyes when I asked, and Rowen had to tell me. But can you blame me? How would I know about this shit?

I lean forward and grab her ponytail from behind the couch, wrap it around my hand and pull her back to me. I'm greeted with a smirk already fixed on her plump, tempting lips.

"I have to go and help out Eli and Rowen. Stay here, butterfly. Don't go outside. One of us will be back later."

"Are you going to kill that guy they have out in the shed?" We didn't keep it from her that we were holding someone in one of our sheds in the woods, but we avoided discussing the details with her about what was going on. So, she surprises me when she mentions me killing someone.

"Yes, I'm going to kill him." I search her ocean blue eyes for any sign of judgment or fear, but instead I find excitement that makes my dick twitch in my pants.

She sits up on her knees and turns so that she's facing me. "Be safe, I'll stay here." Her small hands fist at my t-shirt and she pulls me down toward her to crush her lips against mine.

It takes every ounce of self-control I can muster to pull away from her delicious lips. "I will be, butterfly. I'll see you later."

God, who the fuck is this girl? She doesn't shy away from blood and isn't scared of me even after I just told her that I'll be killing someone. If anything, I think it might've turned her on.

I have met my fucking match.

My little butterfly is beginning to blow my mind. Maybe if I'm lucky, she'll blow my dick later.

Once outside, I hop on the four-wheeler that's parked in the front of the cabin and drive into the woods where we have our interrogation room and my workshop set up.

I park the four-wheeler beside the two others in front of the brown metal shed and knock three times.

Rowen is the one who unlocks the door to let me in.

The large shed we are in is something we have customized for us for these exact purposes.

It isn't a huge space, but it's big enough for the three of us to move around in comfortably and to have our suspect in the room.

Even though we are in the middle of the woods, and no one is around for miles, it's soundproof because better safe than sorry.

An instant smile spreads across my mouth as I take in the sight in front of me.

The man is already chained up. His arms are bound above his head as he's hanging from a hook in the ceiling. His toes barely even touch the ground and he's stripped naked. Pretty bruises line over his body; no doubt from the interrogation he must have gone through at the hands of Eli and Rowen.

"Hello, brothers, what have we learned?" I ask as I intertwine my fingers together and crack my knuckles.

"His name is Joseph, and he's part of a mercenary group that was hired to hand *her* over to someone unknown. The Westside Disciples found out about the fact she's wanted and planned to kidnap her and turn them over themselves in exchange for a pretty penny. This is the information we got from Vlad. Joseph here isn't willing to talk to us," Eli says from where he's standing behind the man, his hand fisting his hair at the root.

"Well, it's not your lucky day, Joseph, you should've talked to my brothers. They're the nice ones." My words cause a chuckle from the three of us. I gather my long hair into a bun on the top of my head and strip out of my shirt.

"Joseph, who hired you?" I ask casually as I open my toolbox and take out a pair of plier cutters.

He doesn't respond, exactly as I anticipated. My back is turned toward him, but I hear the sound of a fist connecting with his face and the groan that follows. I turn around just in time to see him spitting blood on the floor. "Fuck you! Fuck all of you! You'll never get away with this!" Rowen shakes out his fist from the punch.

"Have fun, brother. We're going to get pizza. We've worked up an appetite." Eli pats me on the back and then he and Rowen are gone.

I close the door but leave it unlocked in case they decide to come back. I don't want to be interrupted while I am playing with my new toy Vlad has brought me.

"We can either do this the easy way or the hard way. It's your choice." He glares at me, spitting more blood onto the floor. Rowen definitely has a mean right hook, and I'm almost positive that punch knocked a tooth out.

"Alright, hard way it is, I guess. Personally, that's my favorite so I don't mind." This is my favorite part of having someone in the workshop.

I choose not to participate in the interrogations—that's Eli and Rowen's domain. But when they don't acquire the information they need, that's when I get to come in and have some fun.

"Who hired you?" I give him one last chance to answer my question before starting on my work.

"Your mother," he spits. This little fucker.

With a wide smile and the fakest laugh I could force, I grab his nipple and twist it, causing him to cry out in pain. Stretching his nipple out as far as it will go, I slide my plier cutters over at it.

"You're fucking crazy! What the fuck!" He tries to kick at me, but it's useless since his ankles are duct taped together.

With a sigh, I squeeze down on the pliers, cutting his nipple off, and earning a loud screech from his pathetic self. His scream makes my dick hard.

"Who hired you, Joseph?"

"F–f–f–uck you!" he whimpers. I move the pliers toward his second nipple and snip it off in one clean cut.

I stand back to admire the blood that's now flowing down his chest.

Tossing the pliers to the floor, I pick up a serrated blade next from my toolbox.

"Only you can stop this. Give me the information I need, and I'll make your death quick and painless." Unfortunately for him, I have the patience for torture and a slow death.

Grabbing his right ear, I twist and pull it away from his head, slicing it off with the serrated blade while he keeps screaming like a little bitch.

Even if he decides to tell me what I want to know, I have no intentions of letting him die quickly. He was after my butterfly and that's unacceptable. No one gets to hurt her besides us.

I'm not sure how much time has passed, but I'm covered in his blood and now have an ear, six teeth, two nipples, five toes, and two fingers all perfectly lined up on the metal tray beside my toolbox.

He's still screaming and crying but hasn't given me one single piece of fucking information.

I'll admit; I'm getting a little agitated. Most people sing like a siren at the first sight of their blood, but not him. He's keeping everything he knows to himself and it's pissing me the fuck off.

"King!" The sweet melodious voice has me looking over my shoulder to find my defiant butterfly stepping inside of the workshop.

Tate walks in, still wearing the same t-shirt as earlier and has flip-flops on, carrying a box of pizza in her hands.

"What the fuck are you doing here? I told you to keep your ass inside." I narrow my eyes at her, allowing myself to look over her bare legs.

Tate rolls her eyes and waves me off. "I brought you some pizza; I thought you might be hungry."

"Did you walk here?"

"No, I stole one of the four-wheeler keys from Rowen," she says nonchalantly with a shrug of her shoulders. With a raised eyebrow, she looks around me at the crying, hanging man who's covered in his own blood. She allows her eyes to look over my bloody body. My dick twitches at the way she looks at me. There's no fear in her eyes, only lust.

That's my fucking girl.

She walks further into the studio and sets the pizza box on a table away from the blood. "Is this the guy who shot at you?" I nod, my eyes carefully watching her movements. "Did he give you any information yet?"

"Nope, he doesn't want to talk to me."

She scoffs. "After you've done all that?" She giggles, waving her hand over the table where I have arranged all his body parts that I've cut off.

"You should go back inside. I'll meet you when I'm done."

"But what if I want to play too?" She places her small hands on my chest and moves her fingers around to spread the blood further across my skin.

"You want to play, butterfly?" Her pupils dilate when she covers her hands in blood, her arms wrapped around my neck, and she rises on her tiptoes to reach my face where she crushes our lips together. My hands grip her perfectly round ass and pull her against the growing bulge in my pants.

"You're dead! Both of you!" Joseph roars, fighting against his chains.

"Actually, by the looks of it, you're the one that'll be dead soon," she says with a giggle, her hands moving down my chest and to my belt where she quickly begins unfastening it.

"Hold on, butterfly." I still her hands. "Joseph, I'm trying to fuck my girl, so this is your last chance to tell me who hired you."

"Kill me! I'm not telling you shit!"

I shrug my shoulders. "Okay, fine. What should I use, butterfly?" I lead her toward my toolbox. She looks over the different tools, then with a smile, she picks up one of the scalpels.

"Use this, then hurry up and fuck me."

"Anything for you." With another kiss to her lips, I step in front of Joseph and slice into his skin, peeling a layer of the skin on his stomach away. His screaming is cut short when I dig my scalpel into his throat and drag it from left to right. His eyes widen and his warm blood sprays out and covers me.

My dick is painfully hard now and straining against my jeans. Luckily for me, Tate chooses that moment to wrap her arms around me from behind and frees my cock.

Turning to face her, my own eyes widen seeing that she's already naked. "Good God, you're so fucking sexy." I pick her up quickly, her arms around my neck and legs around my waist. "I'm going to fuck you so hard, butterfly."

She's already rubbing her core against my stomach, and I can feel her wetness and smell her sweet arousal even over the copper scent of blood.

While she holds onto me tight like a spider monkey, I unchain Joseph's lifeless body and let him fall to the ground with a thud.

Unwrapping her arms from around my neck, I chain her up just like Joseph was, and step away from her reach, letting her hang.

She's so small that her feet are nowhere near the ground.

I thought I was already fully hard, but my cock hardens more at the sight of her hanging there naked with blood coating her creamy skin.

"Stop playing games, King. Fuck me!"

I laugh. "Yes, butterfly. Whatever you say." I step toward her, grab her legs to wrap them around my waist, and roughly impale her on my cock.

She throws her head back and cries out, her moans like music to my ears, egging me on even further.

God, what a fucking sight we must be. Covered in blood, her chained, me fucking her wild.

"Rowen was right, you do get so fucking horny from the sight of blood." I pull out only to slam back inside of her, my hands gripping firmly onto her globes of her bottom to keep her in place as I ram her over and over with my cock, not even giving a single fuck if it's painful or too much. She could take me; she would take me.

"Isn't that right, butterfly?" When she doesn't answer, I pull out, only allowing my tip inside of her.

"Yes! Yes! Now, please, fuck me!" she begs breathlessly.

In one quick thrust of my hips, I am buried to the hilt inside of her tight wet pussy.

She feels so fucking good.

"You're so fucking tight and warm," I say through gritted teeth. There's nothing I love more than the feel of her pussy. If I am to die right now, I'd die a very fucking happy man whose balls are deep inside of the woman I can never get enough of.

"Come on, King. Give it to me harder, I know you can," she sasses, provoking me and knowing exactly what she's doing to me.

But I give her what she wants. I pound her tight little pussy even harder as she squeezes me like a vise. I know what my butterfly needs, and she craves a rough, deep fucking, not a light fuck. She needs it just as rough as I do.

"Will you bleed for me, butterfly, like you did for Rowen?"

"Yes! Oh God, yes!" Her lips part, and I see the look of sheer excitement in her eyes. After one more thrust, I pull out and step away from her, letting her swing. I return to my toolbox to grab one of the unused scalpels that I have neatly laid out.

"Good, then bleed for me, butterfly. I want to see how pretty you look when you're bleeding only for me." She swings toward me and wraps her legs around my waist, and I let my cock find its way home back inside of her warm pussy.

I don't move though, I just keep her impaled on my cock as I press the scalpel into the skin underneath her right breast, her soft skin parting like butter.

A gasp escapes her lips, her warm cunt clenches around me and strangles my length as I carefully carve a butterfly into her delicious skin. She's panting and writhing, and I can feel her drowning my cock as she becomes wetter. I know this is painful, but she really seems to enjoy it. It's turning her on.

Her flesh parts beautifully for me. My cock throbs inside of her at the sight.

Dropping the scalpel, I lean down and lick over my carving, sticking my tongue in her parted flesh.

She hisses at the sting; it may have hurt but she likes it. Her eyes are closed, and by the way her pussy is throbbing and squeezing me, I know she's trying to keep herself from having an orgasm. She's getting off on the pain.

I smile at the small butterfly I have carved into her skin.

A butterfly for my butterfly.

I like my carving better than her tattoo.

My hands return to her body, and I bring her chest as close to mine as I can, smearing her blood on me. Keeping my grip around her tight to keep her in place, I piston-fuck her, our lips connecting, and I swallow every scream. And my little butterfly sure loves to scream for me.

My fingertips trace over the blood on her torso, and I smear it over her perfect skin that I can't wait to further cut and watch her bleed.

Especially when she bleeds as beautifully as she does.

It's just for me.

For us.

I smear the crimson on my fingertips up to her neck and grip it firmly. She throws her head back while I pound into her like a crazed man.

Like if I don't fuck her as hard as I can, then I'd disappear into nothingness.

Right now, in this moment, she's my very lifeline.

She's helping me ride the high that I am on. And I am always high on adrenaline after killing, and now fucking her is only intensifying the feeling.

With one hand around her neck and the other stroking her clit violently, her delicious pussy clamps around my cock and holds me captive. "That's it, butterfly, come for me. Let me feel your pussy drench me." With a loud, piercing cry, she does just that. She explodes around me, and I assume the feeling of both pain and pleasure is too much for her because tears stream down her face.

I continue strumming her clit until I am roaring my release and emptying everything I have inside of her greedy little cunt.

Pulling away from her, her legs slip from my waist. She goes back to hanging from the chain. The corners of my lips tip up as my hazel eyes rake over her small frame. I watch as the mixture of our cum spreads down her thighs. Taking her body in my arms, I remove her from the chains and hold her bridal style against me. Her limp body sags against my chest, her arms like tight bands around my neck. Keeping her in my arms, I step into my shoes and carry her out of the shed and into the darkness of the woods, both of us naked and bloody as I make my way to the cabin.

"God damn, King. Put some clothes on," Eli groans with an eyeroll the moment I enter the cabin and into the living room. He's sitting on the couch with his legs spread out on the coffee table and a laptop set on his lap.

"What the fuck happened to you two?" Rowan enters the living room, his eyes raking over my naked, bloody butterfly who's fighting against sleep in my arms.

"Turns out my little butterfly is even dirtier than I thought." I wink, getting a laugh from them both.

"Put your dick away and then tell us how it went with Joseph," Eli grumbles.

With a chuckle, I head toward the stairs. "Yeah, just let me shower and put her to bed and I'll come back down." I'd walked up three steps when I turn around and shoot Rowen a warning look. "Learn to sleep alone, she's sleeping with me tonight."

"Fuck off." He flips me his middle finger.

The fucker has had Tate in his bed for two weeks straight and I've been aching to have her beside me again.

Upstairs in my bedroom, I enter and go to Tate, leaning down and trailing kisses over her gorgeous face to wake her up. "Come on, butterfly, let's shower." With a yawn, she nods and allows me to set her down on her feet.

We step inside of the shower together and take turns washing each other off. Halfway through our shower, Tate drops to her knees in front of me and swallows my dick down her throat.

Fuck.

This woman is going to be the death of me.

After showering, filling Tate's mouth with my cum, and tucking her into my bed, I return downstairs to find Eli and Rowen in conversation about Joseph.

"He didn't say anything. No matter what I did, he held strong and wouldn't give away any information as to who hired him or what the mission was exactly." I groan, stepping into the kitchen to grab myself a bottle of beer from the fridge.

"Security hasn't gotten back to us yet either. They're still looking into Sebastian Riley, so for now we're stuck." Rowen is the one who speaks while Eli continues typing away at his computer.

"If it turns out he's cleared, we're right back to the beginning. He's our only suspect right now."

With a frustrated sigh, I run my hands through my hair, listening to Eli speak. Blinking with an idea, I turn my attention toward Rowen. "Is there anyone in the city from her past that would want her and have the resources to hire mercenaries? Whoever it is that wants her, we don't know why, or what they plan to do once they have her," I say, raising the beer bottle to my lips and chugging half of it.

"She didn't have friends or family here. It was just shitty foster homes that didn't care about her." Rowen slumps his shoulder in defeat. With a sudden gasp, he raises his head and snaps his fingers together. "One of her first foster brothers became obsessed with her. I remember her telling me about him when she caught him lurking around our foster home."

"What's his name?" Eli sits up straighter, his fingers flying across his keyboard.

"I don't remember, fuck! He was weird. She was moved a few months after she was placed in the same home as him. But even after she left, he stalked her for a long-ass time. They were only in the same home for a few months."

"Tate had a stalker and you're just now remembering this?" I roll my eyes, earning a glare from Rowen.

"Fuck, he has a weird and unusual name. His name is Bingo, Jackpot, Spades, something fucking weird." Rowen bounces his leg, snapping his fingers together repeatedly, "Ace! Ace Jackson!" The two of us crowd Eli on the couch, watching as he searches for Tate's foster brother.

"What the fuck?" Eli mumbles, standing from the couch. He holds his laptop in his left hand and scrolls with his right.

"What's wrong? Did you find him?"

"That's what's wrong. The only trace of an Ace Jackson is a rental agreement for an apartment he leased… nine months ago—the same date Tate came here." He turns the screen for us to see.

"This is the only trace of him. I can't even find any juvenile files on him. He was in foster care, yet there's no record of it." Eli could find anything on anyone. Between him and our security team, they could uncover everything about a person. Sealed juvenile records or not, he could unseal them.

So, for him to not find anything besides a lease agreement is fucking odd.

What is the little fucker hiding?

TWENTY-SIX

Tate

It's been three days since I watched King kill a man.

I should've been disgusted or terrified.

I should've asked him to stop or run away.

I should've done anything other than what I did.

No, instead I fucked him right next to a dead body, with blood covering him head to toe.

I even let him chain me to the bloodstained chains that the man had been hung to while King tortured him and then killed him.

God, what was wrong with me?

Am I really that fucked up?

That's the second murder I've witnessed, and I feel the same way now as I did all those years ago when I witnessed Rowen kill our abuser.

Nothing. Absolutely nothing.

No remorse, sympathy, nothing.

I see the way the three of them watch me when I walk around the house. I think they're expecting me to break at any moment and to be afraid of them or of what they're capable of, but honestly, it only makes me want them even more.

All three of them.

That brings me to another realization, I want all three men. I'm fucking two of them and it's only a matter of time before I take Eli's cock too, and we all know it.

Lusting after three men is stirring up memories from my marriage that I've done my best to avoid.

You're a whore. I hear his voice in my head whenever King or Rowen kiss me.

Only whores wear red. I look down at my red fingernails.

You're nothing. He'd look at me with disgust.

When my men look at me, there's no disgust in their eyes, only pure lust and something I can't exactly pinpoint.

Love, maybe? No, that's not possible. But why not? Why couldn't they love me? I *am* good enough.

Sebastian has no control over me anymore. As far as I'm concerned, he's dead just like Lee.

Strong arms wrap around my waist from behind, and I know who it is before he even speaks.

Eli.

I know all of their scents by now, and his is cedarwood. I love their scents; it's oddly comforting.

With a sigh, I relax against his chest, pressing my back against his front. With gentle fingers, he brushes the hair from my left shoulder over to my right, placing a kiss to the crook of my neck. "What's going on inside that beautiful mind of yours?" He grips my waist and turns me around, so I'm facing him.

The dynamics between Eli and I are ever-changing. Since the night he showed me the ballet studio he created for me, we've been getting closer. And it feels really good getting closer to him and seeing the sides to him that he tries to hide. I see the ruthlessness in him, but I also see the softer side that I'm sure no one outside of these walls gets to see. Most of the time, his expressions are stoic. He's calm and collected. He has complete control over his emotions and is careful with how he responds to situations. Everything he does is precalculated.

Eli is the one that has the most control of his emotions and rarely shows how he's feeling.

King is loud, sensitive, and puts his feelings on display and rarely gives a fuck about anything.

Rowen is the one with the temper problem who gets angry easily and would rather punch someone or break something than talk about his feelings.

They're all so different, yet so similar, and I've never wanted anyone as much as I want them. I'm crazy, I know, but with them, it's exciting. I don't know what to expect from one minute to the next. The unknown is something I'd usually fear, but not anymore.

I wrap my arms around Eli's neck and stare up into his chocolate eyes. He kisses the tip of my nose and brushes my raven hair behind my ears, holding my face with a tenderness that makes my heart beat twice as fast. His thumbs lightly brush over my cheeks, and in an instant, his lips are on mine, and he's kissing me tenderly.

It seems that the only time he shows any hint of emotion is when he's around me. Or even Rowen and King.

He's opened himself up around me and is allowing me to get to know him day by day.

"Talk to me, hellion," he whispers, his breath fanning over my lips as his forehead rests against mine.

"Is it wrong that I want all three of you?" I ask with a sigh, searching his eyes for any hint of judgment, but I don't find any.

"Do you feel that it's wrong?" His thumb brushes along my bottom lip, pulling it away from my teeth.

Do I feel it's wrong? I want to say no, but I keep hearing Sebastian's voice in the back of my mind telling me that I'm nothing and worthless, and that I'm a whore, even though I've never once given him a reason to truly believe that I'm a whore.

I've never cheated or let my eyes stray, unlike him.

"You're doubting yourself." Eli's words snap me out of my thoughts, and I blink, looking up at him. "You're hearing *his* voice, aren't you?" I don't miss the malice in his voice when he refers to Sebastian. He doesn't want to mention my sorry excuse of a husband, and neither do I. "Tell me what you're hearing. What would he say to you?"

"He would tell me that I'm a worthless whore. He'd hit me until I was bloody and covered in bruises, and only when my voice was hoarse from screaming for him to stop, he would." His jaw visibly clenches and his eyes darken.

"You, my hellion, are anything but worthless." He captures my lips in a searing kiss that leaves me feeling dizzy when he pulls away. "Do whatever you feel is right, Tate. If being with all three of us feels as right as I believe that it does, then continue being with us. If something starts to feel awkward or weird, then talk to us or one of us. We're all here for you, and I know I speak for them too when I say that you're ours for as long as you'll have us." I am not used to this side of Eli yet, nor am I used to having any man be so open with me about his feelings.

My romance with my own harem is a quick burn, and I am still questioning how it's possible that in the short amount of time I've known these men, for once, my soul feels complete. I'm whole, and I have them to thank.

Does it really matter that I've known them for such a short amount of time?

No, because I feel that I've known them my entire life. The exception is Rowen, because I've known him since I was ten years old.

Our souls are connected, and they have been since the first time I laid eyes on the boy with emerald eyes and hair as dark as night.

"Come." Eli takes my hand in his, leading me away from the kitchen stove where I'd been standing with an empty pan preparing to make breakfast when he entered and distracted me.

It's seven in the morning and King and Rowen have to go into town to meet with someone from their organization that may have a lead on the men that ambushed us and are trying to kidnap me. It's Eli's turn to stay home with me; they don't trust leaving me alone, and for good reason.

Apart from someone trying to kidnap me, I tried to escape once, and I wasn't confident that I wouldn't try again. I'm still confused about my feelings and unsure what I want to do.

Eli leads me upstairs to his bedroom, closing and locking the door behind us. With quick hands, he lays me down on his four-poster king-size bed, the silk bedding cool underneath my exposed flesh. He stares down at me with hunger in his eyes, and slowly he removes his clothing while I lie frozen watching him.

I've seen Eli shirtless countless times, but seeing him nude is unlike anything I am prepared for. His torso is covered in tattoos, and often I wondered how far down they went, but as I stare at his glorious naked body, I get my answer.

His tattoos stop at his torso, his muscular legs free from any ink.

My eyes roam over his perfect body taking in the stunning sight before me. I'm aware that I'm openly ogling him, but he doesn't seem to mind.

My eyes land on his massive cock that's standing proudly between his legs. The veins in his shaft look angry, and I know my eyes are wide as I stare at his third leg.

At the same time, my pussy clenches and my mouth salivates. He's large. Extremely large, and instantly I'm worrying about how he'll fit that massive thing inside of my body.

I wince at the thought.

As if sensing my worry, the corner of his lips curls up as he rakes his eyes over me.

Smug knowing bastard.

The bed dips with Eli's weight as he climbs on and makes quick work of removing my panties and t-shirt. I'm lying underneath him, and in an instant, he's stealing the air from my lungs with a bruising kiss. "Let me kiss away any traces of him. Let me worship you in ways he never did." Goosebumps prickle my skin at his words. "I want to erase every negative thing he's ever said to you, every cut and bruise he's ever left on your body." His fingers trail down my body until he reaches my already damp core. He spreads my folds and flick over my clit with his thumb.

"Let me care for you the way you deserve to be cared for." His words have me choking up. I can't speak or else I'd start crying and the last thing I want to do right now is cry.

He starts with my face, kissing over every inch of my face and trailing his lips down to my neck and shoulders. He moves lower and takes my left nipple in his mouth, his hand massaging my right one and flicking the pebbled bud. He kisses over my body, not missing a single inch of skin.

Eli moves lower until he reaches my core, my legs automatically spreading for him. Another smug smirk curls on his lips. His warm tongue licks up my slit, a gasp escaping me. He sucks one of my pussy lips into his mouth, tugging on it before moving to the other one.

"Stop teasing me, Eli," I groan, needing a release from the ache and build up that's growing in my stomach. His breath fans cross my clit and I shiver, raising my hips up to reach more of his mouth.

"I've got you, little hellion. Always." Without another word, he gives me what I want.

He slides two fingers inside of my wet pussy and sucks my clit into his warm mouth, his skilled tongue flicking and circling my sensitive bundle of nerves.

Sixty seconds is all it takes for me to see stars and cry out his name, but that doesn't stop him from eating me.

My thighs squeeze his head, my fingers tangle in his hair with my nails scratching over his scalp, and my back arches off the bed as he eats me like a starved animal.

Two fingers pound into me rapidly, curling inside of me to perfectly hit my G-spot with each thrust, bringing me closer and closer to the edge of another orgasm.

His velvet tongue laps at my dripping cunt and sucking my clit.

He pulls me into another explosive orgasm that has me floating on cloud fucking nine.

I don't think I can take another one, but Eli thinks otherwise.

Once again, he doesn't stop, he takes my moans as encouragement and picks up the pace of curling and thrusting his fingers into me. I am wetter than I've ever been, I can feel it all the way down to my ass cheeks. Eli pulls his fingers from me just as my pussy convulses and I squirt all over his face. He doesn't pull away, instead he stays there with his eyes on my wet pussy as I throb.

Realizing that I just squirted and came all over his face, I look down at him to see his soaking wet face, a hint of embarrassment tinting my cheeks. Suddenly he's kissing back up my body and hovers over me, pinning me to the bed with his hips and his forearms on either side of my head. He crushes his lips against mine and I feel the stretch at my entrance when his mushroom tip starts pushing inside of me, invading my body.

He kisses me through it, swallowing my gasps and groans, as he inch by inch, slides inside of me. The feeling of fullness consumes me once he bottoms out and stills. The burn from the stretch slowly fades away, but I have a hunch that when he'll pull out, there will be a little bit of blood. I am too full of him, and I love it.

Slowly, he pulls out and slides back inside of me, bottoming out once again. His hips rock against mine, his hands holding my hips down as he fucks me into the mattress.

"Fuck, baby, you're so tight," he groans, his thrusts slow and steady. He's keeping his movements light for me to allow me the chance to get used to the thickness of his cock.

Holy hell is he thick.

He has the body of a bodybuilder, fucks like a porn star, and is blessed with a magnificent cock.

Can cocks even be magnificent?

Eli is the complete package.

His movement quickens as I become adjusted to his girth. The stinging pain quickly turns into pleasure. My legs wrap around his waist as my back arches off the bed, his fingers interlocked with mine. My mouth hangs open and a sling of moans and cries of pleasure escapes.

A light sheen of sweat covers both of our bodies, my next climax quickly building with every thrust against my G-spot. His right hand disappears between us to rub my clit viciously.

I clench around him in a desperate attempt to delay my orgasm.

"You're so goddamn beautiful." His lips crush against mine, my nails raking down his back and my toes curling. "You gave yourself to me, and now, I'll never be able to let you go. You're mine forever. All of ours."

"Yes! Yes! I'm yours!" I can't hold back; he's fucking me so deep and hitting the right spot with each push that delaying my orgasm is no longer possible. With my body shaking, I scream my release as I come all over his fat cock for the first time.

Eli stills, looking at me with another of his infamous smug smirks. Bastard. "Now I need to fuck you hard, okay, baby?" I nod my response. He pulls out of me long enough to flip me onto all fours, and with his hands on my hips, he snatches me back and impales me onto his cock that's glistening with my release.

"Oh fuck," I cry. My pussy is sensitive, but I want more of him.

I need him.

Like an addict needs their next high, I need him.

I'm addicted.

At this point he's my lifeline, and I need every inch of him that he was willing to give me.

His thrusts knock the air from my lungs.

I lower my head to look between my spread legs to watch his cock disappear inside of my body. Every push and pull is enough to make me feel lightheaded and shake with the promise of another release.

My lower stomach aches with my building release, and with his next thrust, I am screaming through yet another climax.

I've lost count of how many orgasms I went through; he's too damn good.

He holds my hips firmly keeping me pulled back against him to meet every thrust. One hand controls my hips, the other plays with my clit until I am becoming dizzy from my climax.

I'd have bruises on my hips from his grip, and I welcomed it. I wanted to be marked in all ways possible by each of them.

I was already scarred from both King and Rowen, and now it's Eli's turn.

With a grunt, Eli stills, and his cock twitches inside of me as he jerks his release.

He rolls his head back and roars, his warm seed filling my pussy.

Eli removes himself from my body, my core contracting with the loss of him. I could feel his cum seep out of my pussy, but that's not what surprises me.

What surprises me is the feel of his tongue licking me from clit to ass and ass to clit.

He covers my throbbing pussy with his mouth and sucks.

Hard.

Gasping, I am sure how to feel. He'd just come inside me, and now he's sucking his jizz out of my hole. I clench, pushing more of his cum and my cream out of me for him to swallow.

With a mouthful of his own cum, Eli shifts me from my hands and knees and lays me down on my back, his chocolate eyes raking over my sweaty flushed body like a predator.

His lips and chin glistens with cum, both of our releases, and once again, I clench my pussy at the sight of him holding his own cum inside of his mouth. He hovers over me, lowering his mouth to me and on instinct my lips part for him.

He spits the cum into my mouth and I swallow instantly, our lips attacking each other and our tongues tangling.

I lick over every inch of his mouth that I can get, trying to get more of the taste of him. I want to savor the sweetness of my cream and the saltiness of his cum.

I want more, but I am not confident enough yet to try taking his cock inside my mouth. He's much too large. My lips will probably crack and split trying to fit him inside.

The slight taste of cooper hits my tongue; I know I was right about bleeding. Looking down at his cock, I see his creamy coated cock with hints of red. It isn't much blood, but I did bleed a small amount during the several toe-curling orgasms he gave me.

Eli lays on his side, wraps me in his arms and kisses my forehead.

Such an intimate gesture. With a yawn and without a word, I let myself drift to sleep in the comfort of his arms, being held against his warm body.

"Dance with me." Eli holds his hand out toward me as the smooth voice of Sam Cooke plays in the background.

We'd woken up from our postcoital nap about two hours ago and took a shower together. Not only is his bedroom and bathroom larger than the other bedrooms, but he has a waterfall showerhead that I fell in love with. As well as a personal shower massager that I'll have to let him use on me once or twice in the near future.

I would've today if I wasn't aching too much.

We'd eaten a late lunch and while I was cleaning the kitchen, he was in the living room playing music.

I place my hand in his open palm, and he pulls me against his taut chest, his hand going to the small of my back.

Slowly he moves us along with the rhythm of the music.

His brown eyes hold mine captive, an unreadable expression on his face as we dance.

Just like everything else he does, he's the perfect dancer.

"You were a dancer." It isn't a question, but I nod anyways. He knows about my ballet background. "You are a dancer," he corrects. "Why did you stop dancing?"

"Sebastian made me. He felt that I wasn't spending enough time at home after we got married, so I quit dancing. The company didn't want to let me go, so they asked me to become a teacher. He agreed to that, but he controlled everything about my work schedule. I taught because I couldn't dance anymore," I explain, and he silently nods, both of his hands going to my hips and grips them firmly.

I slide my hands up his arms and wrap them around his neck as we sway to the music.

"You've been through so much in your life. Yet here you stand in front of me, a woman who isn't afraid to do whatever she wants and be herself. You're incredible, Tate."

"You're getting soft on me," I tease, nudging him playfully.

"Maybe. But I'm being honest with you. You're an angel sent to me, sent to all of us, and I'm glad we'll get to keep you for as long as you'll have us. But tell me, how are you such a strong person after all that you've endured? Most people would be weak and afraid."

I sigh, that's something I wonder myself many times. "I was used to being pushed around by everyone my entire life. One day, I decided enough was enough. And I did not want to be the victim anymore. I took control over my life." He brushes my hair behind my ears as he listens to everything I have to say. "Before I met you three, the only time I ever felt safe in my life was when I was in that foster home with Rowen. Despite what we were forced to do, he protected me the best he could. He took my beatings when he could, and when he couldn't, he'd hold me while I cried and wiped my tears away. Every night he was the one who cleaned the blood off me." My words come out in a strained whisper. I didn't know I'd struggle this much with talking about my past, since no one ever knew about it.

As far as anyone was concerned, my parents died in car accident during my teens, and I was living with an aunt and uncle.

That's the story I told Sebastian. It's the furthest thing from the truth, but he had already seen me as broken and impure, and I never wanted him to see me as anything other than that. I let him think I was a virgin for crying out loud.

"I was weak and living in hell when I was with Sebastian. I was his own personal Barbie doll that he'd dress up and control. I did what he wanted, when he wanted, or else I'd have to face the consequences." We are no longer dancing, but he continues to hold me against his chest, his fingers brushing through my hair slowly.

"I hated being that weak woman, and that's why I killed Lee. I was tired of being weak and controlled by everyone around me." I know that most victims of abuse develop PTSD, or they shy away from people.

I, on the other hand, have not been shy toward the male attention that I've received recently from my guys. I still don't know how to describe or explain my connection toward them, since the first day I laid eyes on them inside of the VIP room, I was drawn to them like a magnet. I couldn't see their faces at that point, only their eyes, but their eyes lured me in and provided me with a sense of comfort that I'd never once had before. Even if they did kidnap me and try to use me as a pawn.

With them, I know I'll be okay.

I still have my doubts about Eli, but I'm certain of how I feel toward King and Rowen.

"Was it hard for you to leave your life behind?"

"No, it was actually easy for me once I got out of the victim mentality. I'd been planning it for three months before I left. His temper was getting worse, and I knew my only way out was death." I should've realized the day I agreed to marry the devil himself there was never going to be a way out. I was his forever. He'd never let me go. The only way to be free was to make him believe I was dead, that he finally killed me. In a way, he did.

"I'm glad you chose death, because that led you here and you've changed our lives in such a short amount of time. You've changed us."

I lean up on my tiptoes and press a chaste kiss to his lips. "Okay, now stop being sappy. I'm here to stay." He chuckles deeply. His laugh is manly and speaks directly to my cunt that clenches in appreciation for the melodic sound.

The cabin door opens and in walks Rowen and King who are shoving each other and laughing. "Ah, there's my butterfly." King rushes toward me and wraps his arms around me from behind, shoving me further into Eli's chest.

Eli groans in annoyance at having King's arms around the both of us, but he makes no attempt to move. Rowen joins in on our group hug and all three men kisses over my face, eliciting a burst of giggles from me. This is what happiness feels like.

"Stop, my dick is getting hard and unless my butterfly plans to give me relief, then I suggest you let go," King says, causing me to grin and wriggle away from the middle of the hug fest. Eli and Rowen pull away quickly too, clearly wanting no part of King's boner, and I can't blame them. I don't right now either.

"Sorry, my vagina is off limits for the next day or two. I'm way too sore to get anymore dick."

"That's fine, but how's your mouth?" King smirks, taking me in his arms and kissing me crazy.

Rowen takes me away from him and kisses my forehead, trailing kisses down until his lips connect with mine. "Hi, angel." My lips curl up in a smile. "Did you miss us?"

"Actually, no. Eli kept me too busy to miss either of you," I joke, eliciting snickers from all three of them. Eli wraps an arm around my shoulders and kisses my cheek.

"Damn right I did, baby." The laughter dies down and I watch the three exchange a look with each other. "We're going to my office for a little bit. Watch TV or something." Eli walks away from me, leaving me standing in the middle of the living room with my eyebrows raised.

Placing my hands on my hips, I roll my eyes in annoyance. "Fuck that. If you have something to discuss that involves me, then you're going to talk with me in the room."

"Angel, I think it's best that we discuss this alone. We'll fill you in on anything that needs your attention." Rowen says, raising his hand to brush a strand of hair behind my ear.

"That's not going to work for me. I've spent too long having men tell me what to do, and you're not going to discuss me while I sit pretty in the next room." I cross my arms over my chest, standing my fucking ground. They can speak in front of me, whatever it is that they need to discuss. "I watched King kill a man. I've earned the right to be in the loop about what's going on." They share a look to each other, and without waiting for any of their responses, I walk right past them and down the hall toward Eli's office.

Taking a seat on the corner of the desk, I look toward the three men in front of me and wave a hand, gesturing for them to begin speaking.

King and Rowen take the two seats in front of the desk and Eli sits behind it. "We had our security team looking into Sebastian. I know you don't believe that he's got anything to do with this, but we had to look into him anyways." I nod, remaining silent to allow Eli the chance to explain what he needs to. "You were right, he's not involved with anything." He leans forward and brings his computer to life, turning one of the dual monitors to face King and Rowen and the second one to face me.

"He completely checked out. As far as him and everyone else are concerned, you are dead. His financials are clear, there's no affiliation with any gangs or mercenary groups, he's clear a hundred percent," Eli says. I am not even angry that they looked into Seb after I told them he wasn't involved. They were only trying to keep me safe, and I appreciate that.

"Sebastian was taken in for questioning. Obviously, there wasn't a body for them to find. The police believe foul play was involved, but Sebastian was cleared as a suspect."

A cold laugh erupts from me. "Of course, he'd be cleared. His father is the chief of police, and his grandfather is a fucking senator. He comes from a powerful family; he can get away with anything."

"Is his family aware of your past? I'm sure they looked into you considering they are as wealthy as they are," Rowen pipes up, leaning forward to rest his forearms on the desk.

"They did, and all that they found was exactly what I told them." When I left the last house I'd been living in, I had a hacker friend of mine change my past and create a new one. I wanted to start fresh with my life and didn't want anyone to ever learn the truth about what I've been through. "I had a friend who erased my past and reinvented me on paper."

"Does your friend have a name?" My eyes shoot to Eli's, my eyebrows pulling together.

"Why? I haven't seen him in years."

"Tate, who's the friend that helped you?" His dominant tone sends chills down my spine.

With a roll of my eyes, I answer him, "His name is Ace." The three of them look at each other. "What?" I snap; I know there's something they're not telling me.

"Ace Jackson, your former foster brother who was stalking you?" Rowen scoffs.

Everyone has always had misconceptions about Ace. Especially my foster families and caseworker. "He never stalked me. He helped me when I needed it. He looked out for me," I defend, pointing my finger to each of them. "Ace is a friend, and you three need to stop thinking what you're thinking."

"What are we thinking, butterfly?" Hazel eyes meet mine, and I fight the urge to smack that smug grin right off King's beautiful fucking face.

"You're thinking that he's behind the ambush and the one that wanted me, but he's not. We're friends, he's not trying to kidnap me." I was willing to defend Ace until my dying breath, because without a doubt I know there's no way he would do this when he's never done anything to harm me. Ace may be a little… different, but he's never been dangerous toward me. He's not a threat, regardless of what they think. I'm not exactly going to share further details about my relationship with Ace, but I know he'd never hurt me.

"Rowen says he stalked you. I'm inclined to believe him." Eli raises an eyebrow, his plump lips curling into an amused smirk.

"What exactly has he done for you?" Rowen asks, and I narrow my eyes at him.

"He didn't stalk me! After we parted from the home we were at, he'd come to check on me sometimes. He'd bring me food, clothes, any other things I needed," I huff in frustration. He gave me my first tampon for crying out loud! I didn't know how to use it and had no one to show me. The home I was at was disgusting. They wouldn't wash my clothes or allow me to, and I was bleeding through everything. Three days later, he returned with a box of pads and a sandwich I know he stole. "During the time I was placed in the same home with Rowen, we stopped meeting up. He tried to see me during that time, but he didn't want to make things worse, plus I had Rowen who was protecting me." I sigh, turning to face my green-eyed savior. "After you killed Greg, I ran away just like you said, but I had no place to go. I was thirteen and scared, so I went to Ace. He helped the best he could." That's not entirely what happened, but they don't need to know that. Not when they're keeping who knows how many secrets from me.

"Those people you lived with, the ones you told everyone were your aunt and uncle, how did you end up with them? If you were with Ace after you left Rowen, how did you end up in another foster home?" Eli asks, and I gulp. Luckily, he continues speaking before I can create a lie to tell.

"They died in a house fire." Eli sits back in his chair, pulling a file from the top drawer of his desk. "Willa and Bill Adamson, along with their son, Colton, who was visiting from college, were killed in a house fire during the middle of the night. Tragic accident." He looks up at me, accusation clear as day in his chocolate eyes. "You were so lucky to be out of the house when the fire started." I look at each of them to scope out their expressions.

No surprise that King is already staring at me with pure amusement. I was learning quickly that the fucker liked death and blood just as much as I do.

With the sweetest smile I can muster, I climb off Eli's desk and walk toward the door. "You know what, you're right. You three should discuss this privately, I'll just be in the living room." King extends his arm, wraps it around my waist and quickly pulls me to sit on his lap.

He locks his arms around me, holding my back against his chest. "Butterfly, did you set your foster family on fire?" I'm not answering that. I wriggle against his grip.

"Did Ace have anything to do with it?" Rowen asks. I don't miss the venom he spits when he says Ace's name.

"Why would Ace have anything to do with it?" I roll my eyes, crossing my arms over my chest. These motherfuckers are not going to blame Ace for my actions.

"Explain yourself, angel." Rowen looks at me.

They're not looking at me with judgment. Curiosity dances in their eyes.

Even though I am not going to be judged for my actions, I don't want to tell them what led me to setting the house on fire.

Up until that point, I have never killed anyone myself, though I was no stranger to death. I've seen death too many times in my life. It doesn't scare me.

I turn my head and look Rowen in the eyes, hoping the look I am giving him would express everything I couldn't say.

His eyes soften, and he reaches across to take my hands in his, tightening his grip. He pulls me out of King's arms and into his lap. He turns me so that I'm straddling him.

Whoever's t-shirt I'm wearing rides up on my thighs. His hands trail up my exposed thighs and keep going until he's shoving his hands into my hair, tangling my dark locks around his fingers, pulling me closer to him to rest his forehead against mine.

"Did they hurt you?" His voice is low, in a whisper for only me to hear.

I don't respond, only nod my head.

They didn't record me like Greg did, but Bill and Colton liked to sneak into my room after Willa passed out after taking one too many sleeping pills.

Then they'd take turns raping me.

They made me a victim once again after escaping Greg. They lured me into a false sense of security.

They enrolled me into a good school and into ballet, and they took good care of me.

Out of all of the homes I'd been in, theirs was my favorite at first.

I'd been living there for nearly a year when Colton came home from college to stay for the summer.

The night after driving lessons with Bill was the first time Colton snuck into my room.

The next time he came into my room, he wasn't alone.

I'm not sure if Willa knew or not.

They'd only come into my room after she was asleep, and when she was awake during the days, they'd act as if nothing had ever happened.

If she did know, she was great at pretending she didn't.

She might've been innocent, but there's not a doubt in my mind that she would've blamed me had she known. It went on long enough, and the week before I turned eighteen, I snapped. I couldn't take it anymore.

I was so fucking tired of being a victim.

"Remember, Lee, this is our secret. We're not blood related, so it's okay that we do this, but still, no one would understand our connection," Colton said as he undressed himself. He was home from college for the summer again, which meant he was back to making his nightly visit to my room.

Bill had his visit last night, so tonight was Colton's turn since he wanted "alone time" as he told his father.

My queen-size bed had dipped with his weight as he climbed on top of me. I closed my eyes once I started aching between my legs.

I laid on my bed staring at my ceiling, not bothering to cover my naked body or even spare the monster in my room a second glance.

I was numb. So completely numb, that even when he wiped the tears away from my cheeks that I hadn't realized rolled down, I barely registered his touch.

I felt nothing.

"You know you want this, don't pretend that you don't." I ignored him until I heard the soft click of my door closing, and the sound of his footsteps against the old creaky wood floor disappeared down the hallway.

I stayed on my bed for what felt like hours. I'm not sure the exact time that passed, but when I finally sat up, I went right into the bathroom and stepped into the shower and used my berry bodywash to scrub myself until my skin was angry red and raw.

Just like how I would've felt on the inside if I could feel anything.

After showering, I dried myself and dressed in a white sundress that Willa had bought me today at a thrift store.

I braided my blonde hair in a perfect French braid that went to the middle of my back.

I was in the darkness of my bedroom, standing in front of the full-length mirror staring at myself.

I hardly even recognize myself anymore.

The life was gone from my face, instantly, I wondered if there ever had been life in my eyes. It was hard to remember when I felt completely content and wasn't afraid of what the night would bring.

My hands moved down the length of my body, and with shaky hands I caressed my swollen belly. The moonlight was casting its glow into my bedroom window and shining on me, I was practically glowing with the moonlight shining on my white dress.

My baby chose that moment to make its presence known by moving and kicking against my ribs. I was nine months pregnant with my rapist's child, and they still wouldn't leave me alone.

I wasn't even sure who the father was. There were three men that could be the father.

I don't remember going outside.

The last thing I remembered was staring at myself with disgust and wishing my child wouldn't have a pathetic excuse for parents.

Then I blinked and found myself in the garage picking up the red gas can and carrying it through the house, pouring gasoline everywhere.

I'd been watching myself do these things, but I didn't feel connected with my body. It must've been an outer body experience?

Such a shame, once such a beautiful house, a home. Now it's nothing but hell, a house filled with secrets and things I wished to forget, but never would.

The scars of my past and present were engraved in my brain, there's not a single chance I would ever forget the hell I've endured in my short seventeen years of life.

Tiptoeing through the house, I poured gasoline everywhere.

Upstairs and down.

I used the electric lighter that Willa keeps in the living room to light a piece of newspaper and tossed it on the floor, watching as the flames and gasoline came together, engulfing the house in bright beautiful orange, red, and yellow flames.

Covering my mouth and nose with the sleeve of my dress, I ran outside, running to the end of the driveway so that I could stand back and admire the flames.

The flames didn't care what objects they attacked and burned, they matched exactly how I felt inside.

I'd been hollow inside and desperate for someone to make me feel anything other than pain, and every time I was let down. It's time I accepted that no one is coming to save me. I'm my own savior and I can and will protect myself.

I made a vow to myself right then at that moment.

They're going to burn in hell for their sins.

Every single one of them.
No matter where they go, no matter what they do, they will burn.
They can run, but they can't hide.

Sebastian preyed on my vulnerability, and I often wonder why I was never able to kill him. I could've so easily set our house on fire or killed him while he slept, yet I never could bring myself to go through with it.

In the beginning I felt safe with him, even when the abuse started, I still found ways to justify it because at the end of the day, he'd tell me that he loved me.

I had food to eat, a car to drive, and a fancy roof over my head. I told myself that's all that mattered, and his abuse was worth it. I justified it in every single way possible. And now I'm worried that I'm letting my vulnerabilities be seen again and letting myself be lured into another false sense of security with these three. They want to know my secrets, yet they give nothing in return. I've been too desperate for someone to love me, to see me, that I let my guard down so easily.

You'd think after all I've experienced in my life, that I wouldn't be so quick to trust.

The reality is I don't know them. They're strangers. They know so much about me, they know so many of my ugly past secrets, and I'm in the dark when it comes to them.

I can't even tell you what they do for a living, or how they have nearly everyone in this city afraid of them.

As if sensing my negative thoughts, Rowen cups my face in his hands and presses a faint kiss to my lips. "Angel, talk to me," he whispers against my mouth. I don't answer right away. I'm trying to gather my thoughts.

I often have these moments. These episodes where I lose where I'm at because I'm getting swallowed up in a memory that becomes triggered by something small.

I hate that my mind does this. I want to turn my brain off and stop losing myself in memories. I don't want to remember anything.

"Tate?" His fingers are trailing up and down my thighs, but I can't feel his touch.

"Nothing, I'm fine." I place my hands on his to still his movements. With my eyes never losing sight of my hands, I slowly take his right hand and slide it underneath my t-shirt and allow his palm to press against my stomach.

Against the stomach that has been home to three babies that were conceived in horrible situations.

"Talk to me, you got lost in your head just like you used to," Rowen whispers.

Just like I used to.

Just like I still do and can't stop.

Some people have anxiety attacks or blackouts; I have moments where I lose sense of reality and become engulfed so deeply in a memory that I forget everything else.

"It's nothing, I'm fine." My soft voice isn't convincing, but I feel vulnerable right now and the last thing I want to do is express my feelings or let them see how damaged I truly am. Pressing a soft kiss against the corner of his lips, I climb off his lap and managed to successfully walk out of the office without looking back.

I've reached the kitchen when a hand grips my wrist and turns me around, arms wrapping around my body and holding me tightly against his chest in a suffocating hug.

Inhaling deeply, I allow myself a few seconds before I fight against his hold. "Rowen, please, I'm fine. I don't want to talk."

"You're not fine, baby. Did you forget that I know you." He lets me go, taking my face in his rough hands, brushing my hair behind my ears.

"No, you don't. You knew me, and there's a difference. You knew me thirteen years ago; you don't know me now." I pull away, I don't want to be touched right now.

I can't be touched right now.

His arms wrap around my body and I fight against his cobra grip. He's keeping me pressed against his chest and forcing me to breathe in his intoxicating scent and feel the warmth of his body. I hate him.

"I do know you, T. Don't pretend that I don't."

"No! You don't! You knew Lee, and she's dead. You don't know me!" I yell, aware that King and Eli can likely hear me since the office isn't that far away.

"You were thinking about something, tell me what it was. Whatever it was, it has you acting—"

"Like what?!" I cut him off before he can finish the sentence. "Like a crazy bitch?!" I pound at his chest, but he's not loosening his grip on me. "I want to go home!" I scream in his face. I surely look like a fucking psycho having a meltdown like this. That's how I feel at least.

"You are home, Tate. You're looking for a fight and I'm not going to give it to you." His right hand wraps around my throat, tight enough to block my airflow, and instantly, I stop fighting him and my attention zeroes in on him and only him. I know he's not doing it to hurt me. He's doing it to calm me. I realize quickly that I *need* pain to feel normal. It's all I've ever known.

Rowen backs me against the wall, his left hand gripping my waist. "You. Are. Home. You are ours, and you better fucking understand that. I fucked up once by not running away with you but, baby, I'm here. I'm

not running, and you don't need to run anymore either. I've got you."
His face is so close to mine I can feel the warmth of his breath across
my lips. He says his words through gritted teeth, and I lose it.

I fucking lose it.

Salty tears stream uncontrollably down my face. My legs shake and
give out, Rowen wraps his arms around me and falls to the floor with
me, holding me against him while sobs rake through my body.

Every single emotion I've ever felt is being exiled.

I cry for the little girl that lost her innocence at a young age.

I cry for the girl who wanted to be loved so badly that she found
herself in the arms of a man who beat her.

I cry for the girl who doesn't know how to be loved, but still
desperately wants to be loved and to love, even if she isn't sure how.

Rowen holds me tightly in his arms, so tight there's no way I can
break any further, I can only heal.

He protected me in ways he didn't have to. Even as a child, I believed
I loved him. I felt something for him.

I feel something for him, for all three of them, that I had never
felt before. I'm not yet sure what the feeling is exactly, but there's
something blossoming within me.

TWENTY-SEVEN

Eli

We could hear Tate's screams and cries from my office, so King and I stayed behind to allow her and Ro to have their moment. They have a bond that none of us can deny.

They were forced into something disgusting and inhumane as children, and for as long as I've known him, he's always had a soft spot for her.

Even if he hadn't seen her, he still thought about her daily.

I still remember the night he told me about her. It was six months after we'd met, and I'd woken him from yet another nightmare. I did that nearly every night, but he finally caved and told me all about the dreams that haunted him. He told me about how he was forced into child pornography by his foster father, and how he was forced to rape a blue-eyed girl when she was only ten. He told me everything, and through the years, he still brought up Tate. Well, Lee, since that's who she was at the time.

"What are we going to do about Ace Jackson?" King asks as he takes the file from my desk that I and our security put together on Tate.

"I've already given his name to security. We'll have a complete report back soon. In the meantime, I'm still digging through her past. Anyone who knows her as Lee is a suspect." I can feel my resolve slipping. I enjoy control in all things. Due to our line of work, I especially have to be in control. And this situation is something that I can't fucking control. We'd initially run a background check on Tate when she'd arrived in our city. But we decided to dig deeper and uncover every possible secret we could find. And I'll admit, Ace did a good job of deleting her background, but he's no match for our security team. They can uncover files that have been deleted.

I'm becoming furious with the fact we don't know who wants Tate or why. We have no information and we're not any closer to getting it either.

The only suspect we had was her husband, and he's been ruled out. For now, he'll stay put in that mansion of his where he beat her repeatedly. But once the dust settles, you bet your ass that we will be paying him a visit and giving him just what the fuck he deserves. We must wait.

I push back from my desk and stand. "I'm taking Tate into the city with me tomorrow. I have a meeting I can't miss." King nods, not needing me to explain to him what I need him and Rowen to do. He's capable of reading between the lines. If I'm at our office, that means he and Rowen are doing the groundwork today. I need both of them this time. No one can stay behind to babysit Tate, they've been doing that enough lately.

"Ro and I will go tomorrow and find out what we can about Ace. We'll visit his apartment to see if he's home. I have a few others we're going to meet with as well," King explains.

"Who are the others you're going to meet with?"

"The Westside Disciples have a new leader. They're operating under the radar, and they have left our city alone. But I think someone within their organization may know something about the contract placed for Tate."

Fuck. This is news to me. Last I checked, the disciples were deteriorating after the death of Malakai. King has access to more information than I give him credit for.

"Alright. Take Ro and stay strapped." I don't have to tell him to stay alert, he's loaded already, but at least it gives me a piece of mind.

I never want to lose either of my brothers, and after Rowen was shot, I'm being even more cautious.

With a nod, King leaves my office and I follow behind.

The common areas are empty, so I assume Rowen has taken Tate upstairs.

Whatever this thing or relationship it is that the three of us have with her has moved way too quick. We've known her a short amount of time, sans Rowen, but yet here we all are, each of us sharing a different type of relationship… a relationship that is more sexual than anything else.

Not that I'm complaining when she's got a pussy as sweet as she does. She tastes like salted caramel, and that's suddenly my new favorite flavor. I know if I'm not careful, I'll become addicted. And I cannot become addicted.

This may be fun, but I can't let a woman become my weakness. I may say a few nice words to make her swoon, but I'm not stupid enough to allow her to get too close or keep her around for too long. My brothers have feelings for Tate, and they'll be crushed when it's time for her to go, but for now, we'll enjoy the time we have with her. For however long that may be.

I don't trust Tate. I know she's keeping secrets, and something feels off. I haven't been able to shake the lingering feeling I've had from the moment we brought her to our cabin.

Unease is settling in, then realization hits me like a slap in the face when I hear my father's words in my head.

She's a distraction. Eliminate the distraction, son.

Instead of thinking about pussy, no matter how great it is, we should be thinking about our business and working on getting a new supplier.

Typical Eli to get distracted by loose pussy.

Those damn Disciples were able to sneak in and take miles of our city and our supplier because we were too distracted with the last wet cunt that got our cocks wet.

That distraction was eliminated in the same way we eliminate every distraction or enemy.

Death.

"You okay?" Rowen asks, eyeing me suspiciously. I'm standing outside of Tate's bedroom door, my hands in fists at my sides, my eyes narrowing in on the door.

He always did know me better than anyone else and he can always see right through the mask I wear to shield my emotions.

"She's a distraction." The words taste like poison, no matter how true they are.

His shoulders pull back and he straightens to his full height.

Ro and I nearly stand eye to eye to each other, but I have one inch on him.

One single pointless inch.

King is the tallest of the three of us. That man is a fucking giant.

"What are you talking about?" he says through gritted teeth, his usual bright green eyes now darkening.

"She's a distraction, Ro. We've been spending all of our time on her and finding out who wants to kidnap her when we should we worrying about our business."

"We can do both, you know we can. We have enough resources."

"We can't afford another distraction, and you know it. That's how Malakai went undetected in our city for fucking months because we were busy buried in pussy." Women are a weakness and that's a weakness we can't afford.

We couldn't then, and we can't now.

Not when we have too many enemies who would love to wait until we're down and then attack.

Maybe she's the enemy. You don't know everything about her. Get rid of her.

I shake the voice from my head. Clearing my throat, I say, "We can't let a used pussy distract us, brother. Eyes on the bigger picture." Wrong thing to say to someone who's a ticking time bomb.

I know how Rowen feels about Tate, and he's never forgiven himself for the shit that went down during their childhood. He's protective over her.

I should've expected the punch, but it still takes me by surprise. My head jerks back, and I stumble, instantly feeling the warm blood draining from my nose.

I deserved that. I know better than to badmouth her to him.

"She's not a fucking distraction. Just because you got your dick wet doesn't mean you get to throw her away because you're done with her. You don't make the fucking decisions, Eli." He opens the door to her bedroom and slips inside, closing it quietly in my face. I assume she's sleeping or else he would've slammed it instead.

He leaves me standing there with a bloody nose and feeling regretful for the things I said.

He is so fucking right, and I hate it.

She might be a distraction, but it's my own problem if I can't control it.

Truth is, she calls to me like a siren and I'm afraid of being weak. She has the power to ruin us, to bring us all to our knees and bow at her feet. But I can't shake the split feelings and thoughts going through my mind. I can't shake the voice in my head telling me she's hiding something.

Secrets are what will tear us apart.

My father taught me to never be weak, never show weakness, and never be afraid of doing what needs to be done.

I've always done exactly that, and I'll do it again this time.

Tate has become a blind spot, a weakness we can't afford, and a liability.

I will do what needs to be done, with or without Rowen.

The distraction will be eliminated.

"Good morning, sir. Coffee?" Elena, my receptionist with a mile-long legs, struts into my office, an eager smile plastered on her face.

My eyes drift away from my computer screen long enough to rake over her legs when she turns her back toward me at the coffee station there in the corner of my office.

I don't get the same feeling that I usually do when I look at a beautiful woman.

Yes, Elena is beautiful, but no woman compares to the raven-haired temptress that's staying at home being babysat by our prospects who hoped to one day soon become bodyguards.

Tate was supposed to be coming to work with me today, but I couldn't handle seeing her face. Not today when I already have too much on my plate to worry about.

I take the coffee from Elena and dismiss her with a wave of my hand.

The disappointed frown that forms on her lips as she leaves my office does not go unnoticed. Usually, she'd prepare my coffee then get down on her knees and suck me dry, but not today.

Rowen, King, and I started our company Hale Enterprises ten years ago with the money we made from selling dope on the streets. We've grown a lot since those days, as has our business.

Hale Enterprises specializes in a little bit of everything, from real estate all the way to technology.

I'm the face of the company, the one who handles the day-to-day legitimate operations.

King handles the real estate, he buys struggling companies that are facing foreclosure, frees them of all personal and business-related debt, and ensures we can use their company to launder money through.

Rowen is the one that handles the finances. He's always been the smartest with numbers, so he handles our accounts for our illegal and legal activity.

Sinners is only one of the many businesses that we own out right.

We all wanted a place to relax from time to time, so when King pitched the idea of a masquerade strip club, it was too good to turn down.

Our elite client list would have to agree too.

Today I have a meeting with one of our overseas partners, a meeting I couldn't miss.

We're expanding Hale Enterprises into Europe, and so far, our England building is yet to be completed within the timeframe that we set. We already have a team over there waiting for a building so they can set up shop and begin conducting business.

And yes, you guessed it, our international operations will be just as illegal as they are stateside. So, you see the importance of needing construction completed in a timely manner.

At exactly ten in the morning, the Skype call pops up on the screen of my laptop just as Elena walks into my office to take her seat in front of my desk, same as she does every time I have a meeting. I can't be bothered with note taking so she does it for me so I won't forget anything.

She's a great assistant, and a great lay too.

But she is nothing compared to Tate.

Tate. Fuck. My dick twitches in my pants at the thought of having her spread beneath me again, moaning my name and leaving scratches down my back. I wonder how she'd look on top of my desk or against the window.

Stop it, Eli. Think with your head and not your dick. She's going to be eliminated.

Fuck. I can't fucking think about her, I don't deserve to think about her.

Clearing my throat and hoping the voice in my head can shut the fuck up, I sit up straight in my chair. I select the green answer button and Callum's face appears on my screen instantly.

"Talk to me, Cal. Where are we at with the production?"

"Hello to you too, you grumpy bastard." He chuckles. "I'm great, thanks for asking."

"I don't have time for this. What's the latest update?" He's fidgety like he always gets whenever he's nervous about something he needed to tell me. He is avoiding whatever it is. "Spit it out," I demand, and so he does. He goes on to tell me that the building is still waiting certain permits that was delaying the build. That, and the contractor happened to quit out of the blue.

"We need more money and more time. The only way to complete the project is to pay everyone off to speed up our inspections and permits. The contractor wants more as well, he did his own research and knows how much the company is now worth." Of course, he does. Greedy bastard.

From my peripheral view, my cell phone lighting up and vibrating across my desk catches my attention. I pick it up, making no show of the fact I was on my phone and no longer giving my attention to Callum. Elena can fill me in on his sorry excuses later.

Countless calls and text messages are coming in from both Rowen and King, and even a few from some of our other staff members. The text that catches my attention and causes me to nearly crush my phone from gripping too tight is a text from King.

King: *911. Bella's.*

911 is what we use when there's an emergency. We try to be vague over text for the most part, not sending anything that can't reasonably be explained.

"Email Rowen about however much is going to be needed to get the job done by the original deadline." Before Callum has a chance to respond, I slam my laptop shut and stand, my knuckles white from how tightly I am holding my phone.

Elena stands looking at me with worry in her brown eyes. "Is everything okay? Can I help with anything?" We walk toward each other, her small porcelain hand gripping my bicep lightly.

In the past I wouldn't hesitate to bend her over my desk and take advantage of her long ponytail, but now I can't stop picturing Tate's face morphing in pleasure and the way her eyes get glossy and roll in the back of her head when she has an orgasm.

Fuck.

I'm a weak little pussy for feeling anything toward a girl. A girl I barely know but can't stop thinking about.

I shake her face out of my mind, and wrap my hand around Elena's delicate wrist with every intention to remove it. Instead, I pull her body close to me and attack her lips in a kiss that feels so fucking wrong.

But I am a red-blooded male after all, so even though she wasn't the one I wanted, that didn't stop my dick from getting hard. And that didn't stop me from bending her over the couch and trying to fuck her. But for the first time in my life, I can't perform. I can't get hard.

Fucking Tate.

She's ruined me for anyone else.

I leave Elena on the couch half naked and begging for me. Yet I don't care. Her pussy isn't the one I want.

Tate is the only one that I had ever fucked bare before. I hadn't planned on it, but I wanted to know how it would taste getting to suck my cum out of her pussy. Just as I imagined, it was fucking magical. It tasted like heaven on earth. It tasted even better because it was mixed with her cream.

I want to spread her legs and eat her sweet cunt like it's my new favorite dessert.

When speeding, it takes me twenty minutes to get from my office to Bella's, an Italian restaurant that we purchased years ago to save it from going under. It's actually one of the first businesses that we acquired, and Fabio, the owner, has been a trusted friend and ally to the Triad for years.

When we were younger, Rowen, King, and I would often work for Fabio in exchange for a few bucks or a meal. He was always kind to us, and we returned the favor when our business took off and we began making money.

He helped us, we helped him. It was meant to be a gift, but the stubborn fuck that he is wouldn't accept it, so we made a deal and he's now one of our most trusted partners.

I'd barely shifted my car into park when I open the door and run out toward where King and Rowen are standing on the sidewalk in front of Bella's, talking to a police officer.

The building is surrounded by cop cars and ambulances.

"What the fuck happened here?" I demand, coming to their side.

"Eli." A detective walks toward me, extending his hands for me to shake.

"Detective Roberts. What's going on?" I shake his hand. Just like nearly every other cop in the city, Detective Lyle Roberts is also on the Triad's payroll.

"There's been a shooting. Three people were DOA, there's no suspects. Unless you have someone in mind that would want to attack Bella's?"

"Who died?" I ask through clenched teeth, my eyes snapping toward Ro and King.

"Two cooks and a waitress," Detective Robert says, opening his notepad and flipping through a few pages. "Alba, Bruno, and Giovanni are the deceased." Somewhere in the distance, his name was called, and he turns his head. "Excuse me." He walks toward the group of officers who are wasting time taking pointless statements of bystanders.

"What the fuck do we know?" I snap, needing answers and needing them right fucking now. Fabio is like family, his staff is like family, and now we're out for blood for whoever killed three members of his staff.

This isn't random, it's personal.

Rowen shoves his phone at me, showing me a text message.

Unknown: *You took what's mine, so I took what's yours.*

"Tate." I scoff, handing the phone back.

"Yup, and I'm going home now to check on her," King states coldly, not bothering to wait for a response before he takes off, leaving the two of us behind.

"What are you planning to do, E?" Rowen asks. Sometimes I hate that he knows me so well.

"Fuck, I don't know."

"Don't ruin a good thing while you're stuck in your head trying to figure it out. Oh, and clean yourself up before you go home. I can smell the pussy on you, and she will too." He looks me up and down with disgust, a look he's never given me before. He shoves past me, hitting my shoulder with his as he too leaves me alone to deal with this mess. I didn't fuck Elena. I tried, but I couldn't. Though I know I smell like her cheap perfume.

I had no choice but to stay behind and talk to both Fabio and Detective Roberts to get more information on the shooting.

From what they had to say, two men entered the restaurant and open fired. Three people were killed. Both cooks were outside unloading a grocery shipment. While they were unloading, they were shot in the head and then came the waitress.

After Detective Reynolds left, Fabio took me into his office and showed me the surveillance video. It was hard to watch considering they were people I knew. They never stood a stance. They didn't even see it coming.

The two men wore all black including their ski masks. From what I could see, there was nothing about them that could be used to identify them. This wasn't random, this was very much planned. And whoever was responsible for this, was also responsible for ambushing us. The text Rowen received is proof enough.

As if I needed any more of a reason to distance ourselves from Tate, this is it.

I went back to my office afterward and spent hours speaking with my security team that we'd hired to run in depth background checks on everyone we did business with. Anything that was buried that someone didn't want us to find, that's exactly the type of things that our security team found.

They found the deep dark secrets of everyone we encountered.

They'd sent me the information they tried to obtain on Ace, which was barely anything. All that they were able to find was his address, which we already knew, and his bank statements. As great as my security team is, there's not one piece of fucking information that's useful.

Up until nine months ago, Ace Jackson didn't exist. He'd been a ghost up until he opened a bank account and rented an apartment. No one deletes their past unless there's something they don't want someone to find. Whoever this fucker is, he's good.

Clearly I wasn't aware exactly how great his skills were.

It's not a coincidence that he happened to show up on paper the exact moment Tate arrived. I believe now more than ever that this shady fuck is out there stalking her again.

The only charges that appear on his account are minimal charges from coffee shops. We searched the surveillance footage from each location he visited, and found the footage was wiped clean, so we have no idea what he looks like. He could be anywhere at any time, and we'd never know what he looks like.

First, I suspected Tate's piece of shit husband, they're always the likely suspect, but that fucker checks out.

He was a suspect in her disappearance, but thanks to his family connections, he was cleared of any wrongdoing.

When Tate found out he was cleared, I didn't miss the look on her face. She was angry but wasn't surprised that he was cleared. Her plan for him to be charged with her murder failed.

The further I research her background, the more I realize she is hiding something, there are still many parts of her story that's left to uncover. And just like everyone else, I had my security team check her background too. That's how I knew about the suspicious fire that killed her foster family.

Ace must've been the one to cover it up. It was hidden well, but not well enough because my team was able to uncover it.

I've seen his work, I know he's capable of deleting someone from existence, he did it to himself. So, why not do it for Tate? Why leave just enough crumbs to be followed?

Closing my laptop, I stand from my desk and gather my belongings to leave for the night. It's nine at night now, and I still have an hour drive ahead of me to get back to our secluded cabin, and I'm not going to get the answers I need here staring at my screen. I need answers, and there's only one person who can provide those answers, and she's sitting in my house right now.

Having to drive two hours round trip is yet another inconvenience of having Tate around. It keeps her safe, but it isn't as convenient as our penthouse in the city is.

With an eyeroll of annoyance, I take the elevator down to the parking garage. The building is empty, all my staff have left hours ago. I do my best to let them leave early and get home to their families at a decent hour.

I am halfway to my car when my phone chimes with a text message. While continuing to walk, I open the text, a smirk finding my lips as I read it.

Unknown: *You have twenty-four hours to deliver what's mine. Time is ticking.*

Sliding behind the driver seat of my custom blacked out bulletproof Range Rover, I bring the engine to life and speed out of the garage, hitting a few buttons on my steering wheel to call King on my Bluetooth.

"Hey man, what's up?" he answers on the first ring.

"I just got a text from that unknown number. Whoever the fuck it is, they're giving us twenty-four hours to turn over Tate."

"Over my dead fucking body. We're not letting her go anywhere." I am silent. "Right?" He pushes, picking up on my silence and instantly his alerts are high.

"We can't be distracted, King. We're spending too much time on her, and there's still too many questions that we need answers to."

"We're not fucking distracted. This became our fight when they fucking ambushed us, and now the attack at Bella's. We have to fight back, but I'm not going to lose her in the process because you're too fucked up to realize she could be an asset."

"How exactly can she be an asset to us?"

"You didn't see the look in her eyes when she watched me kill Joseph. My little butterfly is as bloodthirsty as the rest of us. She can fucking help us. You don't need to treat her like some little damsel in distress." His words make me pause. I'd never thought of her being an asset for us. I labeled her as a liability, and that was final.

Sighing, I rake my fingers through my hair, scratching my scalp. "We'll use her as bait to find out who the fuck is behind this. She can lead us directly to the person or persons responsible, and we will kill anyone involved."

It's his turn to sigh, clearly, he doesn't like the idea of his precious butterfly being used as bait to lure out the fucker hiding in the shadows, but this is one way she can be useful and prove herself.

And we need her to be useful, especially now considering it's her life on the line.

Do I trust her? I'm not certain yet. She's keeping secrets, secrets that I intend to learn very quickly.

TWENTY-EIGHT

King

"Eli wants to use Tate as bait to lure whoever's behind this into a trap. He got a text telling him that we have twenty-four hours to turn her over," I tell Rowen immediately after I end the call with Eli.

I run my fingers through my beard, pacing back and forth in the living room.

Tate went to sleep about an hour ago, so it's only Rowen and I still up, waiting for Eli to get home.

"What the fuck?!" he roars, and I shove him in the shoulder.

"Shut the fuck up, she's sleeping. Do you really want her to hear this?"

"He thinks that she's a distraction. I think he's planning something behind our backs."

"What do you mean? What the fuck could he be planning?"

"I don't know, man, but something's up. You know what happened to Stephanie." He covers his face with his hands. "He fucked someone before he met us at Bella's. He came from the office, so it was probably

Elena."

My blood is boiling at all the information he's revealing. There's no way in hell I am going to let anything bad happen to my butterfly. If anyone is going to hurt her or make her bleed, it's going to be me.

What the fuck is Eli's problem? I understand his need for control, but Tate is nothing like Stephanie.

Stephanie was a dancer at Sinners that the three of us had a fling with a year ago. Technically it was more than a fling since it lasted several months.

In the beginning it was regular sex with no strings attached, but then things changed. We all let our guards down, and it was Eli who had his dick inside of her when we got the call that one of our shipments went missing and six of our men were killed. He was supposed to be there, but when she came over, he couldn't turn her away.

We were all too distracted with pussy to realize what was going on right under our noses.

Stephanie was a rat, sent to us by an enemy to learn our secrets and keep us occupied. She did her job well, and she died for doing the job.

Since then, Eli has only let himself indulge in his assistant and an occasional dancer.

He blames himself for the death of our men.

He doesn't know that Rowen and I are aware that he used to visit Sinners every Wednesday night and book a VIP room to get laid, but we knew from the moment it began.

Now he's labeling Tate as a distraction just like Stephanie. Actually...

"Holy fuck." I groan, my shoulders slumping. "We need to use her as bait."

"No! That's out of the question. Don't tell me you agree with him," he spits. I hold my hands up in surrender.

"There's a lot we don't know about her, and if Eli thinks that she's like Stephanie, there's no stopping him or telling what he'll do. It'll be up to us to prove that Tate isn't working with an enemy."

"You can't be fucking serious!" He laughs humorlessly. "I know her! She'd never try to infiltrate us!"

"You haven't seen her since you were kids. You don't know her now, and we need to protect her as much as ourselves." I say with a sigh. "Just listen to me." I sit down on the couch, leaning forward to rest my elbows on my knees. "I don't think she's a rat, but we need proof, especially to please Eli. We need to give her access to her contacts and see what happens. Tomorrow night, we'll use her as bait. We'll prove Eli is wrong."

"She's not involved. You and Eli will both see that tomorrow." Rowen takes a seat on the couch across from me. I don't believe she's guilty of anything, but at this point you can never be too sure. And using her as bait will at least allow us to find the person who's been after her, and Eli will see she's not a distraction. It's a solid plan that we must perfect.

"I want to keep her, brother. But I don't know what Eli is planning."

"Me too, man. Me too." He lets out a long groan of frustration. "We'll take a few steps back and clear our heads. Let's give her back her cell phone and see who she contacts. We'll keep tabs on her."

"Eli has her phone, and he's already installed a tracker and a recording system. He'll be able to see everything she does. We'll give it to her in the morning and see what happens." I stand, going into the kitchen to fetch two bottles of beer from the fridge. "You have to admit, it is a little weird that she let us take her from the club so easily and only that once she tried to escape." I return to the living room, handing Rowen one of the bottles.

"I don't know, man. It's Lee, she's the girl I swore to protect."

"No coincidences. Why would she come back here? If she really did have to escape her husband, why come here? There's nothing but shit memories for her here."

Before Rowen has a chance to respond, our attention snaps toward the front door to find Eli walking inside with a dreadful expression that matches ours.

"My office. We need to talk; I got another text." He walks right past us and towards the hallway. Rowen and I both jump up and follow him.

"Tomorrow night at nine o'clock, we're going to Confess nightclub, and we're taking Tate with us. We're going to use her to lure out whoever is responsible for the shooting at Bella's. This is personal."

"It became personal when they ambushed us." Rowen scoffs, taking his usual seat in front of Eli's desk.

"You were shot in that ambush and could've died. It was personal then, and it's personal now with the shooting at Bella's that claimed three innocent lives," Eli says.

"What's your plan, Eli?" I ask, not liking any of this, but I understand what needs to be done.

He reaches inside of his desk drawer and pulls out Tate's iPhone that we took from Sinners the same time we took her. "We can track her through this, and she'll never know. We do as this unknown fucker says, but we'll keep an eye on her at all times. I want to see if she knows the person and goes willingly. If she does, then we'll know that she was part of this. If it turns out she's not part of it, then we'll rescue her and have our answer, and at least we'll be able to get the person responsible too," Eli explains his plan.

"And which way are you hoping that this plays out?" Rowen asks with venom laced in his words.

"I guess we'll see. Either way, someone will end up dead."

I don't want it to be my butterfly, but I understand what needs to be done. If she's a part of this, sent to us as a decoy to learn our secrets and weaken us, then I'll kill her.

For her own sake, I pray to whatever God would listen that she's innocent.

She's too pretty to die, and as much as I want to see her bleed, I don't want that to be the end before we even had a chance to begin.

The next day, I avoid Tate like the plague. Eli gave her the cell phone back during breakfast then excused himself to do some work in his office. Rowen is off in the gym working out his frustrations, and I'm in our workshop making sure everything is clean for whatever poor bastard I get to chain up here tonight.

I have fond memories of Tate's bloody body hanging from the chains while I fucked her into countless orgasms.

She looked so beautiful impaled on my cock and bleeding from the butterfly I carved into her skin.

My cock twitches at the memory.

The workshop had already been cleaned, and the body was removed by our clean-up crew, but I always like to arrange my tools in the certain ways that I like them and ensure the room is spotless.

Eli and Rowen always laugh at me for being such a clean freak about it because it's going to get dirty again anyways. But I like it spotless so I can make it dirty.

I like to paint the white walls with fresh blood.

At this point, I'm immune to the constant smell of disinfectant.

I'm ready for whatever will happen tonight.

TWENTY-NINE

Tate

Something is wrong, but I don't know what.

All day the guys have been avoiding me. I've pushed for them to have a conversation or any type of interaction with me, and they've rejected me every chance they could. Their excuses are frivolous, and I know there's something they're not telling me.

They were up late last night talking. I wasn't eavesdropping, well, actually, I was trying to, but I couldn't hear anything from where I was on the stairs and then eventually, they went into Eli's office and stayed there for who knows how long.

I ended up going back to my room and waiting up for as long as I could, hoping one of them would end up in my bed, but that didn't happen. I fell asleep and woke up to a cold empty bed.

This morning at breakfast, Eli gave me my cell phone. I wasn't sure why, and when I asked, he said it was for emergencies.

I'd placed the phone on my nightstand, and that's where it's been all day long.

I should call Cassie and let her know I'm okay. I'm sure she's worried that I haven't been home in a couple of weeks.

I'm sitting up on my bed reaching for my phone when the door opens and in walks Rowen carrying a black dress bag and a shoe box.

Setting my phone back down, I stand and cross my arms over my chest, raising my eyebrow at him in suspicion.

"What's this?" I ask.

He sets the items on the bed and gives me a smile that doesn't reach his eyes. "Get dressed. We're going out tonight."

"Out? Where? Is it safe?" I reach for the bag, pulling open the zipper to reveal a white dress that's absolutely stunning.

"We wouldn't take you anywhere that wasn't safe. I think we could all use a night out. Be downstairs in an hour." He turns and walks toward the door.

"Wait!" I hurry across the room toward him. "What's going on, Rowen? You guys have been acting weird all day."

He takes my face in his hands, holding me as gently as you would a fragile porcelain doll that would break if he were too rough. His eyebrows pull together in a deep frown that matches his lips. "Nothing, everything is fine."

"Say that again, but make it convincing this time."

He sighs, his forehead resting against mine and his arms wrapping around my waist. "There was an attack at one of our businesses yesterday, and some people that we know were killed." My heart drops down into my stomach.

"Oh, Rowen, I'm so sorry." I put enough space between us that I could look up at him. "Is this because of me?" He doesn't respond with words, instead, he places a chaste kiss to my lips that I know answers my question. Once again, this is my fault.

"Get dressed." Without another word he exits my room, leaving me standing there with a knot in my stomach at the havoc I've caused. He was shot because of me, and now his associates are dead because of me.

How many more deaths would there be because of me?

We must find out who's responsible. I've never been more motivated for anything in my entire life. Failure wasn't an option; we have to find the person or persons responsible.

An hour later I am walking down the stairs dressed in the thigh-high white dress that fits me like a second skin, and am wearing the new shoes they'd bought me.

Black Louboutin stilettos.

I feel like a fucking badass. Like a brand-new woman.

I hadn't worn designer anything since leaving Sebastian. With him, it was designer everything all the time. I'm positive if there was such a thing as designer toilet paper, he would've bought it.

My black hair is in a curtain of curls around my shoulders, my lips painted bright red and my makeup subtle. It's nice to get out of the t-shirts that I've been wearing every day and actually dress up for a change.

All three men are standing downstairs waiting, their eyes instantly on me taking in my appearance. My confidence grows while standing under their gawking stares.

I couldn't help it, I let my own eyes wander over each of them.

They wear matching black suits with black dress shirts and shoes.

Eli's hair is slicked back, Rowen's is messy, and King's hair is pulled in his usual man bun that looks even sexier when paired with a suit.

They are all handsome, but they already know that.

I can tell by the smug knowing grin on each of their faces when our eyes connect.

"Need a towel to wipe your drool?" King jokes, giving me a wink while he extends his hand toward me and helps me down the rest of the stairs. "Let's go, butterfly."

Vlad and Nico are our drivers for the night, and to my surprise, we aren't taking one of their usual cars. When we step outside, my jaw drops when I see the sleek black limo parked out front.

King helps me inside and sits beside me with his arm around my shoulders, Rowen and Eli taking the bench seat to the left of us.

"Do you have your phone?" Eli asks, he is barely able to look at me. Yeah, something is most definitely going on with them.

"Yeah, I do." I open my black leather clutch and pull out my iPhone, holding down the button to power it on.

I was expecting to have countless calls and text messages, so I'm surprised to see that there is not a single notification.

Is no one worried about me? Not even Cassie?

My lips curl down in a frown. "Did anyone delete anything on my phone?"

"No."

"Nope."

"No one's touched it."

They all deny it, which means that no one truly cares about me enough to check on me. I probably should've expected that, but it still hurts.

"Something wrong, butterfly?" I shake my head, sliding my phone back into my clutch, snuggling closer to King's side.

We arrive at Confess, a hot new nightclub that Cassie has been begging me to go to ever since they opened. The large building is completely black, and there isn't a single tell that would reveal it's a nightclub.

There's a black and white sign outside with CONFESS written in large bold letters, but that's it.

Nothing like you'd ever expect.

My three guys climb out first then Rowen turns to help me out. He and Eli are by my side while King stands behind me, watching our backs and watching for threats.

Rowen slides open the large metal door, instantly revealing a set of stairs that Eli leads us up. The further we walk into the building the louder the music becomes.

They must have great soundproof walls, because I couldn't hear anything from outside.

The club is nearly pitch black, a faint yellow glow comes from each step to show us the steps, so we don't fall, and I have to watch exactly where I step, meanwhile my guys walk like pros.

They probably own this club too and have been here a few dozen times. I can hardly walk in the near darkness.

We reach the top of the stairs and there stands two very large men dressed in all black, I'm guessing they're the bouncers.

Instant recognition sparks on their faces when they see my guys. They waste no time sliding open another metal door that reveals a second set of stairs, this time the stairs are going down.

The stairs lead us down into the main floor of the club where all the people are. The music is loud, the floor packed, and the lights are low but enough that I can see.

We stand in the middle of the crowd and my white dress is lit up like a glow stick.

Neon lights.

I look at King with a smirk. I look around, seeing many others wearing white and glowing.

"Come on, let's get some drinks." Rowen grabs my hand, pulling me through the crowd. I turn my head to look behind me to see that King and Eli aren't following behind. I'm curious, but it's too loud to question it right now.

Rowen leads me up another small set of stairs that lead toward what I assume is a VIP section. I take a seat on the plush red sofa, my eyes staring down at the party beneath us, hoping I'll see my two guys.

"Relax, they'll join us soon." He places a hand on my thigh just as a redhead waitress wearing black leather shorts and a bedazzled bra appears by our side, unloading her tray of drinks on the table.

She doesn't speak, but I didn't like the smirk she gives Rowen either. *I know he's hot, but back off, bitch, he's mine.* I wanted to yell, feeling a little more territorial than I'd like to admit. I was never the jealous type, at least I thought that I wasn't, until now it seems.

The redhead pulls back the sheer curtains, giving us the smallest amount of privacy, and I relax against his side. He leans forward, picks up two of the shot glasses from the table and places one in my hand. Smiling at him, I take it.

If tonight really is about getting out of the house and having a good time, I am all for it.

"Cheers." We clink our glasses against each other, and both throw back the contents.

Tequila.

I welcome the warmth that instantly fills my stomach.

"Do you own this club too?" I ask, reaching for the crystal decanter on the table in front of us, filling my glass with more of the amber liquid.

"We do, yes. It's a newer investment. We don't come here nearly as much as we visit Sinners." I bring the glass to my lips and tip my head back, swallowing the warming liquid.

Rowen spreads his legs and pulls me to sit on his lap, his hands pulling my dress up to my waist as he guides my legs to wrap around his.

I lean back against his chest, my core completely open with my dress around my waist. "What are you doing?" I ask breathlessly, his fingertips ghosting over the thin material of panties that cover my already aching core.

"You know what I'm doing."

Oh.

I move my head to the side and let it fall back against his shoulder as he cups my pussy through my panties.

"Is it turning you on being like this in public?" His hand finds its way inside of my panties and without warning he shoves two fingers inside of me. A satisfied moan leaves my lips, my hips rolling forward against his hand as he begins pumping his fingers in and out of me slowly.

All too soon Rowen removes his hand and sucks those same two fingers that were just inside of me into his mouth.

That is so fucking hot.

His fingers return to my panties, but inside of entering me like I want, he circles both my hole and my clit in a teasing manner.

"Do you like this? Knowing we can get caught at any second. Someone can come up here and see us or hear you." His breath is warm against my ear, and I can hear the huskiness of his voice that becomes prominent every time he is turned on.

We can be caught, but no one could hear me over the music.

"Rowen, please." I beg, needing his fingers to return home desperately. He's teasing me, and I am too horny right now for that.

"Do you like it, angel? The idea of getting caught doing something you shouldn't?"

"Yes, yes I do. Now, please." I grab the hand that was inside of my panties and move it down where I need it.

At my entrance.

A chuckle rumbles through his chest that I felt against my back before I heard it.

He gives me what I want and slides two fingers back inside of my slick wetness.

"Fuck," he rasps, "You're so fucking wet for me, angel." With his thumb on my clit, he plays me like an instrument, his skilled fingers curling inside of me and hitting that one spot that makes my breathing quicken, and my eyes roll back.

Two minutes is all it took for Rowen to send me floating on cloud nine with an orgasm that shook my entire body. He has to hold me down with his left arm to keep me from convulsing off his lap.

Rowen doesn't stop pumping his fingers even as the orgasm swallows me whole.

He continues, acting as if it doesn't matter that I'm screaming and writhing on his lap, or that my pussy is probably squeezing his fingers so tightly he may lose circulation.

My eyes close, his fingers pushing into me rapidly and sending me into a second orgasm before I can even finish riding the waves of the first.

I am too wrapped up in my own pleasure, lost when his lips kiss the sensitive skin beneath my ear, that I didn't notice when the curtain was pulled back and we had an audience.

"So much for no sex." Someone grumbled under their breath, but it wasn't said quietly enough that I couldn't hear it.

My eyes shoot open and instantly land on Eli who is staring at me with a mixture of darkness and lust in his eyes. I watch with an open mouth as he shrugs out of his jacket, rolls up the sleeves to his black dress shirt, and falls to his knees between Rowen and I's spread legs.

Eli stares at me with such a burning intensity that I need to look away but can't.

He holds me hostage with his stare.

Rowen removes his hand from my panties, and I shudder at the loss, only to groan a second later at the instant burn and snap of fabric when he rips my panties off.

With my panties out of the way, Eli's mouth is quick to cover my cunt and suck it so roughly I swear he's successful with sucking my soul from my body.

I gasp at the assault, his warm velvet tongue circling and wrapping around my over sensitive clit. He slides two fingers inside of me easily with how wet I am.

What I wasn't prepared for is the delicious stretch of having Rowen insert two of his own fingers inside of me.

They both pump me in perfect rhythm.

"Fuck, let me in on this," King grumbles, and I hear the rattle of his belt. Turning my head to the side, I'm met with his cock that's standing proudly. I part my lips, and he feeds his cock inside of my mouth.

"Fuck, butterfly. You look good with a mouthful of cock." He groans, his hand moving to the back of my head.

Someone, I don't know which one, pulls my dress off of my shoulders, exposing my perfect tits thanks to Dr. Hudson.

Sebastian always complained my breasts were too small, and on our first anniversary he gifted me with breast augmentation surgery. It was the only thing he made me do that I didn't mind.

Now King is enjoying the gift too.

His hand kneads my left breast and rolls my nipple between his thumb and index finger.

I pull my head back and allow my tongue to circle his swollen tip, licking the bead of precum that has formed. I flick my tongue over his metal piercing and bite down on it, tugging it between my teeth.

He growls his response; I know he likes a little pain with his pleasure.

King slams his cock into my mouth and down my throat at the same time Rowen and Eli's fingers slam knuckle deep into my aching pussy.

King keeps his dick down my throat, cutting off my air supply. Tears prickle my eyes as I begin gagging.

Can you imagine dying like this? Death by cock.

Man, what a way to go.

My air is restricted, my throat full of cock, and my pussy being eaten, and finger fucked with such a perfected rhythm. I am in heaven.

I've never felt more pleasure than I am experiencing right at this moment.

"You look perfect with my cock in your mouth and Eli eating your sweet cunt." King groans, bucking his hips against my face while he fucks my mouth. I'm swallowing King's dick while Eli is between mine and Rowen's legs eating me like I am his last meal, and they both have fingers knuckle deep inside of me.

My next orgasm is quick, and only when my eyes start rolling back in pleasure and my body begins shaking does King pull back and allow me to suck in gulps of oxygen.

By the red stains on his perfect cock, I know my lipstick is likely smeared all over my face.

Good thing I wore waterproof mascara or else I'd have black streaks down my face with my tears.

King slips his stone cock back inside of my mouth just in time for his salty cum to shoot down my throat, which I swallow happily.

Eli sits down beside Rowen on the couch and frees his monster of a cock. He grabs me from Rowen's lap by the hips and pulls me to his lap so I am straddling him.

With his bruising grip on my hips, he pulls me down, impaling me on his massive cock. A groan of relief leaves both of our lips at the same time.

My arms wrap around his neck, my fingers tangling in his hair, as he begins to guide me up and down, bouncing me on his cock exactly how we both need.

It's rough and quick and not about me at all.

He's hate fucking me, and I'm too selfish to care.

Rowen kneels beside us, his dick already out and needing to be sucked. "Wrap those pretty lips around me, angel. Let me feel how good you can suck me." He wipes the tears from my face. "If you're a good girl, I'll let you swallow my cum."

I comply, taking him deep down my throat without a single complaint. It's only a matter of minutes until the three of us are coming together.

Rowen fills my mouth, Eli fills my pussy, and I soak his cock in return.

"I'm going to go to the restroom and clean up." I announce, pulling my dress into place to cover myself. I wipe underneath my eyes, while King wipes around my mouth to fix my smeared red lipstick.

He grabs handfuls of my ass, pulls my body against his, and steals the air from my lungs with his kiss. My lips part, and he takes that as an advantage to slip his tongue inside of my mouth and swirl it around. No doubt he can taste the saltiness that lingers from both his and Rowen's cum, but he doesn't seem to care. He sucks my tongue anyways.

King lets me go, and I gasp for air. "I want to play when we get home," I say with a devious smirk, hoping he'll restrain me again while he fucks me.

"Anything for you," he promises.

Picking up my clutch from the table along with another shot of tequila, I raise the glass to my mouth and swallow another shot.

"I'll go with you." King takes my hand and intertwines our fingers together, leading us out of the VIP section and down the stairs through the crowd.

We make it to the restroom, I reach for the door, looking over my shoulder at King.

"Wait out here. I'll be a couple minutes to clean up." He leans his head down and placed a kiss so intense to my lips. As much as I love kissing him, it does nothing to ease the feeling in the pit of my stomach that makes me feel like the other shoe is about to drop. King has always been affectionate, but never this much.

His kiss almost feels like goodbye.

What does he know that I don't?

"Don't be long. I need more of your delicious mouth." Yet again, he kisses me breathless, his tongue pushing through my parted lips and licking the inside of my mouth, kissing me until I'm lightheaded from the sensation.

Panting, I walk into the bathroom, thankful that it's empty.

Standing in front of the vanity, I open my clutch to take out my tube of lipstick and powder compact. I open the compact and dip the cotton puff into the powder, dabbing it over my face, covering the blotchy spots from my now dried tears.

Once I'm finished, I place it back into my clutch and grab some napkins from the dispenser, wetting them before wiping them over the inside of my thighs and carefully along my sensitive core.

The beeping of my phone startles me.

I haven't had it in a couple of weeks, so I'm alarmed when it begins beeping.

Quickly throwing the napkins away, I wash and dry my hands before I reach for my phone and unlock it.

That's odd. A new text message with an image attached.

I click open the message, my brows pulling together in a frown as I look at the image on my screen.

It's a picture of King who's standing outside of the bathroom where I left him. It's a picture taken from a distance, and he isn't looking toward the camera. He clearly has no idea that someone was taking a photo of him. I close out of the image and read the text.

Unknown: *You have ten minutes to ditch your bodyguards and get outside alone.*

My blood runs cold reading the message.

Who the fuck is texting me?

I have to warn the guys that whoever it is that's after me is here. I open my contact list and scroll to Rowen's number that he programmed into my phone in the limo on the way here. And as if the mystery fucker knew my intentions, my phone chimes with another alert and image.

This time, seeing the picture, my hand flies up to cover my mouth and instantly bile rises in the back of my throat, I swallow it down.

The picture is of Cassie.

She's bound and gagged, tied to a chair and bleeding from the cuts and bruises over her fair skin.

Unknown: *Warn them and she dies. Time is ticking little one.*

What the fuck? What the actual fuck?!

I'll admit, after the first text I thought it was one of my guys playing a twisted joke or testing me to see what'd I'd do now that I had my phone and was taken out in public. But now seeing the second text that came through and seeing Cassie's scared face, I know it wasn't them.

It's the bastard who is after me.

Fuck. Now he is getting exactly what he wants.

The only way out is through the window. Clearly, I have no fucking choice.

My phone beeps in my hand with another message.

Unknown: *Three minutes. Leave your phone in the trash can.*

Impatient fuck.

I do as the text says and toss my phone in the trash, gripping the hem of my dress and raising it further up my thighs to allow for more mobility, instantly wishing I had panties.

I remove my shoes and climb onto the vanity countertop, reaching for the window that's near it.

To my luck, the window is easy to open, yeah, I have to stand on my top toes to reach it but it slides open easily. I don't know how far the drop is going to be or what part of the street the window will take me, but I have no choice.

Maybe that's a lie. We always have a choice.

I am choosing not to let another person die because of me.

I'm figuring out how to climb out the window when an ear ringing beep starts, and a white light begins flashing.

Fuck!

I cover my ears looking around the bathroom.

The fire alarm.

The alarm is going off.

Uncovering my ears, I am able to hear beating on the door.

"Tate! Tate! Unlock the fucking door!" I can hear King's booming voice through the door and over the deafening alarm.

Wait, I didn't lock the door.

He can't get in.

An eerie shiver shot down my spine as realization hit that this was all planned. Everything was fucking planned! Their plan all along was to give me away to the person who wanted me. That was their plan when they took me from Sinners, and that is still their plan now. Nothing has changed.

God! How stupid can I fucking me?!

I have two options.

Either open the door and confront King with what I know or climb out the window in hopes to rescue Cassie, even though there's a good chance I myself can die.

I take too long to decide, the choice is made for me by the smoke that's beginning to creep in from underneath the door and fill the room.

Fuck it.

Standing on my tiptoes, I stretch up to the window and grab onto the sill, using all of my strength to climb up the wall with my bare feet and pull myself out of the small space.

Halfway through I lose my balance and go falling, screaming as I fall.

I land on my back in a dumpster full of trash bags.

The smell blows around me and instantly I begin gagging. It broke my fall, but the smell itself is bad enough to kill me.

Groaning, I spread my hands out around me in attempt to grab onto anything I can to be able to pull myself out. My fingers touch something warm and wet, my entire body freezes.

What the fuck is that?

Please don't let it be wet garbage. Which is highly likely considering I'm still in the fucking dumpster.

Cautiously turning my head to the side, my eyes widen as I am met with lifeless brown eyes.

Bringing my hand to my face, I see what it is that I touched.

Blood. His blood.

Looking back at the body, I recognize him instantly.

He is… he was one of the bodyguards Eli left behind to stay with me the other day while he went to work. He was supposed to take me with but left before I even woke, and I didn't question him about it.

I hadn't talked to the guard, but his face tells me he's young and regardless, I instantly feel bad because I know it's my fault. Everything is my fault.

This is yet another dead body because of me.

I wipe my bloodied hand on my pretty white dress and close his eyes, seeing that his throat is slit, and he looks gutted.

Oh god. Bile rises in my throat and this time I can't swallow it down.

I climb onto my knees and vomit everything that's in my stomach, including the tequila which burns on the way back up.

With slow and careful movements, I pull myself out of the dumpster and manage to stand on my bare feet.

My eyes wander around me to take in my location, it's dark, and in the distance, I can hear the sirens of fire trucks.

It's night, but the streetlights are bright enough to cast a glow in the alley I'm standing in so I can see.

The mystery fucker said to be outside. I'm outside. Now what?

"Tate! Stop!" I hear King's roar and look up to see him in the window. Fuck!

I can't risk anything happening to anyone else, so I do what I do best, and I run.

He's yelling my name behind me and when I look back, I see he's made it out the window. He's seen the body in the dumpster and that slowed him down enough for me to run further away. He only allowed himself to look at the body for a second though because he's right behind me and my short legs and bare feet are no match for his long legs.

He's yelling for me to stop, and I don't know why considering they're the ones that decided to turn me over.

A black rusted painter's van with no windows pulls up at the end of the alley. I can hear King's boots hitting the ground as he gets closer to me. I'm just about to reach the open side door of the van when I feel a burning sensation rip through my left side, stopping me in my tracks as I let out a roar of my own.

The bastard shot me.

King fucking shot me!

I feel the warm liquid on my left side, I don't need to look down to know that it's blood that's pouring out of me.

I turn to face him, ready to scold him for shooting me when his fist connects with my face, rattling my brain and making me lose my balance.

I stumble backwards, King is shooting at the van and yelling, I can see his lips move but with the ringing in my ears I can't hear what he's saying.

The van behind me must be shooting at him because I see him keep moving to dodge something.

It happens in a flash.

A bullet hits him in the chest, and he falls backwards, "No! King!" I'm screaming, my legs give out and I'm trying to crawl toward him, but I can't reach him. I don't know why, but I want to go to him.

My vision is blurry, my head swimming and light.

I'm screaming and crying for King and trying to get to him, then suddenly I become weightless.

I'm being picked up and carried bridal style just as white spots are clouding my vision, then the darkness takes over.

This feels familiar.

THIRTY

Rowen

I fucking trusted her.

I defended Tate when Eli told me she was up to no good. Even when I had a gut feeling and knew in the back of my mind that something was off about her, I still defended her, looking for the best in her.

I allowed my guilt from our childhood to consume me and used that as my reason for believing everything she had told us.

Tonight was about luring out this bastard. We thought we had all the basics covered.

We had bodyguards all over the club who were checking every single person who entered tonight. Every single guest was fully fucking vetted. Guards were both inside and out, so how the fuck did she get away?

When we found King in the alley cursing at himself for getting shot at, he told us what happened.

Tate climbed out the window and ran toward the van willingly.

My worst fears were confirmed. She was in on it.

But what I can't figure out is why.

Was she just another Stephanie who was sent to make us weak and learn our secrets for one of our enemies to use against us?

We were missing the bigger picture. We didn't have all the pieces of the puzzle, and I was racking my brain trying to figure this shit out.

Luckily, King had been wearing a bulletproof vest. He'll be bruised, but he's fine.

It knocked the wind out of him, and he's been blaming himself for letting Tate get away ever since we got home.

It's not his fault that she escaped, she had help.

If only we wouldn't have let our guards down.

This is on all of us.

She played us.

The little bitch fucking played us, and when I get my hands on her, I'm going to slit her fucking throat and watch as the life drains from her blue eyes.

I now know that I never meant anything to her.

"There's pieces of her background that are missing. There are too many things that are not adding up. She says that Ace Jackson helped her after she left here, yet there's no record of any of that," Eli says, scrubbing his hands over his face. "I can't find the missing pieces."

We're sitting in the living room of our penthouse, going over all of the files for everyone we know about in Tate's life. "There's two years missing. She doesn't reappear again until she's fifteen, and the family she lived with weren't even registered foster parents."

"The ones she killed by setting the fire?" King asks from where he lays on the couch, icing his bruised chest.

"They did something to her in that house. She had the same look in her eyes that she did when we were children and in that house together," I speak. The night she broke down crying in the living room and I held her while she cried against my chest, she let me see how broken she really was.

I saw her broken pieces. I recognized it because the broken parts of her mirrored my own. Her pain called out to mine, and I believed she was something she's not.

The girl I knew is gone.

"She could already be dead for all we know." Eli sighs.

"Yeah, nice job with shooting her, asshole," I mumble, looking at King.

"It wasn't a death shot. At least I don't think." I don't like how nonchalant he is when he says that.

I understand that all our emotions are fucked up right now, but that doesn't mean we can ever deny that we all feel something for her.

I did, or do, and they do too; I know it.

We've shared women before, but we never nicknamed or branded them. Not even Stephanie received that treatment.

Tate did.

Still, this doesn't stop me from wanting to find her and make her tell me everything before I paint the walls with her blood.

We're sitting in silence when King's phone beeps with a text. Grumbling, he sits up from the couch and grabs it from the coffee table. His eyes scan the screen and then he's laughing maniacally, holding the phone out to Eli.

Eli takes the phone; I watch as his features harden before he passes it to me so I can read the text message.

Fuck.

Unknown: *How well she played the role I needed her to play. Next time think with your head and not your dick, it makes you weak. I'll be seeing you.*

I hand the phone back to King, my attention turning toward Eli. "Check her phone. She must've contacted this person, maybe we can get a name or a number."

He nods, grabbing his laptop from the table and sitting beside King on the couch, setting the laptop on his thighs, his fingers flying over the keyboard. "I'm going to fucking kill her," he says through gritted teeth. "We're going to find her, and I'm going to fucking kill her." He turns his screen around and sure enough, there are text messages in her inbox from the same unknown sender.

Unknown: *Where are you? I'm waiting where we discussed.*
Tate: *They're with me. How can I get out?*
Unknown: *Bathroom window. Throw your phone away.*
Tate: *I need a distraction.*
Unknown: *Handled. Five minutes.*

It was a damn good thing that Eli installed the security on her phone. The tracker showed her location at the club, proving that she left her phone behind before she ran off into the fucking sunset with this fuck.

"Fuck!" My anger is boiling over. "Why?! Why the fuck would she do this?" I roar, standing from the chair to pace the living room. "That's what makes no fucking sense! She didn't gain anything by being part of this... whatever the fuck this is!" I spread my arms out, my blood boiling in anger.

"Someone wanted her to get close to us. Learn our secrets," King says with a shrug.

"But she didn't learn anything! She never even asked questions about our business. She's lived here nine months, and we've been the ones watching her, not the other way around. Was anything about her suspicious during the time we were watching her?" I yell, pacing the room.

Eli and King look at each other with hesitant sighs.

"Exactly," I say, hanging my head down in defeat.

I throw myself into the chair, placing my elbows on my knees and burying my head into my hands.

"She's innocent," King says, but I don't bother looking up at him.

If she's innocent, then that means this fucker has her and now she's weak and may die because King shot her.

My blood begins boiling again.

In a flash I am standing toe to toe with him, and we are both exchanging punches with each other.

"You fucking shot her!" I yell, catching him with a right hook.

"That's enough!" Eli shoves me away, standing between us. "Fighting each other isn't going to solve shit. We don't know anything for a fact."

"Then when we find her, we need to listen to her side of the fucking story. She's been honest from the fucking beginning." We jumped to conclusions, and now she's gone. If anything happens to her, it'll be on us. We're the ones that failed to protect her and didn't bother listening to her side of the story.

"We don't know anything for fact, Ro. You're blinded by your connection to her," Eli huffs. I don't answer him. He's wrong. He's so fucking wrong.

We fucked up, and he can't admit it.

This is on all three of us.

Is she innocent? That's the lingering question.

There are too many unanswered questions that I intend to get the answers to.

THIRTY-ONE

Tate

My head is throbbing.

I can feel my blood and pulse thumping inside my skull.

I don't know how long I've been unconscious. When I open my eyes, it's foggy and I can feel the sun shining down on my face.

My mouth is dry, my muscles ache and my entire body feels stiff.

Blinking, I bring my hands up and push the heels of my palms into my eyes and scrub away the fog.

With a groan, I slowly sit up and stretch my aching arms above my head.

With rapid blinks, I clear my vision enough to be able to look around my surroundings, hoping to find something to tell me where I am.

I'm in a small, cemented room, with one single window that has steel bars over it.

There goes that idea for an escape.

With my hands against the cold cement wall, I use it to help me stand, my legs shaky and unsteady. I feel the ache in my side when I stand, and a soft cry leaves my lips.

I take a slow step toward the door, only to fall to my hands and knees suddenly.

What the fuck? Why can't I move?

Looking down at my legs, I see the ankle cuff that is around my left ankle, connecting me to a chain to the wall. I sit up and grab the chain, pulling on it in hopes it'll break.

I'm chained to the fucking wall. Who the fuck does that shit? What the actual fuck?

I'm still wearing my dress.

The white now nearly completely brown with all of the stains on it.

Dirt, blood, garbage, vomit, and who knows whatever else.

I brush my hair out of my face, cringing at the crunch of my matted hair. It's like a bird's nest on top of my head. Gross.

I use the wall for support again to help me stand and lean against the wall. I carefully pull my dress up until it's underneath my breasts and my left side is exposed so I see exactly what the situation is.

There's a bandage wrapped around my stomach. With slow fingers, I unwrap it to see my wound. I've been shot, and I can see my pink skin tissue inside the hole in my body. Bile rises in my throat, I swallow it down and close my eyes, carefully putting the gauze back into place and then pull my dress down.

Someone cleaned and dressed my wound. It doesn't appear to be bleeding anymore, and from the looks of it, it's a straight through shot. At least the bullet isn't inside of me. I may not be bleeding and may have a bandage, but I know I'll need to get to a doctor. I'll need a professional to look at it to prevent infection.

I wonder what else happened to me while I was unconscious. I'm not wearing any panties, and I can't tell if the ache between my legs is still from Eli, or from someone else.

I need to get the fuck out of here, that's for damn certain.

How the fuck am I going to get out of here? Where even is here?

King was the one that shot me, meaning this was part of their plan, so I know that they're not coming to rescue me.

I am alone, and no one's coming for me.

How the fuck was I dumb enough to get myself into his situation?

I must've fallen asleep, because when I open my eyes again, I'm met with darkness. The only light in the room is coming from the pale moonlight that's shining into my cell. It takes a while of blinking and rubbing for my eyes to adjust to the darkness.

"Good, you're awake." The rough voice from within the darkness startles me.

A chill shoots down my spine, and slowly I lift my head to look straight ahead at the figure that's in the room, standing against the wall across me, hiding in the shadows of the darkness.

Bastard.

"Where's Cassie?" I have to unstick my tongue from the roof of my mouth just to speak. My mouth is so dry and tastes like hot fucking garbage.

My mouth feels the same as my skin.

Dirty.

My voice is hoarse, I barely even recognize it.

The fucker steps into the path of the moonlight, revealing his face to me. I study his features, searching for anything that would jog my memory, but nothing happens.

I don't know him.

He's a stranger that I'd never seen before in my life. So why does he want me?

"You were told five minutes. You took longer than that. Nice job, Lee. Your friend is dead because of you." Tears prickle the back of my eyes, but I will them not to fall. I am not going to give this bastard the satisfaction of watching me cry.

He doesn't deserve my tears or to see me weak.

Cassie.

Fuck!

She's dead because of me. He killed her anyways, and he has me captive with zero chance of anyone coming for me.

"What do you want from me?" With a wide smile, the fucker walks across the room toward me and kneels in front of me, reaching his hand out toward my face. I slap it away, leaning as close to the wall as I could, hoping the wall would swallow me whole.

"Me? Nothing." He brushes the loose strands of hair from my face and stands, shoving his hands in his pockets, staring down at me. "But he will." Without another word, he turns and walks toward the door, opening it and walking through it.

The metal door slams shut, and only once he's gone and I hear the click of the lock do I let out a shaky breath that I've been holding.

He? Who's he? And what does he want with me? I had so many questions that were going unanswered.

Cassie is dead.

King is likely dead after getting shot in the chest and going down the way he did.

Now what? Am I next? I am frustrated. So, fucking frustrated. With a deep breath, I scream.

I scream until my voice turns hoarse and sleep takes over.

"Tate! Tate!" Hands gripped my shoulders firmly and shook me awake. I was gasping and covered in sweat. Cassie was staring down at me with

wide eyes that were full of concern and warmth. "Tate, you have to talk to me. Please, tell me what's going on." She's perched on the side of my bed, brushing my damp hair out of my face.

We'd been living together for three months now, and every single night she's woken me up from a nightmare. She asked me every night about my past, and I could never bring myself to tell her.

Until now.

With tears in my eyes, I sat up in my bed slowly, rested my back against the headboard, and sucked in deep breaths to calm my erratic breathing.

"Tate, please. Every single night you scream, and I wake you up, please talk to me." Sighing, I nodded, brushing my hair behind my ears.

"Okay," I agreed. It's not fair to her that I wake her up with my screaming every night. So, I opened myself up to her and told her everything. Well, not everything, but enough so that she understood why I was the way I was.

I told her about Sebastian and his abuse, and how I had ran away from him and about my fear that he would find me one of these days. I explained that he was the reason I always looked over my shoulder, and that he's the reason why I'd been afraid to be out in public for too long. I shared everything that I could.

"Oh my God, Tate!" she gasped after I finished speaking, and pulled me into a tight hug. "This explains so much! But girl, you're giving him power over you. By looking over your shoulder and living in fear, you're still letting him control you. You're not free, and you won't be until you take back control." I stared at her with curious eyes.

"I take a self-defense class twice a week, and you're going with me next time. And then we're going to have lunch and sit outdoors. I'm going to help you take control of your life." She wiped away the tears that I didn't realize were streaming down my cheeks. "I've got you, Tate, from this point forward, it's you and me against the world. You're in control."

I wake with tears in my eyes. My heart is aching at the fact Cassie is gone.

The sweet innocent girl who did nothing wrong is dead because of me.

She helped me in so many ways. When I was afraid of my own shadow, she taught me to not be afraid and to start living.

Because of Cassie, I was able to stop living in fear and for the first time I was able to start taking control of my life and truly be free. Free from Sebastian and free of the fear that he's lurking in the shadows.

Not only did she help me with taking control over my life and learn self-defense, but she also helped me to find a therapist that specializes in working with victims of abuse.

I'd never thought about going to therapy before that, but it really helped me.

Thanks to Cassie, I am no longer afraid of the monsters that lurk in the dark.

My days and nights are blending.

I'm going in and out of consciousness, never knowing what day or time it was.

The chain around my ankle prevents me from reaching the window or the door, when I'm awake and try to move.

At this point I'm not confident in my ability to walk. I stand to at least stretch my legs, but I feel them getting weaker each time I stand.

I need to walk and properly stretch them, which I can't do being chained up like a fucking animal.

There's a bucket near me that I use to relieve myself.

The fucker comes in—I assume once a day—to empty it, and each time he does, I try and make conversation.

I want to know the *he* that he was referring to, and I want to know what the fucking plan is here.

Surely, he can't keep me chained up forever... right?

As if he could sense me thinking about him, he chooses that moment to enter my cell. He doesn't bother closing the door anymore because he knows I can't get out anyways, but he still keeps it locked when he leaves; I know this because I hear the click of the lock after he leaves.

He steps inside of my fucking prison cell and sets a bottle of water down in front of me. The sun is shining through the window, and I know it's morning.

He gives me a bottle of water each time the sun is up, and this is the fourth time he's done it.

Which I guess means I've been here for four days.

Four days. It feels so much longer than that.

I take the water and bring it to my dry mouth and take slow sips. It has to last me the entire day, so I don't want to waste it. No matter how incredible the wetness feels on my tongue, I must make it last.

Along with the water, he gives me a piece of stale bread and medical supplies to keep my gunshot wound clean. I still can't fucking believe that King actually shot me.

He truly fooled me. All of them did.

I have alcohol wipes, ointment, gauze, and medical tape. It's keeping my wound from getting infected, at least, I hope. It's stopped bleeding, but I need proper care.

I'll wait until he leaves to remove my dress and rebandage it. I don't need him to see me naked.

He disappears into the hallway long enough to empty my piss bucket, and when he brings it back into my cell, I can't stop myself from trying to strike conversation again in hopes of getting answers.

"How long?" I croak, my voice raspy and my throat dry. "How long will I be here?" He looks at me, and I don't like the way his blue eyes rake over my body.

"Until he decides that you're ready to behave." He turns and walks toward the door. "Oh, and until he kills those guys you were spreading your legs for like a whore." He spits on the ground.

I've asked this same question every time I see him, and this is the first time he's answered me. I'm taking that as a sign to continue my questioning. "Why would he kill them? They're the ones that allowed me to end up here."

"No, Lee. You let yourself end up here by being a whore. Keep your legs closed, that's all you had to do." His words are laced with pure venom. "He wanted you pure and only for him. And now you're dirty, so that's how you'll be treated until you learn your lesson. You'll stay here until he's ready for you to come upstairs and join us." He stalks toward me, squatting down in front of me, taking a fistful of my hair in his hands. "We'll start by changing your hair. Blonde is much better on you." He drops my hair as if it burned him and glares at me with disgust before standing to his feet. "Don't worry, those thugs you were fucking will be out of the picture soon enough, and then he'll be ready to see you again." With him so close to me for the first time, I am able to study his features. I search for any hint of recognition. He seemed to know me, but I don't know him.

"Why didn't either of you take me yourself? Why hire *them* to do your job?" I couldn't even say their names. I knew if I did, my emotions would show.

"They involved themselves, but details don't matter. They made a deal, they kept you for as long as we asked and then they brought you to the club exactly as they were told to do. They turned you over without a fight. It all went as planned." I have more questions, and I open my mouth to speak, but no words come out. My head is swimming in confusion.

He's lying.

My guys didn't sell me out. This is a setup. At least I hope it is. I need to believe that it is.

They wouldn't do that to me. Rowen wouldn't do that to me. I don't know who to believe anymore.

I see the ghosts of the past haunting him every time I look into his eyes.

There's no way he'd turn his back on me, not when he's carried the blame with him for years over what happened to us as children.

"You're lying," I hiss.

With a sigh, he pulls the pack of cigarettes from his jeans pocket and sticks one between his lips, lighting it with a match. "Think what you want, they're the reason you're here." He unbuckles his belt and zipper. I watch with wide eyes as he frees his disgusting dick from his boxers, pointing the ugly worm straight at me.

"Stay the fuck away from me!" I crawl closer to the wall to get away from him.

"Don't flatter yourself, I'd never touch a dirty little whore like you." I'm covering my face with my hands and shaking uncontrollably when I feel the warm liquid touch my skin.

He's pissing on me! This motherfucker is pissing on me!

I lower my head and cry, covering my face to avoid getting his pee in my eyes and mouth. "You're going to fucking regret this! I'll kill you!" I yell, causing him to laugh.

I don't notice him stepping closer to me because I'm still covering my face. I don't see him until he shoves the cherry of his cigarette against my right knee that's pulled to my chest. I cry out at the pain, bile rising in the back of my throat at the burn. I can smell my burning flesh.

And since there's nothing in my stomach, I only dry heave. My body is shaking, I can't control it.

He stands and smiles down at me darkly.

The bastard smiles at me. "He'll see you soon, little bird."

Little bird.

He called me little bird.

Only one person in my life has ever called me that before.

My jaw drops, my heart is beating so rapidly in my chest that I swear it will rip right through my flesh.

I know who my captor is.

I escaped him once, and there's no way in hell I'd survive doing it again.

THIRTY-TWO

Eli

We fucked up.

I fucked up.

I labeled Tate as a traitor and said she was just like Stephanie, and that's not true.

She wasn't sent to us to become a distraction or to become a weakness, or to even learn our secrets and turn on us.

We took her that night at the club and planned to use her for personal gain.

We went to her. We took her. We fucked up her life, not that it was going so great anyways.

The texts on her phone were faked. The bastard who took her wanted us to believe that she was guilty, he wanted us to doubt her.

Why? So we wouldn't look for her?

I fucked up.

I should've listened when Rowen told me she wasn't trying to do anything to fuck us behind our backs. But I was too stubborn to listen. I wrote her off as a traitor without proof.

I'm such a fucking idiot.

If anything happens to her, it's all on me.

It's been four days since she's been gone, and Rowen can't stand being in the same room as me. He blames me, but not as much as I blame myself. I sure as fuck won't tell him that though. I made a bad decision. But we can't sit around and dwell on it. She's gone, it happened, so now we need to figure out a way to get her back.

I need to get her back.

She probably hates us.

I can only imagine what she's been thinking after King shot her. Knowing her, she's probably thinking the worst. And she has every right to, because I thought the worst about her too.

I should've gone to her and allowed her to explain herself and answer the questions we all had.

We should've fucking talked it out instead of me jumping to conclusions.

Why did she run? That's the lingering question.

If she's truly innocent, why the fuck did she slip out the window and run toward that bastard like King says? That's one part that doesn't make any sense. Why run from us? Security and I both searched her phone. There were no calls, and the only text exchange was from the unknown number, which we know now was fake. The bastard planted the texts on her phone, the timestamp doesn't add up. Which means that someone was in the bathroom afterward who took her phone and sent the texts to make her appear guilty, knowing we'd find the texts and phone.

And he was right.

How did she know to go out the window and go toward the van?

Right after reading the texts King went back to Confess and just like the text said, her phone was discarded in the trash bin. We gave the phone to Detective Reynolds to check for fingerprints, and we've been waiting on results. I doubt he'll find anything; this fucker is good at covering his tracks.

When I find him, and I will find him, I'm going to rip him limb from fucking limb. King won't be the only one who gets to have bloody fun.

"I got something!" Maverick practically jumps up from the table, he's the head of her security team and he was assigned with the task of checking the video surveillance footage from the time of Tate's abduction in search for any signs of the van that took her. We're all sitting in the living room of our penthouse going through every fucking piece of information we can come up with in search for answers.

"What do you have?" I set a file down, giving him my full attention. He brings his laptop over and hands it to me, showing me the black and white video footage.

"There's the van that drove away with Tate. They drove right through a red light that captured their license plate." Finally! Finally, we have a fucking break. I stand from the couch where I've been the last four days and pace around the room while King and Rowen discuss the video footage.

I block them out completely, something isn't right.

That was easy. That was too fucking easy. The fucker intentionally ran that red light, knowing the camera would snap a picture of the license plate, knowing that we would find it.

This is a set up.

He's setting us up and luring us to him knowing we'll come for her. Son of a bitch!

I look up and for the first time Ro looks at me, and I know that he and King are thinking the same thing.

"Get us an address," I say looking at Maverick who's busy typing away on his computer. "This fucker wants us to come to him and fall prey to his trap, so let's do it."

It took a couple of hours and a few phone calls for Maverick to get an address. While we were waiting for him, Detective Reynolds had called me to say that Tate's cell phone was clean.

No fingerprints, which I expected.

Rowen made the calls to gather us a team of backup to go with us to the address that the fucker was luring us to.

We were running into his trap and no idea what the fuck to expect.

It takes less than one hour for our living room to be filled with men who are willing to risk their lives for us.

We have a great team, and I'll be sure to triple the pay for anyone who survives the mission.

We're all fully geared up wearing black from head to toe, bulletproof vests, knives strapped to our bodies, and guns locked and loaded in their holsters and in the back of our waistband.

King being King, of course has an AK-47 strapped to him.

I look over at him with a raise of an eyebrow and he just shrugs and gives me a smirk.

"Mav, go over the information again," I say, adjusting my holster at my sides.

"The van is registered to a Tyson Holbrook. Here is his DMV photo, and all the information I was able to find on him. He's single, lives alone at the address on his driver's license, and is a carpenter, probably hence the van. He's your normal average Joe. Pays his taxes, no large transactions or withdrawals, but he is in debt up to his ears." He explains the information he found for the fourth time, and everyone in the room stops to listen. I've heard it already. I've read over everything.

I've memorized everything, and this isn't the guy we're looking for.

He's a decoy.

Maverick and Rowen show the rest of the guys the images of the house they located online.

I've memorized that too.

I even took it a step further and found the original blueprints and listing for the house and looked at the inside, learning about every single twist and turn. We couldn't afford any surprises, and I wanted to eliminate this fucker's element of surprise. I knew he wasn't working alone, no way in hell he was. Someone else was making him do the dirty work, I just didn't know how many others were involved.

We were going in nearly blind. Not sure what the fuck to expect but knowing what our goal was.

Kill the bastard and get our girl.

We bring her home safe, and that's all that matters.

It takes us an hour to get to the address of Tyson Holbrook.

The house, as we already learned, is secluded. It's outside of town and far enough away from any neighbors that no one will hear us. Not that we care, considering once people learn the Triad's involved, they won't bother fucking with us or calling the police. Everyone knows that we rule this city, and this house is within our fucking limits.

Like that would stop us anyways.

The red brick family style house sits on a hill, the porch lights on and that black van in the driveway.

Someone is home, and whoever it is, they're expecting us.

We've parked our car down the street. The three of us, plus Nico and Vlad drove together. The others are waiting ten minutes before they arrive. We want the unknown fuck to believe that we're alone for as long as possible. We want to have the element of surprise when he finds out that we have backup.

It's nearing midnight, it's so dark that I can barely see my hand in front of my face. There are no streetlights, and it's pretty eerie out here.

As we walk up the small hill leading toward the house, the porch light is enough to illuminate our way toward the house. Nico, Vlad, and Rowen went around to the back of the house while King and I went right up to the front door.

As if the fucker were watching us and knew we were there, the door swings open and, in the doorway, stood none other than Tyson Holbrooke himself.

I recognize his ugly face instantly from his DMV photo.

I resist the urge to punch him right in his fucking face and demand answers from him. There is something in his brown eyes that I didn't expect to see.

Fear.

"He's been expecting you, come in." I look at King and he has a knowing look on his face. He saw exactly what I did on the bastard's face. Pure fear. But from what? It's more than just fear from us being at his front door.

I walk in first and King follows behind me, we're both on high alert, our eyes scanning our surroundings and watching each other's backs.

Tyson gives us his back as he leads us further into the house, and we follow.

The house looks like your typical bachelor pad. It's bare, and only semi clean. It smells musty and I wonder when the last time the house has had a deep clean.

It could sure as fuck use it.

He leads us down a long hallway until we reach a door at the end.

He opens it, and that's when I put my foot down.

"It's time to talk. Where the fuck is she?" I ask through gritted teeth.

"Please, he needs you downstairs." There's no way we're going into his guy's basement without any fucking explanation.

"You need to provide us answers first."

"Fuck this," King growls, grabs his gun from his waistband and shoves it right in the middle of Tyson's forehead. "Where the fuck is she? We know you're involved. Where is she!"

"Please, he'll kill my sister if you don't comply." Fuck. He's innocent in this. Well, not entirely innocent, but he wasn't doing this of his own free will. He was being threatened.

"I don't give a fuck; it should be me you're worried about. I'll kill you right fucking now if you don't tell me where she is." King wasn't playing around, and I knew he would kill him before we got any answers which wasn't a smart idea.

"She's downstairs, go down and do as he says. Please, my sister is pregnant." King lowers his gun and places it back in the waistband at his back.

He yanks the door open further and stomps down the stairs.

"Go." I grabbed my own gun and held it in my right hand, following Tyson down into the darkness of the basement.

We reach the bottom and are met with another door. He opens it and we all three step inside, the steel door automatically slammed shut and we could hear the click of a lock.

What the fuck? Where the fuck are we?

The walls are cement and I swear it just dropped ten degrees. Even with a hoodie on I could feel the chill.

It's like we're in a cemented fucking box with a cold AC blowing.

The hallway is long, and a few plain doors can be seen.

"We're here, now where the fuck is she?" I shove the barrel of my gun

351

against the back of Tyson's skull, just as I feel the cold barrel of a gun being placed against the back of my neck, watching as King draws his own gun and aims it at the fuck behind me who dared to pull a gun on me.

"Drop the guns, both of you, or your precious Tate will die." I lower my gun knowing King has my back and that we still have three people upstairs and a team on their way ready to intervene if we don't reach out to them within a certain amount of time.

I can practically see the calculated wheels turning in King's head and the steam coming from his ears. He doesn't want to risk her life, and he's calculating the risks just like I have already done. He lowers his gun, and I step toward the side with my back to the wall so I can see the fucker behind me and keep an eye on Tyson.

"Thank you for your service," the blonde fucker smiles and puts a bullet right between Tyson's eyes.

Harsh.

"Where the fuck is she?"

"You're too late. She's already dead." The fucker smiles at me.

A bullet flies past my head and the smug smile is wiped off his face only when he falls to the ground, a bullet in the middle of his forehead. He collapses to the ground with a thud. I look over my shoulder to see King with a smug smile of his own.

King shoves his gun in his hoodie pocket and walks toward the bodies, unbuttoning his pants and freeing his dick.

With an eye roll I look away while he pisses on both of their dead bodies.

"Come on, let's find her." I remove my phone from my pocket seeing that there's zero cell service. We've got to find her and get the fuck out.

With our backs together against each other, King and I stalk down the hallway, checking behind each door only to find empty cold cemented rooms.

Empty. Everything is empty. There's no one down here.

We reach the final door with my heart beating so rapidly I can hear it in my ears.

Time slows, it feels as if we're in slow motion.

One door left; I'm saying a silent prayer that she'll be behind the door.

King and I share a look, as I grip the doorknob and turn.

It's locked.

Stepping back, I raise my right foot and kick the fucking door down. Nothing is stopping me from getting to my girl. I let her down once and I won't make that mistake again.

If she forgives me and allows me another chance.

The door gives and the sight makes me freeze in my tracks.

I'm frozen while King pushes past me and rushes toward the pale body on the floor. She's unmoving and looks unrecognizable because she's so damn dirty.

Like a wrecking ball, I'm hit with memories from the past all at once.

"My sweet Eli, I love you so much." My mother whispered, her arms wrapped around me, and I knew she wanted to hug me tighter, but her weak body wouldn't allow her to.

Sniffling, I raised my head to look up at her. "I love you, Mom, please don't leave me. Please, I'll be good and will do better in school." She was trying not to cry in front of me. She was trying to be strong for me like she always tried to do. She never wanted me to see how sad and frail she actually was.

"You are perfect, my sweet boy. Never forget that I love you, and I will be with you always." She kissed my forehead and held me close to her fragile body.

Mom had been sick for a while now. She had cancer and wasn't responding to the treatments. I blamed Steven, her husband for her sickness and her body's inability to fight the sick disease that's taking her from me. If Steven had sucked the life right out of her, out of both of us.

Steven wasn't my father, but he made me call him father or sir. He's the fucking worst and I hate him. I didn't know why Mom has stayed with him all these years. I was young, but I'd been willing to do anything to provide for me and Mom. She'd always declined my offers to help her, never willing to take us away from Steven and his abuse.

I was fourteen, and Mom was leaving me alone with Steven. She was dying, and it's only a matter of time until she goes. Her home nurse says likely would not make it through the night. But I don't know if I trust her. I'd caught her and Steven having sex, so I'd been wondering if she really is giving Mom the best care possible.

"That's enough, Eli. Get out here and finish your chores." Steven's whiney voice interrupted my moment with Mom.

"I will later, I'm with Mom right now." I knew talking back was a bad idea. He always punished me for it. He used to punish Mom, but ever since she got sick, I'd been the one he took his anger out on.

I should've seen it coming, but I was too focused on my mom that I didn't pay him any attention until I felt his grip on my ear and he pulled me away from the bed and Mom. Hissing in pain, I narrowed my eyes at him. He threw me to the floor and stepped inside the room, closing and locking the door.

"I love you, Mom!" I yelled through the door, knowing in my heart that's the last time I would ever see her. I angrily wiped the tears away from my face, cussing at him under my breath for stealing my last few moments with my mom.

I was outside sweeping the porch when Steven stepped outside and stared me down. "Your Mom's gone. She'll be cremated in two days." I already knew she was gone, but that didn't make it any less painful.

She wanted to be cremated, so I'm glad that he's at least going to honor that final wish of hers. I knew he wouldn't give her a memorial, but at least I'd be able to take her ashes and spread them where she wanted to be spread.

"You didn't even let me say goodbye," I muttered.

"What the fuck did you say, boy?"

I threw the broom against the side of the house, suddenly feeling courage to stand up against him. "I said, you didn't let me fucking say goodbye!" He punched me square in the face, and I fell to the ground, holding my bloody nose in my hands.

"What have I been telling you all these years, boy? Women make you weak. Love makes you weak. And you, you are fucking weak! It's time you man the fuck up." So he did what he often did when he felt I was being too weak. He locked me in the cellar for days until he thought I learned my lesson.

According to Steven, love isn't real, it only makes you weak. And all women are temptresses only sent here to make men weak.

Ro's voice brings me out of the memory I lost myself in. That seems to keep happening ever since Tate entered our life.

Love isn't real, it only makes you weak.

All women are temptresses only sent here to make men weak.

I repeat my father's words in my head over and over again until I feel disconnected from my emotions.

Right now, I'm feeling nothing.

I'll go through the motions of trying to set Tate free for Rowen and King's sake, but she's a lost cause. I know that just from looking at her. She's not dead yet, but she will be soon.

She's a weakness that we can't afford. And we have to let go of our weaknesses, no matter how much it may hurt in the beginning.

THIRTY-THREE

King

"Tate!" I shove past Eli's rigid posture and rush toward my girl, my butterfly.

She's laying on her back, her eyes closed, and her body still and unmoving.

I drop to my knees and take her into my arms, not minding that she's dirty.

She's absolutely fucking filthy, and her once white dress is covered in gunk. There are multiple stains on her dress, and it fuels my anger even more to see the condition she's in. Her body is cold, so fucking cold.

I try to pull her closer to my chest, but there's resistance. That's when I notice the chain that's around her ankle.

She's chained like a fucking animal.

"Eli!" I snap, and that seems to be enough to make him snap out of his stupor and realize the situation. He rushes into the room and kneels in front of me, his hands brushing back the matted locks of black hair that are disgustingly tangled on her head. A soft groan leaves her pale blue lips, her eyelids fluttering open slowly, and ice-cold turquoise eyes stare at me, stealing the air from my lungs.

"Fuck you," she whispers in such a broken voice that it causes my heart to ache. A chuckle rumbles out of my chest.

"Don't worry, butterfly. I will once we get you home." She groans in response. My hand strokes over her perfect face, and my heart literally fucking aches seeing her so frail and fragile.

"You came for me." Her voice is only a mere whisper.

"I'll always come for you. Literally." I place my forehead against hers, keeping my arms securely around her fragile body, trying to warm her up.

She smells like a fucking porta potty, but that doesn't stop me from pressing a soft kiss to her lips. She's disgusting, but that'll never stop me from touching her any chance I can get.

Eli's fumbling with the ankle cuff trying to figure out a way to remove it so we can get her out of here.

It doesn't budge, only upsetting him more. I try to distract her, and even that's not working either.

"How did you find me?"

"We have our ways," Eli grumbles, kicking at the chain attachment on the wall, still struggling to smash it down.

Good. I know he knows this is his fault.

"We have to get out of here before he comes back," she warns, grabs fistfuls of my hoodie and pulls herself closer to me, as if she's trying to bury herself inside of me. Little does she know, she's already inside of me. She's dug herself in my fucking soul already and has been since the day I laid eyes on her. "He wants all of you dead." Her eyes glisten with unshed tears.

My poor strong butterfly is terrified for us. I hate seeing her weak and afraid.

"Who are you talking about, baby? The blond fucker? He's dead."

Her eyes shoot open, and she frantically shakes in my arms, tears streaming down her pale cheeks.

"No, not him. The one pulling his strings." She confirms what we already knew. Tyson wasn't the only one behind this, nor was that unknown blond fucker I shot in the hallway. They were both merely a pawn in the game that was being played.

I make a mental note to have Eli and Maverick look into him later and find out everything about him.

"No one is going to die. We're all going to get out of here alive. Rowen is upstairs, and we'll be okay. But first, we have to get you out of here," I say, doing my best to ease her worries. She's unconvinced but nods anyways.

Pulling my hand away from her hip, my brows furrow, seeing the crimson that stains my hand.

How have I not noticed that she's been bleeding this entire time? Slowly, I grab the hem of her dress and pull it up, revealing the bloody bandage on the front and back of her body. With steady fingers I remove the bandage, gasping at the sight of her torn stitches. Whoever stitched her up did a really shitty job.

Fuck. Fuck. Fuck!

"Eli, we have to go now!" I roar, shifting to move off my knees and sit on my butt, laying her small body out across my lap.

"I'm going to check and see if Tyson has a key or anything to pick this fucking lock," he says in a rush, still examining the cuff around her ankle.

Tate's beautiful blue eyes are staring deep into mine. Her hand comes up to my face and her fingers run along my wiry beard. "I didn't have anything to do with this. They set me up." I don't like the way she's looking at me.

It makes me feel uneasy.

"Shh, stop talking, butterfly." I run my fingers along her perfect heart-shaped face, and trace over her features, as if I am subconsciously trying to memorize everything about her face, but she's impossible to ever forget.

Her blood is staining my hand, and this time, I am not getting hard at the sight of it.

This is the only time I don't want to see her blood. I want to scoop it all up to put it back inside of her paling body and make her stop bleeding.

She's going to be okay.

She has to be.

I need her to be.

If she's not, this is on me. This is all my fault.

I'd finally found someone that awakened my soul. Her demons called out to mine the first time I laid eyes on her, and I answered that call. She'd seen the darkness within me, and within herself, and didn't shy away from it. She embraced it, and even when I brought her into my workshop, she wasn't afraid.

She watched me kill a man without flinching. And it turned her on. She let me chain her up on the bloody chains that I'd hung my victim on and cried for more while I fucked her. The moment I carved into her delicate skin, her flesh spread apart like soft butter, that was the moment she officially became mine.

I marked her in the same way she marked my dark and damaged soul.

"King! We have to go now!" Eli comes running into the room, covering his mouth and nose with the sleeve of his hoodie, his eyes wild and frantic.

That's when I smell it.

Smoke.

My eyes widen, and fearfully, I look down at the girl in my arms. Her eyes are now shut tight, and I realize that I wasn't even aware of when they closed. Her chest is faintly rising and falling, but it's getting slower and slower by the passing second.

The only girl I've ever wanted, craved, is dying right here in my arms. She's dying in my arms because of me.

Smoke fills the room and burns my eyes. But I can't leave. I can't just abandon her here in her final moments of death. Not when there's still a chance that she could be saved once we make it out of here.

"We have to get the fuck out of here!"

"I'm not leaving without her!" I hold her tighter to my body.

"If we don't go now, we're going to die."

"Then you go! I'm staying here with her!" I am never fucking leaving her here.

Eli drops to his knees in front of me and snatches her from my arms, slowly laying her dying body down on the cold cemented floor. He places two fingers to the side of her neck, just underneath her jaw where her pulse would be.

I watch as he slumps his head, stands upright, and lets out a string of curses, punching the cement wall.

This one's on us. Both of us.

"I can't leave her." She's gone. And I want to join her. I want to stay here with her and let the smoke kill me like I killed her.

But Eli's not having it.

"Now isn't the time to fucking be poetic, King! We will avenge her. We will find the fucker that chained her here and fucking kill him. But I need you with me to do that!" He grabs a hold of the neckline on my hoodie and pulls me to my feet, giving me no choice but to leave the room and leave my girl behind.

My butterfly.

Covering my nose with my sleeve, we run down the hallway, stepping over the two bodies in the hallway to get to the door.

The door. The locked door. Fuck.

This really was a trap. The bastard lured us here and now locked us in the basement to die of smoke inhalation. I didn't see the flames, but I could see and smell the smoke that was quickly swallowing us whole.

Eli and I work together in perfect sync, kicking and beating at the metal door using a hammer we'd found in the cell Tate's in. We're doing everything we can to get it open.

"Fuck!" My eyes widen seeing the flames that are beginning to follow a perfect trail toward us. I lean down, dip my fingers in the liquid on the floor, and bring it to my nose, inhaling deeply. Petrol.

Had that unknown fucking puppet master been down here while we were here to pour petrol and start a fire? How had we not noticed this earlier?

Suddenly, the door bursts open, and on the other side are Rowen and Nico.

"Where's Tate?" is his first question. I don't answer. How do I answer that? I just push past him, running up the stairs three at a time.

"She's gone," I hear Eli answer before I reach the top. I run out of the house, finding Vlad who's still outside where we left him keeping cover and staying on the lookout.

"What happened, boss?" Again, I don't say a word. I stomp down the driveway and down the hill to where we have parked. I still have her blood on my hands. I need to get the fuck out of here and find the fucker who did this to her. Vengeance will be mine. Even if I am the partial cause of it.

THIRTY-FOUR

Rowen

Something's wrong.

It's quiet. Too quiet.

King and Eli entered the house over ten minutes ago and there's been no sound or movement from the house since.

Vlad, Nico, and I have kept watch outside, checking for exits in case anyone tried to escape. We weren't sure what to expect, but we were prepared for anything. We had to be. We were lured here for a reason, and I have a strong feeling that Tate is in fact here.

She has to be.

We'll get her back, I know we will.

Something's off though.

Our backup team was supposed to be here by now. They were ordered to wait exactly ten minutes before they came to aid us. It's been over ten minutes, so where the fuck are they? I'm on high alert because I can feel in my gut something isn't right.

I walk around to the side of the house where I know Vlad will be. He is keeping watch from the side, keeping an eye out for when our backup team will arrive, but staying hidden in the shadows.

"Have you heard from Conrad or Nate?" I ask as Conrad and Nate both were tasked with leading the backup crew.

"No, not since the last check-in. They were in place and ready to go."

"Then where the fuck are they?" I growl, shoving my fingers through my hair. "Get one of them on the phone. Find out why the fuck they're not here yet." He nods, and I turn my back to go and find Nico.

Although Nico finds me first, as he comes running straight toward Vlad and I. "Nate's crew is down! Conrad just called; Nate's crew was gunned down. All of them are dead. Ambushed while in motion." My fists clench at my sides. I knew something wasn't right.

This entire fucking plan was too damn easy.

Almost as if someone was not only expecting us, but also knew every single move we were going to make. And perhaps the bastard does know our plan and every move we're making.

We have a rat. We have a fucking rat.

"Tell Conrad to meet us at the safe house. The three of us will handle this." Clearly it's time we do some housekeeping. We have a rat in our organization, and there's only one way to handle a rat. And the rat will be handled as soon as we leave here with our girl.

"We need to get inside the house, now!" I order, and they both nod. The front door is locked, but that doesn't stop Vlad from kicking it down. "Watch your back, we need to find them." With our guns drawn, we split up, searching everywhere in the house for any signs of life.

It appears to be empty, but we know for a fact that Eli and King are somewhere inside. We've been watching the house; there is no way they would've been able to get outside without one of us noticing.

With the upstairs cleared, Nico and I descend the one hallway and door we'd yet to check. We take position back-to-back—with me facing the front while he covers my back. I open the door to reveal a set of stairs.

Great, just fucking great.

A basement, my favorite. A shiver goes down my spine. I've hated basements ever since I learned that they were a monster's favorite place to play.

Shivering, and shaking my thoughts away, I look behind me toward Vlad. "Get back to your post. Watch our backs from outside." He nods his head and scurries out of the house.

Nico and I silently tiptoe down the stairs, a second door revealing itself once we reach the end. There were several deadbolts on the front of the door, and carefully, one by one, I turn each of them, raising my gun before shoving the heavy steel door open.

The door swings open, revealing King and Eli on the other side. I jump back in surprise to see them. No doubt the basement is soundproof.

They are alone, which makes no sense. "Where's Tate?"

I raise my hand, and cover my nose and mouth at the smell of smoke. King shoves past me, running up the stairs, and I nod for Nico to follow him.

"Where is she?" I turn my attention toward Eli who still stands in the middle of the smoke cloud.

"She's gone," he whispers groggily, coughing, and then he too pushes past me for the stairs.

She's gone.

What the fuck does that mean? Is she not here?

I follow him upstairs and out of the house where he's sucking in gulps of fresh air.

"What the fuck do you mean she's gone?" I watch as his fists ball at his sides and he stalks down the driveway toward where we have parked.

King's leaning against the car fuming, and I look silently as Eli walks right up to him and punches him square in the face.

"You fucking killed her!" Eli roars, taking another swing at King which was stopped by him, grabbing his fist and delivering a punch of his own. There, in the middle of the road, they both brawl around like children.

"You're the one that left her there!" King screams.

"You shot her! This is on you!"

Realization of what they are talking about hits me like a fucking semi-truck.

She's gone.

Tate's dead.

She was in that house, and now she's dead.

I have to grip onto the car handle to prevent myself from falling.

My jaw literally fucking drops as reality sets in. I couldn't protect her. I swore to her that I would, and I couldn't. I couldn't protect her then, and I didn't protect her now.

"Stop." My voice is failing me. "Stop!" They don't even flinch as they continue their fighting. "Enough! That's enough!" I roar, and both of them shove away from each other and gain their feet at the same time, brushing themselves off. "Are you fucking serious?! What the fuck happened?!" They are too wrapped up in their own feelings and busy playing the blame game.

"Yeah, King, what happened?" Eli shoves him backward, and King pushes back. I step between them, separating them like the children they are. "She bled out from when King shot her." He shot her four days ago. How was she still bleeding?

"She died because of you! If she hadn't been kidnapped, she would've been able to get proper care!"

"That's enough! This is on all of us! We all fucking agreed to use her as bait and now her death is a result of it. We're all to blame for this!" The tears sting my eyes, but the anger prevents them from falling.

Tate survived so much in her life, only to reach her death because of us.

We killed her.

We're all responsible. We have no one to blame but ourselves. Fighting each other isn't going to solve anything for us either.

"We share equal blame, but right now, we need to figure out how the fuck we're going to find the fucker responsible for kidnapping her and then we'll kill him."

Tate is gone, and we can't bring her back.

At this point, all we can do is avenge her death, and that's exactly what the fuck we're going to do.

The hunt is on.

THIRTY-FIVE

Sebastian

Lee is alive.

I didn't believe it at first.

There was no way she was alive. When I woke up the morning after our fight, I had seen the bloody scene in our bedroom. There was so much blood, there was no way that she was still alive.

She was just gone. Vanished without a trace.

One minute I was holding her slim throat in my hands, feeling her pulse weaken, and the next minute I was waking up to a bedroom full of blood.

Apart from the scratches she left on my arms, there was no blood. She wasn't bleeding when I was choking her on the floor. She was fine, well, not completely fine, but she wasn't bleeding.

So where did the blood come from?

Nothing made sense, but I knew I wasn't the cause for all the blood or her disappearance. And because I'm innocent, I called the police and played the perfect role of the frantic husband whose wife was missing.

I knew how it looked, her blood on my hands, no signs of anyone breaking into our home, and they found signs of her in the trunk of my car.

Nothing was out of place in the house. It made sense that the police would suspect me.

It was expected when the police brought me in for questioning. I brought my best friend, Derick, who's also my lawyer, and placed a call to my father. They both knew I was innocent as did I, and since I was a loving devoted husband, I was cleared of any wrongdoing.

I know my father had a lot to do with that, but how I was cleared didn't matter. All that mattered was the fact I was cleared, and the police were out searching for my wife.

My wife that I now know is a lying, cheating, manipulative whore that planned her disappearance.

She fucking planned it, and for who knows how long.

What a sneaky little bitch she is.

When Delilah gave me the packet that Lee had given her in case of her death or disappearance, I should've given it more attention. Delilah and I had been sleeping together for years now, ever since Lee introduced us. She's been keeping tabs on her and telling me everything that Lee would slip up and say.

Poor Delilah's so in love with me that she'd believe anything I told her. She believed me when I told her that Lee is mentally ill and makes up stories in her head. And it's because she felt sorry for me having a wife like Lee that she'd given me the packet of information that Lee had given her before she disappeared. It was the same day I was taken in for questioning that she gave me the folder of information. There were journal entries, video evidence, and photos of her abuse, and I burned it all.

Stupid Lee should've never given the information to poor Delilah.

She had evidence, she had proof that everything Lee had said was true. The way she was questioning me made me so angry, and poor Delilah suffered a sudden death.

You really shouldn't drink and drive; it is very dangerous.

Looking back, I realize how stupid I was to not look further into what Delilah had provided me.

If only I paid more attention, I could've found Lee a hell of a lot sooner.

But instead, I chose to turn a blind eye to it and believed that Lee really was dead and just hoping to fuck me over in death.

The bitch failed. I'm still standing tall.

She took a shot at a king and missed.

I'm going to take a shot at someone who was once my queen, and unlike her, I won't miss.

I didn't have concrete proof about her being alive until one day when a thick manila folder was delivered to my home. There wasn't a name or even a return address on the package. There were no shipping details, which means someone hand delivered the package to my front door.

The folder sat untouched on my desk for several days before I decided to finally open it. And when I opened it, my jaw had hit the fucking floor, and I swear that my blood literally reached the point of boiling.

I'd never been so angry before in my life.

I had proof that Lee was alive.

Inside the folder were dozens of photos of her. Pictures of her working at a strip club, photos with friends, her address, and photos of her with men.

There was so fucking much information inside that folder that my head could've exploded. She played me for a fool, and I fell for it.

Lee's alive.

It's time to tie up some loose ends.

I will find her. And this time, I will fucking kill her.

ACKNOWLEDGMENTS

(Babe, if you're reading this, that means you've read my entire book by now... just remember it's fiction. Do not ask me about anything.) To the curly-headed fucker I share a bed with, thank you for supporting me while I made this crazy dream of mine come true. You stuck by me and put up with all my crazy frustrating moments. I truly appreciate you beyond words. I still can't believe I actually fucking did it! I wrote a book!

To my editor, I can't thank you enough for everything you've done for me. Your feedback, support, motivation, you've been amazing, and I'll never be able to thank you enough. Not only were you my editor, but you were also my therapist. You dealt with my many meltdowns and calmed me through this entire crazy-ass process. And I'll never apologize for killing you with that cliffhanger! ;)

To everyone else who helped bring my first book baby to life, my beta readers, ARC readers, proofreaders, cover designer, readers, everyone THANK YOU!! I could not have done this without any of you! Bringing this book to life was not a solo project, and I'm extremely grateful that I was able to work with such incredible people to make my dream come true. I can't thank everyone enough.

Now it's time to have a Kanye moment and thank myself. For as long as I can remember, I've wanted to be an author. I've always had so many stories in my head, and I dreamed of putting them on paper to share with others. This has been my biggest accomplishment and I'm still awestruck that I did this. I truly hope you've enjoyed this story as much as I've enjoyed writing it. These characters are very special to me, and I can't wait to explore their minds a little deeper in book two! ;)

Xx,
KF

ABOUT THE AUTHOR

Kyla Faye is a twenty-something author of dark, adult erotic, and contemporary romance. When she's not reading about romance, she's writing about it, trying to give a voice to the characters that live inside her head. She has a caffeine addiction and always has a candle burning.

You can find her on social media.

Instagram.com/authorkylafaye
Facebook.com/authorkylafaye
Goodreads.com/authorkylafaye

Made in the USA
Monee, IL
04 April 2024